DELAYED PENALTY

TEAGAN HUNTER

Editing by Editing by C. Marie

Proofreading by Judy's Proofreading & Julia Griffis

Cover Design: Shanoff Designs

Cover Image: Cadwallader Photography

For anyone who has ever felt like they can't do anything right…
You're already doing it.
Keep going.

CHAPTER 1

HAYES

Lawson: New season, boys! WHO IS READY TO GET THE CUP?!

Keller: I was really hoping this group chat would die a quick death now that you're no longer single.

Lawson: Are you kidding me? Ain't NO WAY I'm leaving my boys behind.

Keller: We can dream, though. We can dream.

Lawson: So, what you're saying is… you dream about me?

Keller: Nightmares are dreams too, Lawsy.

Lawson: No, sorry. You can't try to spin this in your favor. You dream about me.

Lawson: Because you love me.

Keller: Hard no.

Lawson: Hard yes.

Lawson: Admit it already. We all know it's true.

Hutch: Please admit it. He's annoying, and it's entirely too early for this shit.

Keller: Fuck no.

Fox: I mean, we know you don't HATE hate him, so why not?

Keller: Because I do HATE hate him.

Locke: You don't.

Keller: Do too.

Fox: Come on, guys…

Locke: There it is. I was waiting for it.

Hutch: Knew he'd say it eventually.

Fox: What? What's wrong with what I said?

Hutch: Always the peacekeeper.

Locke: Such a good club dad.

Fox: I am NOT the club dad! Am I?

Lawson: Eh. Maybe a little.

Keller: Definitely more responsible than half of us.

Fox: Why does this feel like a bad thing?

Lawson: It is.

Lawson: Speaking of dads...Hayes, you there?

Lawson: Because I texted everyone for a totally important reason, and I need ALL of your attention.

Me: I'm here.

Lawson: Good. Now, gather around, everyone...

Lawson: You guys ever had a fart you feel like is going to change your life and you forget you're lying next to your girl, and you just let it rip?

Fox: Wow. Good morning to us.

Me: More like good morning to Rory.

Hutch: Please tell me you didn't.

Locke: It's Lawson. Of course he did.

Keller: Every day, I wonder what random thing will come out of your mouth that makes me wish I never met you. It's not even eight AM, and you've already accomplished that. Kudos to you.

Me: I bet Rory wishes she never met him right now.

Lawson: Wow. Rude. She loves me.

Lawson: At least I hope she still does.

Lawson: IDK. She hasn't made eye contact with me all morning.

Lawson: DID I FUCK THIS UP ALREADY????

Fox: Nah, man. You're fine.

Me: No. Definitely not.

Locke: I'm sure it's not a big deal.

Hutch: I fart in front of Auden all the time.

Lawson: Really?

Hutch: No, fuckwad. I have manners.

Lawson: UGH!

Lawson: What do I do??? I'm freaking out!

Keller: You should move. Far, far, far away.

Lawson: Like to your apartment, Kells? You'd take me in, right?

Keller: I'd take you OUT.

Lawson: I'm flattered but taken.

Keller: *knife emoji*

Lawson: But seriously…nothing to worry about, right?

Keller: Wrong. You have everything to worry about.

Lawson: THAT IS NOT HELPING, KELLER!

Keller: LOL. You actually thought I was going to help you.

Keller: Get bent, Lawsy.

Lawson: STOP IT.

Lawson: HELP ME.

Lawson: HELLO?

Lawson: AM I TALKING TO MYSELF HERE?

Keller: Yes.

Lawson: *cries*

Keller: Your tears fuel me.

I chuckle at the absurdity of my teammates and their antics as my phone continues to blow up. I'm certain Lawson, our resident sunshine guy, and Keller, easily the grumpiest human I've ever met, are arguing back and forth. Knowing them, this is going to last a while, and usually, I'd sit around and watch their bullshit roll in and egg them on, but I no longer have that luxury. I have far too many responsibilities to take care of now.

I toss my phone onto the bed, right onto the spot that was rarely vacant before this summer. Ever since I got *The Call*, though, it's been empty. Unfortunately for me, it will remain that way for the foreseeable future.

How the fuck can one phone call change so much?

I try to shake away the thought as I peel the sheet off me and rise from my massive California king-sized bed. I stop, listening for any sign of life or indication that my new roommate is awake, but I don't hear a thing. The quiet both comforts me and sets my senses on high alert, which has me padding over to my dresser and pulling on a pair of sweats instead of parading around my own damn house in my underwear like I usually would. I can't do that. Not anymore.

I put on a simple gray t-shirt, then open my bedroom door and look right.

It's open.

I close my door and make my way to the bathroom because I'm going to need a minute before going out there and facing…well, my new shitty reality.

No. Not shitty. That's an awful thing to say. It's not *her* fault.

It's *his*.

I shake my head as I wash my hands. Why does

family have to make *everything* so complicated? Why do they have to screw shit up for the rest of us? And I don't mean the *Oopsie, I spent too much money at the casino last night, could you spot me until my next paycheck?* kind of screwup.

I mean the *big* kind. The kind that means my one-bedroom apartment in the heart of downtown that I loved so much? Gone. My spontaneous decisions to go out and get plastered? Not happening. Summer trips to wherever the fuck I please? Never again. Doing whatever I want whenever I want? No longer a thing.

And it's all thanks to my asshole older brother who couldn't keep his life together for more than six months at a time. You'd think after all the shit we went through as kids with our parents, he'd have made better decisions, but *of course* not. He went and fucked his life up, then took mine down right along with him.

I brush my teeth with too much force while my new ward is presumably sitting on the couch, quiet as a mouse, just like every morning for the last few months. I finish my routine in the bathroom, then take a deep breath before moving out into my new living room with quiet steps.

After the court ruling, I knew one thing right away —I needed a bigger place. Now, I feel like a certified adult with a mortgage instead of a bachelor pad in the city.

Fuck, I miss my bachelor pad.

As soon as I round the corner, my eyes drift to the sofa, and as suspected, my new roommate is sitting right in the center of the giant black couch.

"Good morning," I say quietly, tucking my hands into my pockets.

I hold my breath and wait for her to acknowledge me. It's awkward, and I'm still unsure if that's normal. How could I know? I've never had to deal with a kid before.

"Good morning," Flora, my niece and new charge, whispers, flicking her big blue eyes my way for only a moment before returning her attention to the television.

I thought seven-year-old kids were supposed to be loud and rowdy, not sitting on the sofa watching the weather channel before eight AM. Apparently, Flora is the exception.

"Did you sleep okay?" I ask her.

Flora nods, and I let my shoulders relax. I was warned things might be a little rough with her initially, but what I didn't expect was the bloodcurdling scream she let out our first night together. We were still in my apartment, and I was sleeping on the couch so she could have my bed. She shrieked so loudly I bolted upright around two AM and ran into my bedroom only to find her still sleeping, her little legs kicking and her breaths uneven. I watched her for a good thirty minutes until she finally settled down and back into a normal sleep. I didn't shut my eyes again that night, and when I asked her about it the next morning, she said she couldn't remember her dreams. I wasn't sure if that was a good thing or bad.

She's only had one other incident since, but those two times have still been enough to keep me on edge every night. Well, those and my own recurring horror story. It's been the same one since she moved in with me—I'm in a crowded place with Flora, and one second, she's there, then the next, she's gone, and I spend the rest of the dream running around trying to find her until I wake in a sweaty panic.

It reminds me how utterly unprepared I am for this. I never wanted kids—and, frankly, I still don't—but none of that matters anymore. My brother, Aiden, made sure of that, so all I can do is embrace it.

"Are you hungry?" I scratch at my beard, which I desperately need to trim, but I can't seem to find the time to do so. Just like I haven't had time to hit the store. If she's hungry, we'll need to go out for something. I'm used to living in a city where everything is a short walk away. Yeah, we have a few places nearby, but nothing compared to the options I had there. Yet another way my brother has managed to put me out.

Flora nods in response again, and I hold back an irritated sigh. I get it, she's not used to someone giving a shit about her, but giving me just a little help would be nice.

"Want to get donuts?" I ask.

There's the faintest hint of a spark at the mention of donuts, and when she nods again, there's a bit more urgency to it. Flora translation: *She's excited.*

"Go get dressed, then we'll head out. Sound good?"

Another nod as she aims the remote at the television, turning it off before placing the device *just so* on the tray in the middle of the coffee table. She scampers by me, her steps quick as she beelines straight for her bedroom.

She doesn't fling the door closed. No, she gently presses it into place, like she's afraid closing it too hard might destroy it. Or maybe she's just scared of loud noises. I can't tell quite yet.

I follow behind her to my bedroom, swap my sweatpants for a pair of jeans, leave the gray t-shirt in place, and toss a flannel over it. It's a sunny Saturday in September, not a cloud in the sky, and I likely won't need a jacket. When I step out of my bedroom to find Flora waiting back on the couch wearing her squeaky pale pink rain jacket and matching boots, I know there's a good chance I'm wrong about the weather. I ignore it anyway.

"You ready?" I ask.

Another nod.

"Flora…" I say softly. "You have to try to remember to use your words. It might seem silly, but you need to get used to talking to people. Your teacher was very adamant about that."

She goes to nod again but corrects herself. "Yes, Uncle Adam," she says in a whisper-soft voice, her lips barely even moving with the words. It's the bare minimum, but I'll take it.

"Thank you." I clear my throat, then paste on a big grin. "Now, how about some donuts? I'm thinking trash-can flavored with extra slivers of rotten bananas on mine. What about you?"

Her lips tip upward—but only barely—before she slides off the couch and marches past me to the door without giving me an answer. It might be the world's most microscopic hint of a smile, but I swear it's the biggest win I've had all week regarding her.

Flora isn't like other kids, and I don't just mean because she's quiet. She's smart, and I suspect it's the kind of smart that could have her skipping several grades if I wanted to get her tested. It's evident not just in how she carries herself but also in her eyes. They're old. *She's* old. She may only be seven, but she's been

through more than some adults have in their entire
lives, thanks to the shit my brother put her through.

I try to shake away all thoughts of him. If I spend
too much time dwelling on him and his actions and
choices, I'll get angry, which will only lead to me
drinking far too much, which I *really* don't need to be
doing with the season so close. I need to be sharp and
ready to prove that this new predicament I've found
myself in with the kid won't affect my game so I can
stick around, because I really fucking want to stick
around.

I certainly wouldn't tell them because it would just
inflate their already big egos—especially Lawson's—
but I like my teammates here a lot. Initially I was
pissed when I found out I was being traded from the
Carolina Comets. I'd just won a Cup with those guys,
and we were really starting to build something good.
When I got the call saying I was being shipped off to
the Emerald City, where rain boots are required and a
vitamin D deficiency is a real concern, I thought for
sure it was the worst thing that could happen. Turns
out it might have been the best, even if they're *still*
bickering back and forth in our group chat, my pocket
buzzing incessantly. I have no doubt it's because
Lawson and Keller are at each other's throats.

I let the messages go unread as I follow Flora out
the front door, pressing the lock button on the keypad.

We turn right onto the sidewalk, heading toward the shops a few blocks up. I'm not overly proud to admit it, but we've often walked this same path since we moved in two months ago. I don't do well in the kitchen, so stocking the fridge has never been my priority. Thus, donuts for breakfast are almost becoming routine at this point.

It takes us fifteen minutes to walk to the small bakery, and Flora is silent the entire time. No small talk, not even a sigh or a grunt. She's quiet per usual. Hell, her feet barely make noise against the cement. She doesn't even get excited when a couple, each steering two dogs, goes by us.

The bell chimes over my head as I open the small lilac-painted door to B's Bakes, one of the best bakeries I've ever been to, and the dark-haired woman behind the counter whips her head up. It takes only a moment for her to shoot us a megawatt grin.

"Miss Flora!" Bess, the bakery owner, rounds the counter and bends until she's my niece's height. "How are you this lovely, sunny morning?"

"Good," Flora says in her usual tiny voice.

Her shyness doesn't deter Bess one bit. "Well, I'm so glad to hear that. What are you in for today? Let me guess…you want a donut with sprinkles?"

Flora starts to nod, then peeks up at me before giving Bess her attention and saying, "Yes, ma'am."

I can't help but smile. She's learning.

I like that she's learning, that she's listening. I know how this is for me at twenty-five, so I can't imagine how hard it must be for her at seven. She's not only being thrown into this unfamiliar environment but now is saddled with a guy she doesn't even know. That would be rough on anyone, let alone a kid.

I only wish I had known about her sooner.

Given his history, getting the call about Aiden wasn't a shock. But then the people on the other end of the line started using words like *your niece*, *temporary custody*, and *guardian*. That's when my jaw hit the floor. He's lied about a lot of shit over the years, left out mountains of details, but an entire fucking kid? That was a whole new low, even for him.

"Let's get you that donut, then. *Extra* sprinkles." Bess winks at Flora, then rises to her full height, which isn't all that full considering she's five foot three at best. "And how are you, Mr. Hayes?"

I've asked her several times to call me Hayes like everyone else, but she insists on ignoring me. She's lucky I like her enough to let it slide.

"Doing fine, Bess. And you? How're the kids?"

"Oh, a mess as usual." She rolls her eyes. "But that's just par for the course. Quinn, my youngest daughter…" She shakes her head with a cluck of her tongue. "I don't know what I'm going to do about her some days. That's the one who was helping in here a few weeks back, remember?"

How could I forget? I ordered a black coffee, and she somehow managed to mess that up. How is it even possible to take something so simple and make it so complicated? I don't know, but Quinn sure did.

"I remember. Has she been giving you trouble?"

"Since the day she was born." She smiles fondly. "Anyway, enough about me. Your usuals?"

"Please."

"Coming right up."

She gets started on our breakfast—a chocolate donut with *extra* sprinkles for Flora and a toasted everything bagel with cream cheese for me. She pours my coffee and grabs chocolate milk for the kid without me having to ask.

Damn, we really do come in here too often. I can't help it though, and not just because I'm a terrible cook. It reminds me of Scout's Sweets back in North Carolina, and I miss frequenting that truck far more than I care to admit.

"Thanks," I tell her as she slides our breakfast our way. "What's the damage?"

"That'll be ten seventy-five."

I hand Bess my card, then grab the plated donut from the counter, shoving it Flora's way. "Go grab us a table, huh, kiddo? I'll finish this up."

"Okay," she murmurs, taking her plate and milk, then carefully walking over to the table near the entrance, the same one we always sit at. She doesn't make a peep as she slides her chair out and settles into it, folding her hands in her lap, staring down at her donut, and just...waiting.

So odd.

I turn back to Bess, and there is no mistaking the look on her face—pity.

Her heavily purple-painted lips are turned down as she asks, "How are things really? With Flora, I mean."

"They're great," I lie, mostly because I know I can. Bess won't question me, not with Flora standing right there. Sure, she'll ask about her, but she won't lecture me because she doesn't want to upset the kid.

I don't want to upset her either. It's why I've been tiptoeing around everything for the last two months. It's easier that way.

"I see. And have you found a sitter for her? For during the season?"

It's no secret to Bess that I play hockey. This area we moved to is a hotspot for players with families, so I wasn't entirely surprised she recognized me. Then she told me the real reason she knows who I am—her son plays for Tennessee, and he was ranting about a play I made last season for weeks. I laughed, she laughed, and she gave me two donuts for the price of one.

That's the hockey world for you. It's small, and even when players on opposing teams don't get along on the ice, you're family off it.

"I'm working on it," I tell her, and it's not a complete lie. I *am* working on it…sort of. Sure, I have no idea where to start when it comes to finding childcare, but it is in the back of my mind. That counts for something, right?

"If you get in a pinch, you let me know, all right? I'm sure I can help figure something out for you."

"I'll keep that in mind." I don't mean it in the least bit because I'm sure she has her own stuff to worry about. "Thanks, Bess."

"Any time, kid." She gives me a warm smile, and I throw a twenty into her tip jar.

I tuck my card back into my wallet, then grab my breakfast and meet Flora at the table. I settle across from her, folding my napkin over my lap, just to see how she reacts to it. She watches me intently, then does the same. My lips twitch at the action.

I lift my coffee to my lips, taking a tentative sip since it's still hot as hell. Flora matches my movements.

It's cute, her mirroring me. I just wish I could tell if she's doing it intentionally or if she's simply learning. With Flora, I never know. The kid has the best poker face of all time.

"So, how's school going?"

She lifts a dainty shoulder. "Fine."

I try not to react to her one-word answer.

"And what about Mrs. Aguilar? Do you like her?"

"She's nice," Flora tells me. Then surprises me by following it up with, "I like her dresses. She always wears pretty dresses with flowers on them and matches them to her earrings. Some of the kids in class make fun of her, but I don't. I always tell her I like her outfits."

It's sad to say, but this may be the most my niece has ever said to me at one time, and it's easily the best. She might have spent the first seven years of her life with my asshole brother, but it's clear Flora is nothing like him, and damn am I glad.

"Is that so?" I ask her. "Tell me more about Mrs. Aguilar."

That's how we spend our breakfast—Flora telling me about her teacher and me listening intently, not at all worrying about all the other things I need to do to prepare for the season.

Who the hell would have thought my life would turn out this way?

CHAPTER 2

QUINN

"You got fired? *Again?* You haven't even been there a month!"

I wince at George's tone, then unwrap a butterscotch candy—my favorite—and pop it into my mouth because I could really use something sweet right now.

For a man in his seventies with a heart condition, George sure does like to get riled up. Then again, he's been like that since I started coming to George's Grocery two years ago. It's a little store with everything you need from milk to ice cream to bread but also somehow everything you *don't* need, like the display of whoopie cushions that sit by the register. I honestly have no idea how this place is still in business with its identity crisis, but the people love it.

"First of all, settle down, Mr. Heart Problems," I

tell the old guy I've spent way too much time talking to over the years. "Second, yes, but it wasn't my fault this time."

He huffs like he doesn't believe me, and honestly, I can't say I blame him. I have a bit of a reputation of losing my job to things that "aren't my fault" but, if inspected extremely closely, might actually be.

Aw, who am I kidding? They've all totally been my fault. Generally because I can't keep my own impulses under control. The proof of that can be found in the overdue credit card statements sitting on my kitchen counter.

"What happened this time?" George asks, his arms crossed over his burly chest and covered in thick white hairs.

"Marco."

"Polo," the old man automatically responds.

I smile. "No. He was my assistant manager. And, uh, let's just say we had a...*special connection* and his fiancée didn't appreciate it very much and made a scene during our lunch rush when she found out."

Or at least that's what Marco said after he stripped me out of my dress and had me for dinner on his kitchen counter. Then for dessert on the living room floor. And second dessert in his bedroom. How the hell was I supposed to know he was engaged? I didn't ask, and he didn't offer up the information. I assumed he was single when he asked me out after work one night.

Now that I think about it, the heels sitting by his front door should have been an indication, but I was so lost in the lust I didn't even think twice about them.

George is right. This is my fault too.

"So what are you going to do now?" he asks. "Isn't your car still in the shop? You're going to need somewhere local you can walk to."

"Are you offering me a job, George?"

He laughs. "Not a chance. I know you too well."

I know he's only teasing because George loves me like his own daughter, but I can't deny that his words sting.

"I don't know. I'm sure I could ask my mother for a few hours at her bakery until I find something."

The thought turns my stomach sour. I *hate* asking for help from anyone, especially my parents. It's not because they don't love me or won't help support me; it's *because* of that I won't ask. They're too nice and take too much pity on me. I'm too old to keep asking them to bail me out.

"Or figure something else out," I add.

"Like you figured it out when that last roommate of yours moved out?"

"Hey! I'm working on it!"

"It's been months, Quinn. Your savings isn't going to last you forever."

What he doesn't know is that my "savings" were never big to begin with, and I blew through them two weeks after my last roommate moved out when I *allegedly* ate the cookies her mother sent her all the way from London.

Fine. I did, but in my defense, she didn't label them, so I had no idea they were hers and she *knew* I had a little online shopping issue. I thought they were something random I bought, not a gift from her mother.

But I don't tell him any of that. There is no way I could stomach more disappointment today.

"I've got it handled, so don't you worry a hair on that gorgeous, absolutely stunning full head of white."

His cheeks turn a deep red, and my words do just as I've intended—distract him. Truthfully, I appreciate George's worry and his desire to look after me. It's sweet, and it's nice to have someone who cares. But a big part of me wishes he wouldn't care at all. That way, I wouldn't feel so terrible whenever I disappoint him.

That's what I inevitably do—disappoint people.

I'll be the first to admit I'm not exactly the most stable person ever. I've had six roommates over the last three years and just as many jobs, and I've dropped out of college twice. I'm behind on every last bill in my name, and my trusty, old, cherry-red VW Bug is almost always in the shop for one reason or another. I don't exactly scream "responsible adult."

But isn't that what your twenties are for? Finding yourself and making mistakes? I'm just out here having fun. Is that really such a crime?

I hitch my thumb over my shoulder. "Now, which cookies did you put the most love into this week? I'm on dessert duty tonight for family dinner."

"You mean The Bensons Pile on Quinn Night?" George grumbles, annoyed by my family's monthly ritual of dinner and a show—me being the entertainment.

I don't even want to think about how tonight is going to go once they find out I lost my job again.

"They're in the back," he tells me. "I'm sure we've got some left. But just so we're clear, it's absolutely criminal taking my cookies to dinner when your mother makes the best in the city."

"Thanks, George. You're the best, and even though you've yet to compliment me on my sweet, sweet lollipop earrings today"—I tuck my shoulder-length brown hair behind my ear to show them off—"I still love you."

He might roll his eyes, but I still see the corners of his mouth twitch before I make my way to the back in search of my favorite cookies, which I know he keeps in the back near the beer section. This place is right around the corner from me. There is no way I'm *not* going to know where he keeps the good stuff.

I dig around until I find what I want—butterscotch cookies. They're heaven and just what I need to make sure my mother doesn't go completely off the rails when I tell her I've been fired yet again.

"They have cookies here?"

I lay a hand against my chest to calm my racing heart as I stare at the little girl standing just a few feet away. I swallow down the last of my candy, which I'm glad I didn't just choke on.

"You scared the shit out of me."

Her big, blue eyes widen, but she doesn't call me out on my bad language. Instead, very quietly, she says, "I'm sorry, ma'am."

"It's okay, sweetie." I peek around for an adult, but nobody is nearby. I crouch down closer to her height and give her a reassuring smile. "Uh, does your mom or dad know you're back here?"

"I don't have a mom or dad."

She states it calmly as if every kid doesn't have a mom or a dad, and it completely breaks my heart. I don't even know this girl, but I want to scoop her up into my arms, hug her tight, and keep her safe from all that is evil in this world.

"Are you here alone?"

She shakes her head.

"Are you here with someone else?"

A nod.

My senses start tingling. She's not talking much and looks skittish, as if she will bolt at any moment. If she doesn't have a mom or dad, and she's not here alone, then…who the hell is she here with? A kidnapper?

No, no. Don't go there, Quinn. You've been watching too many Lifetime movies.

But the thought refuses to leave my head the more I look at her sad blue eyes, so I make my decision: I'm taking this little girl to the police station.

I rise to my full height. "Why don't we try to find someone to help you, huh?" I hold my hand out to her, giving her my best *You can trust me* face.

She looks at my outstretched hand, and her little brows crush together when she stares back at me. "I'm not supposed to go places with other people."

"It's okay. I'll make sure you're safe, sweetie."

Her eyes dart around the store. "I don't know…"

"I promise I won't let a thing happen to you. I—"

"What the hell do you think you're doing?"

I jump-spin for the second time today, but it's not a little girl I find behind me this time. It's a man—a *big* man, tall with broad shoulders, reddish-brown hair, and the most piercing silver eyes I've ever seen.

And I know him.

Well, I don't exactly know him, but I know *of* him. Adam Hayes, forward for the Seattle Serpents, and a regular at my mother's bakery. The latter part I only know because he came in the last time I was between jobs and my mother took pity on me—I hate that it's a trend—and was incredibly rude when I messed up his order.

"It's a simple black coffee. How hard is it to not screw that up?"

I *might* have "accidentally" spilled his replacement cup on his shoes. Maybe.

Okay, I totally did, but did he really have to be such a jerk about it? So I got the orders mixed up and added a couple packets of sugar to his. Big whoop. Clearly he needs some sweetening as he's currently scowling at me like I just stole his last piece of cake or something.

"What the hell do you think you're doing?" he barks again, this time moving past me and sinking to his haunches, grabbing the little girl by the shoulders. "Are you okay, Flora?" His voice is softer now, sweeter. Nothing like how he just talked to me.

Even though he's crouched down, the girl still has to tip her head back to look up at him. "I'm okay, Uncle Adam."

Ah, he's her uncle. Not stranger danger. *Thank god.*

"I told you not to move." His voice is a mixture of

anger and panic. "I was just going into the bathroom for a minute."

"I—I'm sorry. I...I..."

He sighs, shaking his head, water droplets from the downpour outside sliding over his forehead and down his slightly crooked nose. "It's okay. Just...don't do that again, all right? I was worried about you. Someone could have taken you." He swings that intense stare of his back my way as if I wasn't already aware he was talking about me.

"The only place I was taking her was to the police station."

He grunts. "I don't need someone who can't even get a simple black coffee right to be taking Flora anywhere."

So he remembers me too.

"Sorry about your shoes." I smile at him, but we both know I don't mean it.

"It's okay. Bess made sure to take the cost of them from your paycheck."

"You know Mrs. Bess?" Flora asks, her eyes lighting up for the first time. Sure, it's only a little, but at least it's something.

I smile at her. "I sure do. *Mrs. Bess* is my mother."

"You have a mom?"

That same ache from earlier lets its presence be known. This kid, who is likely around seven or so, shouldn't be surprised people have parents because *she* should have parents. It's heartbreaking to know that isn't the case.

"I do," I tell her. "And she makes the *best* desserts."

Her lips twist to the side, her brows scrunching together. "Then how come you're here buying George's cookies?"

"Because I'm going to dinner at her house tonight, and she asked me to bring dessert, and because I'm a grown-up with a job"—well, not technically anymore —"I don't have much time to make cookies. Besides, I'm not very good in the kitchen, so it's probably safer for everyone."

Flora nods like it's all making sense now, and her uncle makes a noise. I narrow my eyes at him but don't say anything since little ears are present. If it were just the two of us, I'd let him know what an ass I think he is. I mean seriously, who gets *that* upset over coffee?

"Well, as fun as this has been…" The hockey player rises back to his full height, and holy hell is he tall. I mean, sure, I'm only five foot four, so damn near everyone seems tall to me, but he looks extra big.

And strong.

And muscly.

And *hot*. Seriously hot. Like "stop traffic" kind of attractive.

He also doesn't seem to like me. A pity. I bet we could have a whole lot of fun together.

Just like you had fun with Marco, right, Quinn?

I pack the thought away for another day. It's still too fresh and a wound I don't want to deal with right now, especially not when I still have to face my family tonight.

"We should really get going before it starts raining harder out there." He grabs Flora's shoulder. "You ready?"

She nods. He tugs her along, and I watch them go, my heart aching still. The girl looks so sad. It makes me wonder what kind of scary things the world has brought her way in her short life.

I've started sorting through the cookies once more when I hear the squeak of shoes against the floor.

"Flora, what are you…"

There's a tug on my hand. I look down, and Flora is staring up at me with those sad blue eyes.

"Yes?" I ask.

"Did you try putting love in your cookies? That's what Mrs. Bess does. She told me so herself."

I smile. It's impossible not to with this cute-as-a-button child telling me to put *love* in my cookies to make them taste better.

"You know, I think I heard something about that once upon a time. Maybe I *should* try it out."

I send her a wink, and if I'm not imagining it, the corners of her mouth twitch a *tiny* bit. I don't even know this kid, but something tells me that's a major accomplishment.

"I bet it would make them amazing, just like Mrs. Bess's cookies are."

"They are pretty great, aren't they?" Flora nods, her eyes sparking just the tiniest bit. "Well, thank you for the tip. I'll have to give it a go. Who knows? Maybe my cookies will be better than Mrs. Bess's."

She scrunches her nose up, then shakes her head. "They won't."

Her uncle coughs out a laugh but quickly recovers. "Flora, that's not very nice."

She looks up at him sheepishly. "Sorry, Uncle Adam."

He lets out a deep rumble. "Don't tell me you're sorry. Tell *Quinn*."

His thick, dark brows pull together when he says my name, and I can't help but smile. Man sure can hold a grudge over some coffee.

"Sorry, Miss Quinn," Flora offers quietly.

I grin. "That's okay. I happen to agree with you. Mrs. Bess is the best, isn't she?"

The little girl nods vigorously, the corners of her lips tipping up in a half-smile.

"Tell you what, I'll make sure she gives you *extra*

cookies the next time you're in." I pat her head. "Now, you'd better get going, or that vein on your uncle's forehead will pop."

Said uncle's brows dip closer together, but he doesn't have a response to my comment. "Come on, Flora. We have to get going."

She gives me one last look before returning to her uncle's side, slipping her hand into his outstretched one. This time, I watch them leave, and I can't help but smile at him tugging her along and her tripping after him.

Just before they turn the corner back toward George, he looks over his shoulder, his silver eyes clashing with mine.

I smile.

He frowns.

That's when I hear it.

"I like her," Flora tells him.

He looks down, and I *swear* his scowl deepens.

I like you too, Flora, I want to say.

But I don't. Instead, I pop another piece of candy into my mouth, return to the cookies…and prepare for another evening of disappointing my parents.

CHAPTER 3

HAYES

"So, this whole kid thing…it's the real deal, huh?"

I laugh, glancing over at Fox, our starting goalie, who is on the stationary bike next to mine, pedaling fast. "Considering she's sitting in the room next door, yeah, I'd say it's real."

I was so keyed up after the incident at George's that I needed an outlet. What's a better way to blow off steam than hockey? So I texted the group chat and said I'd be at the rink for some quick puck and a training session, hoping like hell someone would take me up on it so I wouldn't be here alone on a Saturday night like a loser. When I pulled into the parking lot with Flora in tow, I was relieved to find Fox waiting for me.

It's not ideal to bring kids to the practice facility, but the staff have been making an exception given the circumstances. I've not exactly been a model player off the ice over the years, so to see everyone be so accommodating has been surprising. Especially Coach Smith, who has allowed me to bring Flora to a few meetings. I think it's because I was a Carolina Comet once upon a time, just like him, and that's the sort of thing that bonds you for life.

Hockey is weird like that. The organization might seem big to those outside of it, but really, it's small. Sure, we may battle on the ice on the regular, but otherwise? We're one big family. I'm thankful for that as Flora sits in the adjacent lounge with a chapter book, snacks, and a tablet, which she never touches. I thought kids were addicted to the things, but leave it to my niece to be different about that, too.

I pedal harder just thinking of her and the heart attack she about gave me earlier by disappearing like that. It was like every fear I had about fucking things up with her was coming true right before my eyes. Then I rounded the corner and relief flooded through me until I realized the stranger she was talking to was trying to coax Flora to go with her.

Quinn. Bess's mess of a daughter.

I've met her once before, and it was brief, but damn did she leave an impression—and not a good one. She not only managed to screw up my order but spilled it all over my shoes when handing me my replacement, and I swear she did it on purpose.

I won't even get started on all the horror stories I've heard from her mother, like how she lost her roommate and hasn't told her parents but she's making up so many extravagant lies that Bess knows she moved out. Or how Bess is certain there's something going on with her and her boss, and she's worried Quinn will lose her job over it. There's a whole gambit of things the girl is up to, and none of them are good. She seems like kind of a screwup.

A gorgeous screwup with a great ass, sure, but still a screwup. And while I don't have much room to judge on that front because I was a wreck myself before Flora came along, that's not me anymore. It can't be. I have too much on the line now.

"I just…I can't believe it. I never thought *you'd* be someone's guardian," Fox says, dragging me back to the present.

"Fuck, man, me either, but it's happening. The lawyers filed for emergency guardianship with the season starting up, and we finalized it last week. My life is over."

Or at least the carefree life I was living. I used to go out all the time, used to stay up way too late, used to care about three things—hockey, women, and seeing how fast I could drive without getting a ticket. Now I care about shit like school schedules, waking up at a decent hour, and making sure I'm on the straight and narrow so I don't leave Flora without a parent again. She deserves better than that.

"Come on now. Don't be like that," Fox says with a stern look, the Southern accent he typically hides well a little more noticeable today. "Having a kid doesn't mean your life is over."

"Then why does it feel that way?"

Getting the call about Flora—one they were lucky I even answered because the moment I saw the out-of-state area code, I thought for sure it was just Aiden begging for money again—felt like the most brutal delayed penalty ever. It's as if life said, *Hey, Hayes, remember that time you trashed that hotel room because you scored a hatty and wanted to party? Or in the AHL when you skipped out on praccy and got fucked up in Vegas because you were pissed Coach benched you? Or when you threw those statues into the hotel pool and caused fifty grand in damage?*

Now I'm serving time for being a little shit, and I deserve every minute of it.

"Because your life *is* over," a new voice adds.

Lucas Lawson strides through the door. He whips his towel over one shoulder, climbs onto the bike beside me, and begins slowly pumping his legs.

"It totally means your life is over," he continues as if he's suddenly part of this conversation. "That's why I'm not having kids. I like my own time far too much for that. And my own space. And money. And sleep.

That and I'm not good at sharing. I want all of Rory's attention."

Being a proud card-carrying member of the Serpents Singles Club—the official unofficial club for all the single guys on the Seattle Serpents—normally I'd fake gag or make a comment, but it's kind of hard to when it's clear he's head over heels for his girl. Lucas Lawson might have been the one to start the group, but he was no match when it came to falling for Rory Sinclair, a grumpy veterinarian who could give Keller, our resident cantankerous forward, a run for his money when it comes to being irritable.

It's still funny to me that the so-called leader of the singles club is no longer single himself. Nor is our captain, Hutch, who just happened to fall for Rory's twin sister, Auden, last season too. I'm not entirely surprised it happened. Back when I played for the Carolina Comets, a group of guys swore they'd never fall in love, and, well, look how that played out. They're all in committed relationships now.

Not me, though. No way in hell am I going down that path. I made a promise to myself to never, ever drag someone into all the bullshit life has dealt me, and given where I'm at now with Flora, I intend to hold on to that promise even more.

"Don't you have, like, three pets or something?" Fox asks.

Lawson gasps. "How dare you forget about DK! That sweet little baby doesn't deserve that. Between Daisy, Duke, DK, and Rory's demon cat, Hades, we have four, thank you very much."

"You really went with DK, huh?"

"Uh, yeah." He gives me an incredulous look like *I'm* the one out of line here. "Donkey Kong is the best character in Mario Kart, and my little English bulldog is a chunky dude just like the monkey. It's fitting."

"It's stupid."

"You're stupid," he fires back with a proud smirk, even though we both sound like children. "Anyway, I'm Team Hayes on this. Kids ruin everything."

"So Rory doesn't want kids either?" Fox asks.

"God, no. She can barely tolerate me. Do you really think she wants to bring an actual human into this world?" He shudders. "She'd never."

"And you've talked about this?"

"I..." He pauses, his brow furrowing. "Well, no. But I know her. We're on the same page with it. We're..." He shakes his head, then shoves off the bike. "Fuck it. I'm texting her."

He marches out of the room, heading for his phone, which he's no doubt left in his bag in the locker room.

Fox laughs lowly, resuming his pace. "You know, it's still a shock to me every day that he found someone who puts up with him. Especially after his little confession this morning."

"What a way to wake up."

"For Rory and us." He shakes his head. "So, how are things really?"

I repress my sigh. It's not that I don't appreciate Fox asking questions, it's just that I feel like that's all *everyone* has done this summer. My lawyer. My agent. My GM. Coach Smith. Bess. Hell, even my real estate agent has checked in with me several times. And that doesn't even include several guys from the team, *plus* the Serpents Singles Club. Even old teammates from the Comets have been in touch.

It's constantly *How are things with Flora? How are you adjusting? How are* you *doing, Hayes?* Variations of the same thing, over and over. I appreciate Fox checking in, but it's erring on the side of annoying now, especially when I'm just trying to focus on putting one foot in front of the other.

"About as well as they are expected to be when you get handed a kid you never knew existed."

Fox winces, and all I can think is *Same, dude.* That's pretty much been my reaction for the last few months.

The initial phone call about my brother's shenanigans that landed us in this mess? *Wince.*

The judge declaring me sole guardian of Flora? *Wince.*

Having to tell my GM and coaches what's going on? *Wince.*

Realizing how badly this could screw up my chances at a Cup with the Serpents? *Wince.*

Realizing what an ass I am for not putting Flora first? *Wince.*

I know I should think of her first, I really do, but it's been twenty-five years of just me. It's a hard adjustment to make. This whole situation came out of nowhere, and even though I wish they would, things aren't going to change instantly. I need to accept that.

"Sorry, man. I can't..." Fox shakes his head. "I can't imagine how rough it's been. If one of my siblings was going through this crap or put me through hell like this... Well, I'd wring their necks, that's for sure. I don't know how you're doing it."

"I've got no choice."

"You did have a choice. I know it, and you know it, too. But you made the right one and she's lucky to have you. I know it's going to be a big adjustment considering..." He trails off, sliding his eyes toward me in a telling way.

I chuckle. "Considering I'm a fucking mess myself?"

I can't even count the times I've thought, *Am I really the best person to take her in?* To anyone on the outside, the answer is a resounding no. I can hardly take care of myself. Before Flora came into my life, I was barely coasting by. Sure, there was always hockey to keep me a semi-functioning adult, but does that path usually involve trashing hotel rooms and partying all night, showing up late to practice and arriving barely—and I mean *barely*—sober enough to participate? Because that was me.

But I'm also Flora's uncle and her only semi-stable living relative. She needs me. The last thing I was going to do is let her go to my parents, who love a bottle of booze more than they've ever loved me. I don't want that life for her, so I guess it's up to me, whether I like it or not.

Fox points at me. "You said it, not me." He laughs at himself. "But, hey, she's still alive, right? Fed and clothed and all that. Count that as a win."

I'm lucky if I get five hours of sleep a night. Not to mention the fact that I've fed her donuts for breakfast at least four days this week, and for the other three, I made scrambled eggs. She picked shells out for two of those days. And I know without a doubt if it wasn't for my housekeeper, I'd have shrunken her laundry by now. If that's a win, it's a piss-poor example of one. I'm hanging on by a thread, and it's not even regular season yet.

"Any luck with finding a nanny?" Fox asks.

"I...I haven't looked yet." I cringe the second the words leave me.

He stops pedaling. "Tell me you're kidding."

I say nothing, which says plenty.

"Dude." My teammate shakes his head. "What the hell are you waiting for?"

"A miracle?"

"You're not kidding. That's a big ask on such short notice. The regular season is..."

"Just a few weeks away? Yeah, I know."

He's right. I know he is. If I'm struggling now, I'm going to be really fucked here before too long, especially if I don't find someone to take care of her while I'm on the road. Sure, the coaches and staff are being cool about her being here now, but when things are in full swing, there's no way she's going to be able to hang around.

"I don't even know what I'm looking for," I confess. "I've never had to deal with this shit before. Until a few months ago, my biggest worry was not waking up my one-night stand when I snuck out of their place in the wee hours of the morning. Now it's..." I shake my head.

"Sucks, dude, but that's life. As far as what to look for: someone with CPR training and the ability to keep a child alive would be a good start, plus someone Flora likes."

"Wait, am *I* supposed to know CPR?"

"I mean, it would be ideal." Fox grimaces like he's sorry he even brought it up. "Want me to ask around? See if I can help find someone?"

"Who are you going to know around here? I thought all your family is down south."

"That…is an excellent point." We both laugh. "I don't know. Maybe Lawson will know someone?"

"Know who?" Lawson strides back into the room and hops onto the bike like he was here the whole time. "Good news! I was right about my girlfriend. She doesn't want kids either. No little life ruiners for me."

"They aren't life ruiners," Fox argues. "Some people argue they make life better."

"And good for those people. However, I don't want kids, so don't make me have kids, ya feel?" Lawson tells him in a serious tone, which is unusual to witness. He's typically the biggest joker around, but I guess even he has his lines.

"I feel," our goalie says, effectively dropping the subject.

"Now, who might I know?" Lawson asks.

"A babysitter for Hayes. Or would it be a nanny?"

"A nanny for sure. Babysitters are like that old lady down the hall who watches you for a few hours while Mom's at work. Nannies are live-in old ladies who do everything like cooking and cleaning and butt wiping."

"I don't want someone living with me," I tell Lawson.

"Unless you want to schlep your niece back and forth to someone's house, you might not have a choice with our travel schedule." Lawson shrugs. "Besides, it probably won't be so bad. Maybe she'll be a hot older lady, and you can get frisky with her on cold winter nights." The assclown bounces his brows up and down.

There will be absolutely *no* getting frisky, *especially* not with my nanny.

"Want me to ask Rory? See if she might know anyone? A wide range of people are in and out of the vet clinic all day, and she could hit Auden up if she doesn't know someone. That woman has connections all over the city."

"Fucking billionaires," Fox mumbles. Auden is, in fact, a billionaire after building a luxury hotel empire, then selling it for some big, big smackeroos after she got together with Hutch. Something about wanting to put down roots with someone and not be tied to a business she wasn't as passionate about anymore. I don't know. That's her business, not mine.

"But he does have a point," Fox continues. "Rory may know someone. I mean, she has how many people in her office daily?"

"I can text her and ask," Lawson offers, referring to his girlfriend.

"Yeah, I guess." I don't know what else to do.

The only people I know here besides my teammates and their partners are my coaches and the training staff. Well, I guess Bess, too, but I've already determined I'm not asking her for help. She has enough on her plate with the bakery and trying to keep her own kids in line, especially her youngest.

"I liked her."

Flora's words about Quinn from when we left the corner store float through my mind. Maybe it's just because Flora is young and doesn't know better, but I'll admit she did look genuinely happy talking to the woman with light brown hair and the most ridiculous pair of lollipop earrings I've ever seen. She was responsive, asked questions, and even used full sentences. She was downright friendly, and as surprising as it was, it gives me hope that maybe one day she'll be a normal seven-year-old.

I look through the massive window along the wall and into the lounge. Flora is still sitting in the same spot where I left her when I began my training session. Her head is bent, and she's dragging her finger along the page of her chapter book, her lips moving as she reads the words. She finishes the page in record time, then flips to the next, doing the same. Though she's lost in her fictional world, that permanent frown that seems to grace her lips is still intact, and I wish I knew how to fix it. I wish I knew how to bring back that spark she had earlier with Quinn.

"Don't sweat it, man. We'll find someone for you," Fox says, mistaking my quietness for panic.

I guess it's not a total mistake because I do have just a tiny bit of panic. I've been putting this off and putting this off, but I'm running out of time. I need to get this sorted, and I only have two weeks to make it happen.

"And if we don't, just remember—she's tiny. We can zip her up in your equipment bag and take her with us," Lawson says, still pumping his legs hard like he didn't just say the most absurd thing ever.

"I know you said you weren't planning on having children, but I am begging you, Lawsy, *please* keep that promise." Fox shakes his head with a laugh.

I laugh too, though I'm not even remotely engaged in this conversation. I'm still watching Flora, wondering what the hell I'm going to do.

CHAPTER 4

QUINN

"So, Quinnicorn," my father says, using the nickname I insisted on going by during my unicorn-obsession phase. "Anything new with you?"

Almost as if it were rehearsed, like we're some choreographed family band, every single one of my siblings and their partners lifts their head, turning their attention to me. They sit blinking, waiting for me to reveal all my secrets while I sink lower in my seat, weighing my options very carefully because how the rest of the evening goes largely depends on what answer I give my father.

I could tell him the truth—I got fired. Or I could lie my ass off and tell them everything is amazing, tell them I didn't lose my job and my car is running perfectly and I'm not hanging on by my fingertips.

The second I meet my mother's hard stare, I fold.

"I, um…" I take a deep breath, sitting taller in my chair and tipping my chin up. "I parted ways with The Dock."

"Jesus, Quinn," my sister Liza mutters. Her husband, a total asshat if you ask me, shakes his head, throwing back the rest of his wine like *he's* the one who needs a drink. Their four kids—who I much prefer the company of—are playing in the living room, having only eaten a few bites of their dinner before racing off to get back to their video games.

"What a surprise," Ruthie, my other sister, offers, which really isn't helpful at all. Her partner says nothing, which isn't shocking. Kristin is always quiet, and I'm pretty sure she has hated me ever since my semi-drunken speech at their wedding, where I accidentally spoiled their pregnancy announcement.

"Again?" my oldest brother, Daniel, asks condescendingly. His wife gives me a smug smile, rubbing her pregnant belly. Baby number three is on the way, and we're all hoping this one doesn't get saddled with another D name like the other two. Having a Daniel Jr, Danielle, and Danika gets entirely too confusing as it is.

"Didn't you *part ways* with your last job too?" Matthew says beside me. With him being the one I'm closest to in age, you'd think we'd get along a lot better than we do, but we couldn't be less alike. He's the exact opposite of me. Luckily, his equally stuck-up girlfriend isn't here to offer her words of wisdom, which she always hands out without prompting.

Meanwhile, my parents sit quietly watching me. Disappointment shines brightly in my father's eyes, though I'm used to it, so whatever.

My mother, though? There's no disappointment. There's no annoyance. No frustration. There's just indifference, and I'm not sure if I feel worse or better about that.

She turns to Daniel with a smile. "More mashed potatoes, dear? Made them from scratch myself this afternoon."

Oh, okay. I guess we're done with my thing now. On the one hand, I'm relieved. On the other, I'm a little upset. Does she even care that I was fired again? Is she at all surprised? Does she simply expect this out of me?

I stab my fork into my Brussels sprouts. I take a bite, chewing and swallowing with a grimace. No matter how old I get or how they're cooked, I just cannot get behind these little green suckers. Still, I eat them, because I know my mother worked hard on this dinner, and I don't want to upset her even more.

The conversation picks up around the table, and I do my best to tune everyone out, ignoring the not-so-subtle jabs from Matthew about his upcoming five-year anniversary at his company and the disgusted glares from Liza whenever our eyes accidentally meet. It's what always happens at family dinners. My siblings pile on me, then they act like I'm not even there. I guess that's what happens when you're the perpetual screwup—you get tossed aside and ignored.

I look over at the sole empty chair, the one that was occupied by Brody, my favorite brother, over the summer. If he were here right now, he'd tell them all off or start a fistfight with Matthew just to defend my honor. He's always been like that, fiercely protective of me. I remember when I was six and he was ten, Brody found me crying in our treehouse because a kid from school teased me for having braces. The next day, the kid showed up with a black eye and an apology.

I wish he were here now, not to protect me or beat someone up, but just so I could have *someone* on my side. With the season coming up so quickly, he's already back in Tennessee to do what he was born to do—play hockey.

"Quinn?"

I snap my head up, surprised to find my mother staring down at me.

Huh. Guess I tuned my family out better than I thought.

"Would you like to help me with the dishes?"

Honestly, no. Who actually *wants* to do the dishes? But I know that's not what she's truly asking. She wants a minute alone with me, and she knows as well as I do this is the only way she'll get it with my other siblings here since they aren't about to help clean up.

"Of course." I rise from my chair, grabbing my plate and then Matthew's. He doesn't thank me, so I make sure to walk extra close and "accidentally" elbow him in the head.

"Ouch! Brat," he says to my back, but I ignore him and continue following my mother into her spacious kitchen.

When she and Dad moved out this way two years ago, the one thing my mother wanted more than anything was a kitchen big enough to comfortably accommodate all six of her children. I'd say she got her wish with the sprawling space that fits an island, a commercial refrigerator, and not one but *two* walk-in pantries. My entire apartment is the size of her kitchen, but she deserves it and more after raising six children while my father worked absurdly late hours.

I scrape the leftover food from the plates into the trash while she fills the sink and gets the dishes ready. Sure, she has a big, fancy dishwasher, but she refuses to use it when we have these family dinners. She says this is our quality time. I fear this is going to feel a lot less like quality time and more like lecture time. I pull a butterscotch candy from my pocket and pop it into my mouth because I suspect I'm going to need that too.

When she grabs the first plate and her sponge, I step up beside her, taking my usual spot—me drying while she washes—and hold my breath, waiting for what's coming next.

"So," she begins, then there's a long pause. It's the kind of pause that makes the hamster that lives in your brain start running on his little wheel, letting all the questions you don't really want answers to start spinning around. "I noticed you walked instead of driving. Everything okay?"

I exhale heavily. It's not at all the question I was expecting, but I'll take telling her my car woes over explaining why I got fired yet again any day. The last thing I want is to have to explain to my mother I lost my job because I slept with my engaged boss.

"The Bug is out of commission again."

She frowns, scrubbing the plate in her hands extra hard. "Hmm. Want your father to take a look at it?"

Our eyes meet, and we burst into laughter, and the tension I've been holding all day eases just a smidge. We both know my father, who is far more adept with technology than anything hands-on, would have no clue what he's looking at were he to pop the hood of my car.

"Nah. I had it towed directly to the shop." I grab the clean plate from her hand, running the dish towel over it. "Cost me an arm, a leg, *and* a pinky, but it's there."

She's back to frowning. "Do you—"

I hold my hand up, stopping her, because I know exactly what she's about to say—*Do you need money?*

"I'm good," I tell her, continuing to rub at the plate that's so dry it's squeaking. "If I need help, I'll let you know."

But I *won't* let her know, and we both know that too. The truth is, I do need money. *Bad.* I just don't need *their* money. It was embarrassing enough the first, second, third, and fourth time, but I'm not letting there be a fifth. I can't. I *won't*.

Mom scrubs and rinses a few more plates, and I dry them, that tension I've been holding since I was fired creeping back into my neck and shoulders as the strained silence fills the kitchen.

"You know, I could use some help in the bakery tomorrow if you're not busy." She says it so casually as if she's not throwing pity work my way because she knows I'm in desperate need of income.

"That so?" I ask, my attention solely on the dishes as I refuse to look over at her so I don't see the displeasure in her muddy stare.

"Yes. We're getting quite swamped over there. An extra set of hands would be nice."

While my father worked on getting his tech

company to where it is now—a roaring success—my mother held down the fort at home, rushing us kids to and from every sports activity, after-school program, and playdate like it was nothing. But what she really wanted to do was open her own bakery. Last year, when she turned fifty-five, she made her dream come true, and B's Bakes, her final baby, was born. While I have no doubt the business *is* doing well—my mother makes the *best* sweets—I also know she doesn't need my help and is just trying to offer me a job.

And I absolutely love her for it.

"Sure. I mean, if you really need the help."

I dare a glance her way just in time to see her smile softly. "Even if it means being there at five AM to help prep for the morning rush?"

I swallow back the urge to gag. "Yep. Five AM. Bright and early."

So, so very early.

Her smile widens, her eyes softening in the corners. "Good. I'm so excited to work with you. It'll be fun."

She's wrong. Nobody has ever thought five AM was fun. I'm already regretting tomorrow.

"Is it always like this?" I ask my mom before taking a long pull off my second iced white chocolate latte of the day.

We've been busting our asses since five, and I am beat. There's no way I won't have achy shoulders from rolling dough and blisters on my feet from being on them all day.

"Yes," she says. "Why do you think I make someone else bring dessert when we have these dinners? I need a break."

I shrug. "I just figured you wanted to make sure your kids still listen to you."

She laughs. "Well, yeah, that too." She dips her head toward the creamer on the end of the counter. "Refill those while we're slow, will you?"

I nod and finish off my coffee before making my way over to the fixings station. The bell over the door goes off just as I gather the carafes between my fingers. I'm not sure how many times it's sounded this morning, but I do know it's far too many. I repress my sigh, pasting on a smile and turning toward the door.

"Good morn—"

The rest of the words don't come out because Adam Hayes is standing inside my mother's bakery, and he's scowling at me just as hard as he was yesterday.

I ignore him, letting my eyes trail down to the little

girl pressed to his side, her hand tucked tightly into his. Flora's blue gaze sparks when she sees me, and she lifts her free hand in a soft wave. I return it, ready to ask her how she's doing, but the perpetual grump doesn't let me.

"Good morn?" he asks, a dark brow arched, his lips in that same thin line they were pressed into yesterday. "Is that some new hip lingo I missed out on learning?"

I want to tell him we're likely around the same age, but I doubt my mother would appreciate me smarting off to the customers.

"*Ing.* Good morn*ing*," I tell him through a forced grin. "Nice to see you again."

He grunts in response, ignoring me as he approaches the ordering counter.

Damn. And here I thought *I* was supposed to be the grumpy one today having to get up so early.

As they make their way over, I watch as Flora tugs on his flannel jacket.

"Use your words, Uncle Adam," she says softly yet somehow sternly.

He looks down at her with crushed brows. "What?"

"That's what you tell me, right? To use my words?"

I snicker as I set the creamers on the back counter and meet Hayes and Flora at the register to take their order.

"Let me guess, a black coffee to match your mood?"

His lips don't even so much as twitch at my joke. "And an everything bagel with cream cheese."

"Got it." I punch his order into the screen, then grin at the little girl in a simple gray dress, her hair desperately in need of detangling. "And what about you, Miss Flora?"

Her eyes brighten, and she gives me a small smile. "A chocolate donut, please."

"Sprinkles or no sprinkles?"

She nods. "Sprinkles, please, ma'am."

"Ma'am? Good lord. I am way too young to be a *ma'am*. You can call me Quinn."

"Please, Miss Quinn."

I laugh, not having the heart to correct her again. "Anything to drink?"

"Chocolate milk, please."

I'll give the girl this—she may be quiet, but she has some excellent manners, which she no doubt did *not* get from her uncle.

"You got it, little flower." I look at her uncle. "For here or to go?"

He stares back at me like he's never heard that question before. Then he looks at me, at Flora, and back at me again. I look at Flora, but she's staring at her uncle, equally confused by whatever is happening.

Just when he's about to answer, my mother speaks up behind me, and I jump at her sudden appearance.

"For here. They always get their breakfast for here." She rounds the corner, bending at the waist and beaming at the kid. "And how are you today, sweetie?"

The girl tucks herself halfway behind her uncle's leg again. She darts her eyes at me before turning them back to my mother. "Good, Mrs. Bess."

"I'm so glad to hear that." My mother straightens, turning her curious gaze to Adam Hayes, who is...

Holy crap! He's *smiling*!

And it's *hot*.

If I thought he was attractive when he was scowling, that was nothing compared to his grin. It's like he's a whole different person when he smiles. I want to make him smile.

"And you, Mr. Hayes?" My mother lifts a brow. "How are *you*?"

"Please, Bess, just call me Hayes." He says it like he's asked her this before, but knowing my mother, she doesn't care. "And I'm good."

But there's something in his voice...something in his eyes...they don't match the words that just left him. He's lying, and damn if it doesn't make me curious.

"Any leads?"

Leads? Leads for what?

Hayes's eyes find mine for only a moment, almost

like he wishes I wasn't here to witness this conversation, and then he shakes his head. "Nothing yet."

Mom hums. "That's too bad. I—*oh my gosh!*" she gasps loudly, clapping her hands together excitedly.

"What?" I ask.

"I can't believe I didn't think of this before!"

"Think of *what*?"

I look to Hayes to see if he has any idea what she's going on about, but he just shrugs.

"It's genius, really. And it works out perfectly since you just lost your job."

I wince, daring another glance at Hayes, who lifts a single brow in my direction. I duck my head, hoping he doesn't see how red my cheeks have become. I'm not sure if I'm more embarrassed by my mother just blurting it out for all to hear or if it's because she said it so casually since it happens so often.

"You!" She points to me.

"What about me?" I ask, not sure I want to know the answer given how excited she is. That can either be a really good thing or really bad.

"You can help him!"

I jerk my head back. "Excuse me?"

"You can nanny for him." Her eyes are bright with excitement as if she's just coming up with the solution to everyone's problems, and she sort of has.

I don't have a job right now, so *any* income would

be nice, and apparently Hayes here needs a nanny. This would be a win-win, except that I'm not a nanny. I've babysat my nieces and nephews, but that's different. I've known them since they came screaming into this world. I don't know Hayes or his niece. My mother might think it's a genius idea, but no matter how desperate I am, it's not happening.

"No," I say simply, turning to Hayes and ignoring the hard stare my mother's throwing my way. "That'll be ten seventy-five."

Hayes thrusts a card at me, and I take it, swiping it through the machine before handing it back while he takes cash from his wallet—a crisp twenty-dollar bill—and tucks it into the jar like he didn't just spend more on a tip than he did his entire breakfast.

Must be nice, rich bastard.

"We'll have your breakfast out in a jiffy," I tell him with a smile he doesn't return.

He just leads his niece to the table near the front window and settles in the chair opposite her.

"Quinn!" hisses my mom the moment they're seated.

"Mother," I return calmly, turning to pour his black-like-his-soul coffee.

"That poor man needs help, and you know it."

"Why do you care about some random customer so much?"

"Because he's not just some *random customer* and you know it."

Which is why I don't feel bad for him. He makes millions. He doesn't need help from some girl who can't even afford to pay her own rent.

"So he's a hockey player, big deal. Why should that make me feel bad for him?"

"Because he's a good man who took his niece in when she needed it and is now her sole guardian and needs a nanny for her during the season and clearly has no clue where to start. I mean, look at them. Do you really think he has a handle on this situation?"

She waves her hand toward the duo. Flora's attention is trained on her hands, which are folded together in her lap, her little shoulders sunken in. And Hayes…well, he just watches her. They aren't engaging in conversation like every other patron in here. They aren't smiling or sharing jokes. They're just sitting there awkwardly like they're total strangers when they're family. If I were at that table with my niece or nephew, we'd be playing a silly slap game, or I'd be making faces at them, doing anything I could to get them to laugh, but not these two.

And damn if that doesn't make me sad.

"Are they always like that?" I ask.

"Pretty much. I think I can count on one hand the number of times I've seen them talk to one another for more than a few sentences, and they're here multiple days a week. Don't even get me started on that." She huffs, grabbing the donut Flora ordered from the case. I don't miss her pulling out the shaker of sprinkles and adding even more to the top before plating it. "I bet they don't have a single decent thing to eat in that house if he's feeding her donuts daily."

I want to remind her that she used to feed us kids sweets every day, but I don't think it would be wise given how much this clearly bothers her.

"And let's not forget his profession. You know how often your brother is gone. How can he raise a kid on his own with no help?"

I shrug. "I'm sure he'll find someone."

"It's been months, Quinn, and he hasn't found anyone."

I'd be lying if I said that didn't tug at my heart, but I try my best to push it aside. I have my own problems to worry about. I don't need to start feeling bad for some multi-millionaire who can't find a babysitter.

"I just…" She trails off, shaking her head as she begins wiping down the display cases that aren't at all dirty. "Well, I just don't know what he's going to do. I feel so awful for them. I would take her in myself, but…"

If she wasn't working so hard at making her dreams come true with the bakery, I have no doubt my mother would scoop that little girl into her arms and love her all season long. She can't do that, so she's trying to help in the only way she knows how to— fixing the situation for them.

I dare a peek back over at Hayes and am surprised to find him staring at me with hard eyes, brows pulled tightly together. I smile, and that gets him to look away, back at Flora, who hasn't moved a muscle. He sighs, his shoulders rolling forward, and that same sadness from before hits me again. They really do look like they're struggling. It's like they don't have a clue how to navigate this new life of theirs.

"What happened?" I ask my mom.

"Hmm?"

I nod toward Hayes and Flora. "Why does she live with him now?"

She lifts her shoulder. "I don't know. Hayes hasn't told me, and I haven't asked. I figured it was none of my business."

Yet she thinks helping him *is* her business.

"Look, it was just a suggestion," my mother says. "If you don't want to help him, don't. I'm sure he'll find someone, just like you said. He has some time until the season really starts."

Yeah, but not enough time. I know it, she knows it, and I bet Hayes damn sure knows it. He's screwed, and I know a thing or two about that with my unpaid credit cards and utility bills stacking up. And, oh yeah, my lack of income.

Perhaps my mom is right. Maybe this *could* solve both of our problems. Even if it's just for a few weeks until he finds someone permanent and I find a new job somewhere I actually want to work, it'll still help us both out. Besides, what's the worst that can happen? I can handle a few weeks of babysitting. Easy-peasy, right?

"What are you doing?" Mom asks when I grab the plated donut and bagel.

"I'm taking them their breakfast," I say nonchalantly.

But it's not casual enough because my mother grins like she's just won a giant stuffed bear from a claw machine on the first try.

"What?"

"Nothing." Her grin grows. "Nothing at all, dear."

I narrow my eyes at her, sliding past. I blow out a breath, then push my shoulders back, pasting on the best customer service smile I can muster as I make my way out to the floor.

Hayes catches me approaching in his periphery, his brows cinching tighter together the closer I get.

I'm about to ask a hockey player for a job...and I'm pretty sure he hates me.

CHAPTER 5

HAYES

I'm not sure what it is, but the way she's smiling at me is unsettling, like she's going to kill me in my sleep.

Quinn, I mean. Not Flora. She hardly ever smiles, and when she does, it's cute, not like the stiff, toothy expression Quinn is currently sporting.

I was relieved when she turned her mother down on her "genius" idea. It saved me from having to do it. After all the stuff I've heard about her, it's clear Quinn isn't capable of taking care of herself, let alone another human. I appreciate Bess trying to solve my predicament, but I promise her daughter isn't the answer.

She makes her way through the bakery, not stopping until she's at the edge of our table. Then she just stands there, unmoving and still smiling.

See? Unsettling.

After nearly a minute of the awkwardness, I lift a brow. "Yes?"

"Oh!" She shakes her head, seemingly snapping herself out of it. "I brought your breakfast."

She settles my bagel in front of me, then slides Flora's donut across the way.

"*Extra* sprinkles," Quinn says, tossing the kid a wink.

Flora grins, grabbing her donut instantly and taking a huge bite like she hasn't eaten in days.

Fuck, I really need to feed this kid better.

"Will that be all?" Quinn asks, still with that unnatural grin.

"The coffee I paid for would be nice."

Her smile slips just slightly, her eyes tightening around the edges. "Of course. I'll be right back."

She hurries away, and I stare after her as she sashays back behind the counter, her ponytail swishing behind her with every step.

I bet her hair is soft.

I don't know where the thought comes from or *why* it comes, but I push it away as soon as it appears. Who cares how soft her hair is? I don't even know her.

"Uncle Adam?"

I jerk my head to Flora. "Yes?"

"Your phone is buzzing."

She points to my phone, which is indeed shaking across the table. I snatch it up, and the name *LUCAS LAWSON* flashes across the screen. It goes black, then lights up again because *of course it does*. Lawson is just that persistent.

Or maybe he's calling because he found me a nanny.

"And here you go." Quinn slides Flora's chocolate milk—in a mug just like mine—in front of her. "One chocolate milk for the little flower, and one—"

"Can you watch her?"

Quinn pauses, her eyes boring into my own. They're hazel, a perfect mix of greens and amber. I hadn't noticed them before, but I certainly notice them now. Just like I notice the corners of her mouth tipping down in a frown.

"Pardon?" she says.

I lift my phone. "I have to take this call. Could you watch her for a few minutes?"

She looks at Flora wide-eyed, and I see her throat bob with uncertainty. I understand the feeling. It's the same one I had when I met the kid for the first time, looking at her like she was half human, half alien or something. I had no idea what to do with her then, and I still don't know now either.

"Please?" I ask as my phone starts buzzing again.

She nods. "Sure."

The word barely leaves her before I'm out of my seat and pushing through the door. Bess has no problem with people bringing laptops into the shop, but she becomes a grouchy diner owner regarding cell phones—they aren't allowed.

My phone lights up again as my feet hit the sidewalk, and I answer on the first ring.

"What?" I bark.

Lawson being Lawson, he just laughs. "Fuck, dude, it took you forever to answer."

"I was busy. Anyone ever tell you you're annoying?"

"Keller did this morning, but at this point, it's just his version of foreplay."

"Nah. I think he just genuinely hates you."

He gasps. "He could never. At least I hope not." He mumbles the last part, and I have no doubt he's spiraling in his head. He always comes off as this guy with no cares in the world, but deep down, he wants people to like him.

"Why'd you call me ten times?" I pace the sidewalk outside the bakery.

He scoffs. "It wasn't ten. I was only on call five, thank you very much."

"Lawsy…" I clench my teeth, rapidly losing my patience.

"Right. I was calling to let you know Rory asked

around about the whole nanny thing, and she came up with nada. Auden too. She suggested her friend Lilah, but I guess she's taking off to Europe or something while figuring out what she wants to do with her life. I don't know. Sounds like rich people problems."

Rich people problems. As if he doesn't make six million a year playing hockey.

He's definitely more financially conservative than some of the guys, though. He chooses to invest instead of spending his money on lavish things like cars and extravagant homes literally nobody needs.

I can't judge, though. I was the same way until Flora came along, spending my money on whatever the hell I wanted, like high-end watches, expensive bourbons, and dinners at restaurants with no business charging so much. Now, I'm a lot more cautious with my spending. I have to be for her.

I glance through the bakery window to check how she's doing. Quinn is sitting at the table now, sipping *my* coffee before bending her head close to Flora as she says something. I have no idea what they're talking about, but it's clear Flora is having a good time and Quinn is genuinely engaged in the conversation as she says something back to the kid.

Then, a miracle happens—Flora laughs. And I mean *laughs*. She full-on tips her head back, the knotted dark hair I haphazardly threw into a ponytail brushing against her shoulders. I've never seen her laugh before —ever. Not even at the TV or something she's reading in one of her many books. She's smiled a few times, but even those are rare.

To see her laughing like this? It's the best damn thing that's happened in months, and I want to hear it.

"Don't worry about it," I say, marching back toward the door.

"What? I thought you'd be pissed. The season is—"

"I found someone."

"You did? Who? When?"

"I'll call you later."

I pocket my phone, then tug open the door to B's Bakes.

"Welcome to—oh, it's just you," Bess says from behind the counter.

I don't pay her any mind. I'm too focused on her daughter, who is still making Flora laugh. The sound is so…odd, almost like the kid doesn't know *how* to laugh, but I love it all the same.

"Reconsider," I say as I approach the table.

Quinn jumps at my sudden intrusion, one hand going to her chest and my coffee sloshing over the side of the mug she's clutching in the other.

"Crap," she mutters, grabbing a napkin to clean it up. "You startled me, Hayes."

Hayes. It's the first time she's said my name. It's as odd as Flora's laugh, but I find I like it, too.

"Reconsider," I say again.

She slides her eyes over to Flora, then back to me. "Um, what?"

"What your mother suggested earlier. Reconsider it. Please."

"What my mother..." Her brows rise slowly. "Do you mean nannying for you?"

"Yes."

Her jaw drops. "I..." She shakes her head. "I'm not a nanny."

"I know, but..." I look at my niece. "Flora, do you want another donut?"

"I..." She looks sheepish.

"You can have another one, you know that, right?"

She nods, even though she doesn't look like she knows that at all. "May I?"

"Yes. Here." I pull my card from my wallet and hand it over to her. "Go ask Mrs. Bess for another."

She hops out of her chair and grabs the card. "Thank you, Uncle Adam."

She's thanking me for feeding her, and I can't decide if it's the sweetest thing ever or if I want to rip my brother's head off for clearly not giving this girl the basics.

Instead, I tell her, "Of course, kiddo."

She hurries off to the front counter, and I watch as Bess lights up, chatting with her. I take her abandoned chair and focus my attention on Quinn.

"Look, I know we don't really know each other, but I do know two things. One, your mother loves that little girl and would never put her in harm's way, so that's got to count for something."

"My mother also thinks my oldest sister is a saint, but one time when I was six, I swear I saw her eyes turn black."

"Black, huh?"

She nods. "And my oldest brother swore she had a tail when she was born. Sounds like she's the devil to me, but who knows?"

My lips twitch.

"What's two?"

"What?"

"You said you know two whole things. You've already told me one. What's the second?"

"Right." I clear my throat. "You made Flora laugh."

"So?"

"So?" I shake my head with a derisive chuckle. "So you don't know what these last few months have been like. The kid hardly ever talks and barely smiles. She's *never* laughed before."

Quinn rolls her eyes. "That's an exaggeration."

"It's not."

She tips her head, studying me to see if I'm lying, which I'm not.

She settles back in her chair, crossing her arms over her chest. "Say you're being serious and you've never seen her laugh until now. Why does that mean I—a person who has only babysat a handful of times—should be your nanny?"

"Because she likes you."

She looks to the counter where Flora is still talking with Bess, wringing her hands with nerves. Quinn watches her fondly, with a clear hint of admiration. She likes Flora too. I can tell.

"She is really adorable."

"She is," I agree. "But that's not the point. The point is she likes you."

"Plenty of people like me. How do you know I'll do a good job and won't totally screw her up?"

I've asked myself the same question.

I sigh. "I don't, but I have to take what I can get. I, uh, I'm kind of on a time crunch with hockey season starting."

"I didn't realize mascots had such demanding schedules. Surly the Snake must be a huge hit, then."

I narrow my eyes at her because I know she knows who I am. "Ha. Funny. Our mascot's name is Stu, and he's a *silly* snake, thank you very much."

It's a ridiculous creature that looks like some five-year-old drew it, but the kids love him.

She grins. "So, hockey, huh?"

"Hockey."

"Does that mean you know my favorite brother?"

"Benson is your favorite, huh?" I smirk, thinking back on the last time I saw the defenseman and how pissed he was. "Dangled the fuck out of him last year. He chirped me pretty good the rest of the game, but the Serpents still won."

"Don't worry, Tennessee will get you back this season. Just wait."

I like that she's sticking up for her brother even though he's not here. I wish I had the same kind of relationship with my own, but I haven't in the past, and now, I never will.

Which brings me right back to Flora.

"Look, I don't know if you'll do well with Flora, but it's a risk I'm willing to take with the season starting up. It's clear you two have some sort of connection, and she needs that. She needs someone she can feel safe and be herself with. You could be that person."

Quinn sighs, resting her arms back on the table, her lips cocked to the side. She lifts my coffee to her mouth again, sipping it before setting it back down. I'm not sure she even realizes she's doing it, and I want to say something, but I don't want to piss her off. I think she could be coming around, and I need her help right now more than I need the coffee.

"I'm really not a nanny—you know that, right?" She nibbles on her bottom lip, drawing my eyes to the spot, and I momentarily wonder if her lips are as soft as they look.

"So you've said. A few times now."

"I know. I just want to be clear on that so you know I have no clue what I'm doing and I *could* mess this up. I mean, I'm going to try really hard not to, but the possibility is there."

I like that she's admitting she could screw up. Maybe it'll mean she'll pay extra attention so she doesn't.

"The truth is, I'm...I'm kind of in a bind right now." She flicks her eyes to her mother and Flora, then back to me. "I lost my job and my car is in the shop again and I'm wildly behind on my rent and can't believe my landlord hasn't kicked me out yet. I could really use a break."

Fuck, is this a good idea? Am I banking everything on her? It's clear she doesn't have a single responsible bone in her body. Is this truly my best option?

Then I remember the sound of Flora's laughter.

Yes. It's worth giving her a shot just for that.

"I could use this job more than you know," Quinn continues. "If you'll still have me after I just spilled all my secrets to you, I mean."

I nod. "I'll still have you."

She lifts her brows, and I realize how suggestive my words sounded.

I clear my throat. "For Flora, of course," I amend.

"Right. For Flora." I follow her gaze to the kid, who is now being handed a chocolate donut. "Is she always so quiet?"

"Believe it or not, this is the most animated I've seen her yet." I look back over at Quinn. "It's you. At least I think it is."

"I don't know about that." She shrugs, her cheeks turning pink. "Probably just drawn to my immaturity."

Probably, but I don't tell her that.

"I think you could help her and break her out of her shell more. I just need you to say yes."

"Hayes…" Her eyes cloud over with apprehension, and I fear I'm losing her. I can't fucking lose her. I haven't even gotten close to finding someone yet. I can't afford to let this opportunity pass me up.

"A trial run," I offer, looking for any breadcrumb I can find to save this. "You could spend the day with her tomorrow, then see if you're up for it."

"Tomorrow? It's a Monday—doesn't she have school?"

"Some teacher meetings or something. She's off." Which means I'd have to take her to the practice facility yet again, and I really don't want to do that. I need to start focusing on my game, not checking on Flora every few minutes.

"Oh. I mean, tomorrow is so…soon."

"You have anything else to do?" I challenge, knowing she likely has no plans other than wallowing on her couch if she just lost her job.

"That's fair."

"So, does that mean you're in?"

"I don't know…"

"*Please*," I beg, because that's how low I've stooped.

She sighs. "Fine. A trial run tomorrow, then I'll let you know for sure. Deal?"

She holds her hand out to me like we're shaking on a bet or something. If that's what it takes to get her to say yes, I'll do it. I slide my palm against hers, trying not to notice how soft her hand feels against my rough one, then shake twice.

"Deal."

"Good." She clears her throat. "Well, then…" She rises from her chair, pushing her hair back from her face and smoothing her apron. "I guess I'll see you tomorrow."

"I'll grab your number before we leave so I can send over my address."

She nods. "Good. Good."

She hesitates. Flora quietly comes back and slides onto the chair Quinn gave up, digging into her donut and having no clue I solved all our problems.

"Right. Well, bye."

She spins away, then pauses before turning back to me.

"Yes?" I ask.

"Could you…" She tucks an errant strand of hair behind her ear. "Could you maybe not mention the whole 'possible eviction' thing to my mom? I haven't told her yet."

"Your secret is safe with me."

"Good." She smiles and turns away again.

"But, Quinn?"

She stops, looking over her shoulder at me. "Yes?"

"I'll take that coffee now."

Her eyes widen and fly down to the lipstick-stained mug in the center of the table. She rushes forward and grabs it, her cheeks now a deep red, then hurries off toward the front counter, muttering to herself the whole time. I watch her, grinning as she fumbles to get the machine going.

"You like her too."

I snap my eyes to Flora, who is looking at me more

like a seventy-year-old than a seven-year-old, wise far beyond her years. "What?"

"Miss Quinn. You like her too."

"I…" I shake my head because, no, I don't like her. I like the fact that she's going to fix all my problems. That's all.

"Eat your donut, kid," I tell my niece.

And she does…smiling the whole damn time.

CHAPTER 6

QUINN

He offered *me* a job!

There I was, about to go beg for one, then he offered it to me. I won't lie—I panicked for a moment because it all became too real. I don't know if I'm cut out for this. It's going to be a lot of work. 24-7 kind of thing.

But then I thought about how much fun I was having just talking to the kid and how easy it seemed. Sure, I'm not going to like working for her uncle one bit, but I like her, and that just might be enough.

I pass George's, sending him a wave as I walk by the corner store on the way to the address Hayes sent me. I laugh at the double take the old man does seeing me out and about this early. I check my phone to ensure I'm still headed the right way, then scroll through the messages Hayes sent me last night for the millionth time. They were so direct. Straight to the point, all business. I'm unsure if I was unnerved by that or just the thought of nannying in general, maybe a bit of both.

About half a mile up the road, I turn into a neighborhood I've never been in and am surprised to find it all looks so…*normal.* Like something out of one of those Hallmark movies I secretly love to watch. I don't know why, but I pictured him somewhere more remote, a gated community and his house being watched by men in fancy black suits with earpieces. Maybe a little rain cloud perpetually hanging over his house, something with sharp edges and dark shutters and no front lawn.

I did not expect white picket fences and sprawling yards.

I stop at the end of a driveway where the mailbox matches the number he sent me and stare up at the expansive home in front of me. It's unlike any other house on this street, and I don't mean its structure or color—those are all in line with the rest of them.

No. It's the lack of any curb appeal or sign of life aside from the fancy SUV sitting in the driveway instead of tucked safely inside the two-car garage.

But someone *does* live here—Hayes. And Flora, too.

Flora, who I can't wait to see again. I had fun with

her yesterday in the few minutes I watched her while Hayes stepped outside. She told me about the book she's been reading, something about a group of middle school kids whose teachers are supernatural creatures and get into all kinds of trouble. I made some ridiculous and completely unfunny joke about spiking her uncle's coffee with garlic to find out if he was a vampire, and she laughed. I didn't realize at the time how rare it was, or I would have soaked it up more. Maybe I can make her laugh again today so I can appreciate it this time around.

I reach into my pocket, pulling out one of the butterscotch candies I always keep tucked in there, and toss it into my mouth before pushing my shoulders back.

"Here goes nothing," I mutter as I march up the short driveway, climb the three stairs that lead to the front door, and press the doorbell. The chime rings through the house, but that's the only sound. It's quiet. Almost too quiet, like nobody is home.

I wait a minute. Then two. Still, nobody answers the door.

I knock and wait again. Nothing.

I pull my phone from my pocket, checking to make sure I have the right house, even though I'm ninety-nine percent sure I do.

"Yep. This is it," I mutter to myself, then hit the

doorbell again for good measure. "So where the hell is everyone?"

"You know, when someone doesn't answer, that usually means they aren't home."

I whirl around, my heart thundering in my chest. Hayes and Flora are standing at the end of the stairs. His eyes are narrowed, and hers are full of excitement.

"Hayes."

His gaze sharpens even more. "Quinn."

There's apprehension in his tone, and maybe even a little surprise like he didn't expect me to show up on time today.

What is it with everyone always doubting me?

Flora holds up a lilac bag, one I'm very familiar with, as they walk up the steps, her bright pink rain boots clomping against the wood. "We got you a donut."

I remember my mother's comment about how they're in her bakery almost daily. Even I don't eat out that much, and I'm a terrible cook.

"You did?"

She nods frantically as Hayes punches in the passcode for the door, balancing a tray filled with three drinks in the other hand. "Uncle Adam said we should play it safe and get you a glazed donut, but I told him you needed something with sprinkles."

I smile, dropping into a squat to match her height.

"Well, you'll be happy to know you were right. I happen to *love* sprinkles. Want to know why?"

"Why?"

"Because sprinkles make everything better." I boop the end of her nose, and she giggles. It's not the same laugh she gave me yesterday, but it's just as adorable.

I push back up to standing and find Hayes watching us, his brows cinched together, lips downturned.

"What?" I ask, worried I did something wrong.

He shakes his head, then pushes the door open wide. "Come on in."

Flora breezes past him, and I follow behind her, squeezing past Hayes's big frame the best I can without making contact. It's futile though. He takes up too much of the doorway, and my chest brushes against his. He stiffens, scooting back until the door bounces off the wall with a loud thud to avoid more touching.

I trade worrying about his odd behavior for letting my eyes roam around the house. It's...well, it's empty. Almost like a museum. There's a couch, a coffee table, and an entirely too big TV that takes up half a wall, but that's really it. There are no throw pillows on the sofa or pictures on the walls. There's not even a rug to help soften some of the echo.

I notice Flora's boots by the door, so I take off my

yellow ones, smiling at how ridiculous our bright shoes look next to Hayes's dark ones.

"Hey, how about we eat in the kitchen today?" Hayes says to his niece as she begins unrolling the bag of donuts at the coffee table.

"Oh. Okay." Flora hangs her head like she's in trouble, and my heart aches for the kid.

"Just so we have more space," Hayes explains with a smile.

Her little shoulders relax a bit as she pads softly into the kitchen and takes a seat at the table that still has a tag hanging off it. I follow behind Hayes, sliding onto a chair while he heads for the cabinet and pulls out a few plates. I smirk when I see they're still sporting their tags as well. Flora divvies up the goods— chocolate with sprinkles for her, a bagel for her uncle, and a vanilla twist with sprinkles for me.

"How'd you know this is my favorite?" I ask her.

She grins proudly. "Mrs. Bess told us." She looks to her uncle. "Can I have my chocolate milk in a mug like yesterday?"

I don't know why it makes me smile, but it does. I knew she'd like that little touch, making her feel like an adult instead of a kid sipping from her milk carton.

"Of course you can." Hayes pushes away from the table and looks back at me. "I assume since you were drinking mine yesterday, you take your coffee black?"

I smirk. "Black is fine."

He grabs a mug and pours Flora's chocolate milk into it, and we dig into our breakfast. Flora keeps looking at my donut with curiosity, so I pluck a chunk off the end I haven't eaten from and settle it onto her plate. She picks it up, examining it briefly before taking the world's tiniest bite. Her bright blue eyes widen with surprise, and she nods, shoving the rest of the piece into her mouth in one go. It's so silly because it's a simple donut, but I love how much she loves it.

I peek over at Hayes. He's watching her too, just as enraptured by her as I am, his bagel still untouched on his plate. As if he can feel my stare, he slides his gaze my way, and I pause mid-bite.

He looks tired. His eyes are heavy with fatigue and dark circles sit under them. His hair is a mess like he didn't even bother trying to tame it before leaving the house, and his beard is in need of a good trim. His shoulders are hunched forward, and he certainly looks like he's seen better days.

I can see why my mother was so insistent I help him. He's clearly not getting enough sleep or eating well. Not that I really have any room to talk about either of those things, but still. I just have me to take care of, not an adorable kid.

"I like your earrings."

I swing my head over to Flora, touching the silly thing that dangles from my right ear. "You do?"

She nods. "Is that a *Nemo* fish?"

"It is!" I push it out toward her. "It's a clown fish, and he's trapped inside a plastic bag like in the movie."

She twists her lips. "I hate that part."

"Me too. But that's the whole point of the movie— to show you that you're brave enough to overcome anything just like Nemo did."

She grins, then digs back into her donut. I glance over at Hayes, who is no longer looking at Flora but at me. His head is tipped to the side like he's studying me and is unsure about what he sees.

I shift in my seat under his scrutiny. "What?"

"Nothing."

He shakes his head once, then finally picks up his own breakfast, eating nearly half the bagel he's smashed together like a sandwich in one bite. *Who the hell eats a bagel like that?*

"What now?" he asks when he realizes I'm still watching him.

"It's just… Why are you eating it like you're diving into a turkey club instead of, I don't know, like a bagel?"

"What? Eat each slice on its own?"

"I mean, is that not the correct way to eat a bagel?"

I look to Flora to back me up, and she nods. "See? Even the little flower here agrees."

He looks at his niece. "You're taking her side instead of mine?"

She shrugs. "It's weird."

"It's not weird. It's efficient."

"It's weird," Flora insists.

He sighs, setting his bagel down and pulling it apart like a normal human would. He takes an exaggerated bite. "Better?" he asks through a mouthful of food.

Then Flora does it again—she laughs. It's such a beautiful sound, I don't know how I missed it before. Hayes watches her with a grin on his face, and when he sees me looking, he tries to hide behind his to-go coffee. It's no use. I saw it.

We finish our breakfast in silence, but there's an obvious shift in the room. The tension has dissipated, Hayes looking more alert, and I think it has very little to do with my mother's delicious coffee.

I rise from the table, collecting our plates, but when I reach for Hayes's, he tries to stop me. I narrow my eyes at him and snatch it away anyway. I rinse them and then put them in the dishwasher, noting the plastic covering still clinging to the outside.

Man, they really don't use this kitchen much, do they?

"May I go read my book?" Flora asks softly.

When I was her age, I was looking to do absolutely anything other than read, *especially* if I had a bonus day off from school. But not Flora, and somehow, I feel it makes perfect sense for her.

"Of course. Just remember what we talked about."

"Turn the light on so I'm not squinting?"

"Yes, that."

"Yes, Uncle Adam," she says.

She rushes off toward her bedroom, leaving just a crack in the door, then flicks on her light.

"She reads in the dark?"

Hayes sighs, rising from his chair. "My brother, Aiden, was a fucking moron and would make her always keep her lights off so she wouldn't *disturb* him. I caught her reading in there one night with the book pressed against her nose."

"That's…"

"The stupidest thing ever? I know." He shakes his head with disgust. "But that's Aiden for you. Stupid to his core."

There's no missing the contempt in his voice, and I want so badly to ask more, but I have a feeling he'd tell me it's none of my business, and he'd be right.

Hayes finishes his coffee, then drops the cup in the trash before opening the fridge and grabbing a bottle of water. He shakes it at me, but I decline.

"I can't stand the taste of plain water. I need flavor, or I'm not drinking it."

"How do you stay hydrated?"

I lift my coffee. "Go-fast juice."

"That's unhealthy."

"Says the guy feeding the seven-year-old donuts every morning."

He makes a noise, and it's the closest he's come to a laugh yet. "I'm not very skilled in the kitchen either. Guess we're alike in that department."

"Is that going to be a requirement for the job?"

"I've gotten by without it, so I guess not. Besides, she's not that hard to feed. She likes the basics like chicken nuggets and grilled cheese—that sort of stuff."

"I could handle that. Speaking of the job...we haven't really covered what all it entails."

"Keep her alive."

"Gee, why didn't I think of that?" I roll my eyes. "I know that part. I mean, what are her school hours like? Is she allergic to anything? Do you have a schedule for her? What time does she go to bed? What are my hours? What's my salary like?"

He tips his head to the side. "You're asking questions like you're so sure you got the job."

I stand up straighter, ready to fight for it, and he laughs disdainfully.

"Relax. Assuming she's alive tonight..." He gives

me a look that says *She fucking better be.* I hold up my hand, letting him know I got his message loud and clear. "...then you're hired. Flora clearly loves you, and that's a win in my book."

"And you?"

"Do *I* love you? Moving kind of fast, aren't you, *Quinny?*"

I narrow my eyes at the nickname. "I meant how do *you* feel about me working for you?"

He stares at me, his grayish-white gaze burning into me. I sip my coffee, praying he doesn't notice my hands shaking under his stare.

"Well, you're here, aren't you?" is his answer.

He brings his water to his lips, chugging back half the bottle in one go, and I pretend I don't pay any attention to how his throat bobs as he takes the long pull.

When he's finished, he drags the back of his hand over his lips. "Hundred thousand."

My breath catches in my throat because there is *no way* he just said what I think he did. "Excuse me?"

"You asked about your salary, right? A hundred thousand for the season."

A hundred thousand? That's... That's... I don't even have the words. I could get my car fixed and I mean *really* fixed. I could pay my credit cards off. I could buy groceries. And shoes. Oh my gosh, *so many* shoes!

"Plus room and board, obviously," he says.

Wait. Room and board? Is he saying…

"I'll be living here?"

"Well, yeah. I'm going to be on the road a lot."

Shit. I hadn't thought of that, but now that he says it, it would make the most sense if I lived here instead of trekking back and forth. Which means I'm going to be living with Adam Hayes. I know he'll be gone a lot, but what about when he's not gone? Then what? We just…live together? I'm not sure I'm ready for that.

"Besides, aren't you struggling to pay your rent anyway? Solves that issue."

Oh. Right. I almost forgot about that part.

"I guess it does make sense," I agree. "When… When would all this happen?"

"Well, I could give you half the money up front."

I do my best not to let my jaw hit the floor. *Half?* That's fifty grand for doing nothing!

"But as far as you moving in," he continues, "it would need to be sooner rather than later with our upcoming preseason games and prepping for the regular season. I know that's probably not ideal, but…"

I nod. "I get the schedule. Brother is a hockey player, remember?"

Man, Brody will have a shit fit when I tell him I'm living with Hayes. But that's a problem for future me.

"I can do soon," I tell him. "That shouldn't be a problem."

And it will save me from dealing with my cranky landlord. I can hand him the money I owe him, then promise to never, ever darken his doorstep again. He'll be so happy he'll probably cry.

"And the living-with-me part?" Hayes asks, those light eyes of his boring right through me. "That won't be a problem either?"

"You wouldn't be my first roommate."

"No, but I bet I'd be your first male roommate."

He's right. While I've had plenty of roomies over the years, they've all been girls who are like me. Not big, tall men who play professional hockey and are undoubtedly hiding a set of rippling abs under their shirts that are just a bit too tight and toned muscles in their jean-clad legs. I've definitely never had a roommate like that.

He grins wickedly. "Yeah, thought so. I'll let you simmer on that while I'm gone."

"You're leaving?"

He lifts his brows. "Uh, yeah, that's sort of the whole point of the trial run, isn't it? See if you can make it through the day?"

"Oh. Yeah, I guess that's true."

I nibble on my bottom lip, the nerves I've been repressing beginning to rear their heads. I'm going to be all on my own, taking care of a seven-year-old I barely know. I can do this…right?

"I have a team meeting around ten, then I'm heading to the rink to get some skating in before hitting the gym." Hayes pushes off the counter and tosses his empty water bottle into the recycling bin next to the trash. "You have my number, so call if there are any problems. I'll make sure to keep my ringer on. I'll be back later this afternoon."

I nod. "Sounds good."

"Does it? You don't seem sure, and I *need* you to be sure. Flora is…" He looks down the hall to where her door is still slightly ajar. "Well, I want the best for her. So if you think this won't work, I need to know now, not later, so I can figure something else out."

I understand where he's coming from. I do. I want the best for Flora too, and I think—*I hope*—I can do this.

I push my shoulders back, determined to make this work, and nod. "I'm sure." And there's only a slight waver to my voice when I say it.

"And, Quinn?"

"Yes?"

"Think about what I said."

He doesn't have to elaborate. He doesn't need to. I know he means our living arrangement.

Could I live with the ridiculously hot hockey

player? Sure. Am I going to have to remind myself he's my boss and to keep my hands to myself? Probably every damn day. But am I sure I can do this, especially if it means I can pay my bills and not be worried every time I leave the house that I'm going to come back to a padlock on my door? Possibly. I'm just going to have to remind myself of that rule every kid is taught when they're little—I can look, but I can't touch.

Even if I really, really want to touch.

CHAPTER 7

HAYES

"No fucking way."

"Way."

Lawson shakes his head. "I'm calling bullshit."

"Then you'd be wrong."

"Bet you can't even hit 180."

Keller scoffs. "Bet I can hit 220."

"Prove it, and I'll buy drinks tonight. You lose, you buy them."

"Uh, *everyone's* drinks?" Fox asks, raising his hand like we're in a classroom or something.

Lawson nods, not taking his eyes off Keller. "Everyone's."

"Do it," Locke says. "Take the bet."

"I bet he hits 230," Hutch adds.

Now, anyone other than Lawson would realize the entire room is against him and take it as a sign, but of course, he doesn't. Instead, he holds his hand out to Keller, and they shake on the deal.

I can't wait for my free drinks.

This is all completely ridiculous, but it's the perfect distraction from thinking about Flora at home with Quinn. It's the only thing I could focus on throughout the team meeting. *Are they getting along? Is Flora just hiding away in her room? Is Quinn being nice to her? Is Quinn paying attention to her? Will Flora hate me for dumping her off on someone else and compare me to my brother?*

Then we hit the ice, and my mind calmed the second my skate glided across the slick surface. I skated until my legs were tired, then I skated some more, and one thing was obvious—I've missed being out there. I've missed who I am on the ice. It felt like coming home, like how everything did before my brother fucked me over.

Now the guys are being idiots, and I missed this too. Keller smirks over at me before resting on the bench and gripping the bar.

Lawson adds some weight, then steps to the top of the bench, readying his hands to catch the weights if Keller can't lift them. "That's 150. We'll start small."

Keller grunts and holds his breath as he shoves the bar with a struggle everyone other than Lawson knows is fake.

"Dude, you're already wobbling." Lawson laughs,

then adds another ten pounds. "No way you're going to be able to lift this."

Keller lets go of the bar, shaking his hands out like this is exhausting him. He repositions himself and pushes the weight up, again pretending to struggle. He sets the bar back on the rack, and Lawson stands over him with a satisfied smirk.

"You ready to tap out?" asks the golden retriever in human form.

"Nah. Let's do 180."

Lawson's brows shoot up. "You sure?"

"Yep. Stack them on there."

Keller sits up, putting on a show of being out of breath, grinning at me, Locke, Fox, and Hutch. Lawson whistles jauntily while he loads the bar with the new weight. He claps his hands when he's finished, then rubs them together.

"All right. Whenever you're ready, man. Don't want to hurt you, so if you need to call it…"

Keller shakes his head. "Not a chance. Let's do this."

He settles back on the bench, grips the bar, and takes a deep breath. Lawson's grin widens, his eyes bright with excitement like he just won a million bucks even though the bet isn't over.

My favorite part? When that light extinguishes in a

split second the moment Keller lifts the bar like it's a feather.

"What the fuck? H-How… W-What…" Lawson sputters.

"Add twenty," Keller demands.

"Now wait a damn minute. I—"

"Fox, add twenty."

"You got it, Kells." Our goalie slides by Lawson and adds another twenty pounds to the bar.

Once again, Keller lifts it with ease. He keeps going, adding ten pounds at a time until he hits 250, then he slams the bar back down, and this time when he sits up and begins sucking in deep breaths, it's genuine.

He smirks over at Lawson, who is standing there with his hands on his hips and his brows pulled tightly together. "Did I win?"

"You played me," Lawson accuses.

The team grump shrugs. "It's not playing you if I just know my own strength." He nods to us. "Should have listened to the guys when they started betting against you."

Lawson points to each of us. "Betrayal! Betrayal! Betrayal!"

He gives us all a glare, and we just laugh at him.

Keller stands, clapping him on the back. "Poor, poor, stupid Lawsy. I think I'll take that drink now."

Lawson grumbles, shaking Keller's hand off him, then stomping out of the gym to the showers. Eventually we all follow him, rinsing off and heading to our cars, promising to meet at Top Shelf, the local sports bar we tend to frequent. With the game being so new in Seattle, it's nice to have a place to go where we're welcome and feel at home.

After fighting for street parking—and Lawson cutting me off to steal my spot—I stumble into the bar and am immediately greeted by the bartender behind the counter.

"Hayesy!" Chaz calls out. "Where the hell have you been, man?"

Before Flora came to live with me, I used to spend a lot of evenings here. And by a lot, I mean *every* evening. Nothing beats cheap beer and women who will do anything to say they slept with a hockey player.

"Chaz," I say, bumping my fist against his as I approach the counter. "Good to see you, man. How's business?"

"Be even better with you hanging around. Where have you been?" he asks again.

"Busy," I tell him, which isn't entirely untrue. "But now that I'm here, I'd love a cold beer."

"You got it."

"Put it on Lawson's tab!" I holler as he moves to pour my usual IPA, a local hazy brew I love.

Hutch walks in with Fox, then Locke, Keller trailing after them. The captain sits to my left, Keller to my right, and Locke on his other side.

"Keller, you fucker!" Lawson calls as he comes barreling through the door two seconds later.

"What'd I do?" the man in question asks, Lawson shoving him right off the stool and stealing it.

"*That's* for putting the sign on the back of my car."

Keller laughs. "Oh, you mean the one that says *Honk If You Swallow Too?* How many beeps did you get?"

Lawson just glares at him, then turns to Chaz. "Unfortunately, I'm buying everyone's drinks tonight. Give them all light beer, will you?"

The bartender laughs, used to our shit, and takes everyone else's order, then sets about pouring our drinks. When he slides them over to us, Lawson immediately lifts his into the air.

"Serpents Singles, baby! We're back!" But nobody lifts their glass along with him, and he pouts. "Aw, come on. This is our reunion. Why isn't everyone jazzed?"

"First of all, nobody says jazzed except old people. No offense, Locke," Fox says.

"I'm not old," the old man grumbles. "And you're not even single anymore, Lawsy."

"So? Neither is Hutchy."

"Hutchy who didn't even want to be part of this stupid club in the first place," Hutch says with a scowl.

"But is still so, so happy he is." Lawson grins at him, then takes a swig of his lager.

"You two are all in love and shit. Should you even be in this club?" I ask.

Fox pokes his head around Locke. "I thought we established that we're still a club, whether single or not."

"Then how can we be called the Serpents *Singles* if we're not single?" I ask.

"Just shut up and be happy you are even part of the club, new kid."

"Hey, be nice, Lawson," Locke says. "He's not new anymore, and he's not a kid either now that he has one. Sort of." The veteran player turns his attention to me. "How is that going, by the way?"

"Yeah, you never called me back after you said you found a nanny." Lawson pouts like he's genuinely offended I never returned his call, and knowing him, he really might be.

"Wait, you found a nanny?" Fox asks.

I sling back my beer, already annoyed with all the questions, then nod. "I think so. I hope so."

I *do* hope so. As much as I wish it weren't Quinn given everything Bess has told me about her, I genuinely think she could help bring Flora back to life.

Make her a normal seven-year-old who laughs and smiles and is a little wild. Not how she is now, quiet as a mouse and afraid of her own shadow, thanks to my brother.

"Who is it? Is she a babe?" Lawson asks. "I mean, I'm super in love with Rory, so I'm asking for you, not for me, just so we're all clear."

"More like so Rory won't feed you your nuts for breakfast." Keller smirks. "Though I do love the idea of her doing that."

"First of all, that's rude." Lawson looks to me. "Second, is she a babe?" I scowl at his question, and he laughs. "Oh, so she *is* hot."

"I never said that."

He points at me. "Your face just did."

I smack his hand away. "No, it didn't."

"It kind of did." Locke shrugs. "You got all scowly like Hutchy gets when people bring up Auden."

"Yeah, because she's—"

"Mine" we all say at the same time.

"We know," Keller adds. "It's not like we're hitting on her or anything. We're just saying she's got a great—"

"I swear to fuck the next word out of your mouth better not be rack, or you'll be eating your teeth." Hutch glowers at Keller.

"Personality," he finishes. "We're impressed she's so down to earth, being a billionaire and all."

Lawson whistles lowly. "Wow. Okay. Anyone else just get a little tingly watching Hutchy go all caveman just now? I'm starting to get why women love that."

"Fucking hell. Please stop talking, Lawsy." Locke shakes his head, downing his beer, then lifting his hand for another.

"So, back to my question…" Fox clears his throat. "You found a nanny? Or at least hope you did? What does that mean?"

"We're doing a trial run. She's with Flora right now."

"Oh, a trial run. That's a good idea." Fox nods. "Anyone we know?"

I shake my head. "Nah. You know that bakery I go to all the time out by my house? It's the owner's daughter. She was in a pinch, I was in a pinch, and Flora seems to like her, so…" I lift my shoulders.

"Wait. Do you mean that chick who made your coffee wrong, and you wouldn't stop complaining about her and her weird cats-in-pajamas earrings and how someone with that great of an ass shouldn't wear something so stupid?"

I want to roll my eyes just thinking of Quinn and her ridiculous earrings. They're bizarre and don't even kind of match her outfits, but somehow, they still make perfect sense for her.

"It wasn't cats, it was goats, and yeah, that's her."

"So she *is* hot, then."

"I didn't say that."

But she is hot. Very, very hot, a little fact I've been trying hard to ignore.

"You said she has a great ass, so you're clearly into her."

"That's not..." I pinch the bridge of my nose, exhausted by Lawson. And to think, just an hour ago, I was thinking about how much I missed these obnoxious assholes.

The truth is...if I had met Quinn a few months ago, I probably would have liked her wild side. I would have been wild with her. But not now. Now, I just need her as a babysitter for my niece, and that's it.

"Why haven't we heard of her before?" Locke asks.

"Because *you* were gone all summer. And you two dicks were gone too." Lawson sends an accusatory glare at Hutch and Keller, who don't look at all sorry about bailing for the summer.

"We were building a house, then went on vacation. I don't regret a single night I spent away." Hutch smirks into his beer like he's remembering exactly what he did while he was gone.

"I was with family." Locke shrugs. "Someone's gotta be the fun uncle."

Lawson looks at Keller. "What's your excuse for running off to…well, wherever the fuck you were hiding?"

"No excuse. I just wanted to get as far away from you as possible, Lawsy."

We all laugh because we know it's true, though I am curious where Keller was. He answered all the group chats readily, but he's the only one who never fessed up his location. He's always been like that, though. Anytime someone asks him something personal, he deflects. I can't blame him. I do it, too, especially if someone brings up family. There's a mile-long list of shit I'd rather talk about than them. Nobody wants to hear about their fuckery.

"Is she going to live with you?" Lawson asks. "Because if you're crushing on her, that's probably not a good idea."

"For fuck's sake. It's not a crush. Saying someone has a great ass does not equate to a crush."

"I don't know…Rory has a great ass, and I'm definitely crushing on her."

"Booo!"

"Gross!"

"Is that a boner?"

Lawson covers his junk. "You wouldn't see it if you weren't looking, Kells!"

"Shit, he's got you there." Hutch laughs.

The conversation around my new nanny dies down, shifting to something else that's equally absurd. I do my best to pay attention, but it's no use. I'm officially distracted, and all I can think is *Quinn really does have a nice ass.*

The house looks quiet as I pull my SUV into the driveway and shut off the engine, and I'm not sure if I'm unsettled by that or relieved.

I stayed out longer than I planned to. I probably should have gone straight home to Flora after the training session, but I couldn't resist going out with the guys. Even though the guilt is setting in now, I can't find it in me to regret it. I needed the break, to let off a little steam. The camaraderie is the one thing I miss the most during the offseason. Being part of something bigger, hanging with the guys. I'd never tell them that because they'd make fun of me endlessly, but it's true.

It's one of the biggest hurdles of having Flora now —being unable to go out whenever I please. I'm not a homebody and never have been. I can't stand sitting around with my thoughts. I need something—or someone—to distract me. With the kid around now, I don't have that luxury anymore.

I climb out of my new, totally safe and boring SUV —the one I bought because there was no way Flora was riding in my Porsche 911 GT3 RS—grab my gym bag, and head for the front door.

Hand on the knob, I pause.

Are those voices I hear? Is someone here? Did Quinn invite a stranger into my house? Is she already screwing this up too?

I push the door open, expecting to find someone, but I only see a startled-looking Quinn sitting on the couch, the TV playing in the background.

Ah. That's the voices.

But where's Flora? I check my watch. It's only five PM. It's too early for her to be in bed already.

"What are you—"

She holds her finger to her lips, silencing me, then points to her lap.

I pad farther into the room and peer over the couch. Flora is sound asleep on Quinn's legs. She's wearing a crown that looks a little familiar, and she's snoring softly. There's a book lying over her chest like she fell asleep reading.

And fuck, it's adorable.

I smile down at her. "How long…"

"Only about thirty minutes. She was reading out

loud to me, then the next thing I knew, she was out. We had a busy day, so I'm not surprised."

I lift my brows. "You did?"

Quinn nods, her eyes shining with excitement. "We played tag in the backyard, then hide-and-seek—which I won, thank you very much. We drew pictures, made sandwiches for lunch, built a fort in her room, and then decided to build a fort out here, too, because what living room isn't better with a fort? She wanted to read more of her book, so I suggested she read out loud to me to get some speaking practice in." She looks down at the sleeping girl. "Worked a little too well, maybe."

I have no words. I had an image in my head of what their day would look like, and that certainly wasn't it. I thought maybe they'd talk a little, but I figured Quinn would mainly play on her phone while Flora read or played quietly in her room. But it doesn't seem like that happened at all.

"My legs are completely numb," Quinn whispers, still peering down at the worn-out kid.

"Here, I got her."

I round the couch, carefully cradling Flora in my arms. She stirs a little, and slowly, her blue eyes pop open. She blinks once. Twice.

"Uncle Adam?" she asks softly.

"Yes, Flora?"

"I'm hungry."

I laugh. "I can fix that."

"Oh, um, about that..." Quinn winces. "Are you aware you have almost *nothing* in your fridge or cabinets? I used the last of the lunchmeat for Flora's sandwich and gave her some chips I had in my bag *and* the last of my butterscotch candies, which you now owe me a bag of, by the way."

Fuck. I knew I needed to do some shopping, but I didn't realize I needed to do it that badly. I'm glad Quinn could find something for Flora's lunch, but does that mean she didn't eat?

"We're going to dinner, then the store. Get your shoes on." I look down at Flora. "Would you like me to carry you to your chariot, Princess Flora?"

My niece giggles as I carry her to the door. "Yes."

"Wait!" Quinn calls after us, tripping over the many blankets—where the hell did she find all those? —trying to catch up. "Dinner? I—"

"Have been here all day and need to eat. Shoes. Let's go."

Her eyes narrow to slits, her lips turning down, and I know she's a second away from arguing about this. I really don't want to hear it.

"Hayes, you are *not* taking me to dinner."

As if on cue, her stomach growls—*loudly*. Even Flora's brows rise at the noise.

"Your body says otherwise. Now, are you going to

stand here and argue with me, or are you going to get in the car and go to dinner with us? I bet Flora would love to spend more time with you, right, kid?"

She nods eagerly in my arms. I shouldn't be leveraging her against Quinn, but she shouldn't be so damn stubborn, either. I should have also made sure there was enough food in the house today, but that was then, this is now, and I'm trying to fix that fuckup, okay?

Quinn smiles softly, and I know it's a smile for Flora and Flora alone. "All right. I'll come. But I'm getting fries, and you're not allowed to have any."

I squeeze my brows together. "O...kay?"

She rolls her eyes. "Not you. *Her.*"

Flora giggles. "Deal."

I wonder what that's about, but I figure I'll learn soon enough.

Quinn follows us to the car, and I drop Flora to her feet to open the door. She climbs into the SUV, buckling herself into her booster seat—something I had no idea was even a thing until some mom went off on me in the grocery store parking lot—then I hop into the front just as Quinn is sliding in too.

"This is nice," she says, looking around. "Still has that new-car smell."

"You think this is nice, wait until you see what I have hidden away in the garage."

I haven't had a chance to take my sports car out lately, but maybe if this arrangement with Quinn works out, I can change that.

I back out of the driveway, heading toward the little diner I know Flora loves to eat at. We're quiet on our way there, Flora reading a book she keeps stashed in the seat pocket and Quinn sitting oddly still next to me as I navigate rush-hour traffic. We finally pull into the lot twenty minutes later and pile out of the car.

"Hayes!" Tex, the owner, calls as we walk through the door of the retro-looking establishment. This is another place Flora and I come far too often, but the food is cheap, and Flora likes it, so it's good enough for me. "Grab a seat wherever, and I'll be right over."

I let Flora lead us to our table and watch as she slides into the aqua and white vinyl booth. I go to get in next to her so Quinn can have her own side, but Flora holds her hand up.

"May I please sit next to Miss Quinn?"

I look down at the tawny-haired woman trying to hide her smile and shrug.

"All right, little flower," Quinn tells her as she scooches in next to her. "But only if you promise to drop the Miss part. It's just Quinn."

"Okay, Just Quinn."

Holy shit. Flora made a joke! I've never heard her

make one before. It's so...strange. And normal. So fucking normal, and I love it.

I slide in opposite them, trying not to gape at her with surprise. If she notices my delight, she doesn't say anything. She's too busy rearranging the sugar packets so they're all facing the same way and are tucked down into their holder nice and neat.

"Well, I didn't realize we had royalty in the building," Tex says, appearing at the end of the table, his tattoos peeking out from under his black polo as he passes out two adult menus and one kids menu. I don't know why he's bothering with one for Flora and me, as we always get the same thing. "Should I bow?"

Flora's cheeks flush red, and she shakes her head, sliding down in the booth a little.

Tex laughs. "Good to see you again, Hayes. Are the Serpents ready to bring us the Cup this season?"

"I hope so. Looking forward to getting back out on the ice."

Being out there today felt good, but it wasn't enough. Hell, I don't think it'll ever be enough. When I fell in love with hockey, I fell hard, and now it's like an addiction I can't seem to shake.

"Good. We're going to be rooting for you." He claps me on the shoulder. "You want your usual drink?"

"Please."

"No problem." He turns to Flora. "And for you, Your Majesty?"

"Chocolate milk, please, Mr. Tex."

"I had a feeling you'd say that." He grins at her before turning to Quinn. "Looks like we got a crasher. What'll it be, sweetheart?"

Something unfamiliar shoots through me as Tex smiles down at Quinn. I like the guy well enough, but I don't at all like that he just called Quinn *sweetheart*.

"Diet Coke, if you got it."

"Sure thing." He winks at her. "Be right back with those."

I scowl after him, not bothering to pick up my menu like Quinn. She peruses it for only a moment before setting it back down.

"You find something?"

She shrugs. "All diner food is the same. As long as I get fries with my meal, I'm good with whatever." She turns to Flora. "What are *you* getting?"

"Grilled cheese with pickles."

"Pickles?" Quinn wrinkles her nose. "You like those things?"

Flora nods. "I *love* them."

It's one of the few things I try to keep stocked in the fridge, especially after I caught her sneaking them in the middle of the night the first week she lived with me. Since then, I make sure we always have a jar, just in case.

"Well, I knew you had to have at least one flaw." Quinn ruffles her hair, careful not to mess up her crown.

Speaking of…

"Where'd the crown come from?"

"My teddy bear," Flora answers. "It fell off, and Just Quinn fixed it."

Ah. So that's why it looked vaguely familiar.

"I found some super glue in the hall closet and patched it right up. Then, we both agreed crowns belong to princesses, not stuffed animals. Right, little flower?"

Flora nods.

It's not the first time Quinn's called her *little flower*. I have no idea where the nickname came from, but I don't miss the way Flora's eyes light up every time it's said.

"All right. Here are those drinks for you." Tex passes out our cups, then grabs his pen and paper. "What'll it be?"

"Usual for us two," I say, wagging my finger between me and Flora.

"Grilled chicken sandwich with chipotle mayo and tomatoes. Fries for the side. And a grilled cheese with pickles. Got it." He jots it all down before looking at Quinn. "And for you, sweetheart?"

I grind my teeth at the pet name.

"I'll take a bacon cheeseburger, medium rare, with no lettuce, a side of fries, and a big bowl of mayo, please."

He lifts his brows. "A woman who eats. I like it." He scribbles her order down, then tucks his pen away. "All right. I'll get this in. Shouldn't be too long of a wait."

He hurries off to the ordering station, leaving the three of us sitting in silence. It's not awkward, but it's not comfortable either. It reminds me a lot of those oddly tensioned meals I used to have when I was a kid.

I clear my throat. "Did you have fun today, Flora?"

She lifts her head from her sugar packet project, her vivid cerulean eyes shining with delight. "We built a fort."

"*Two* forts," Quinn corrects. "Can't forget the one in the living room."

Flora scrunches her nose. "I don't think that one counts. It kept falling on us."

"Fort building is a very complicated skill."

"Didn't look that hard to me." The kid shrugs.

Quinn crosses her arms over her chest. "Well, if you're so good at it, *you* get the blankets down from the top shelf next time."

"I can't reach. I have little arms." Flora tosses her arms in the air.

"Then quit bragging about your fort-making skills, Little Arms."

Little Arms huffs, but she's grinning while she does it. It's the most playful I've ever seen my niece, and I'm almost jealous of Quinn's ability to come in here and bond with her as she has. It's not that I want to be building forts with a seven-year-old or anything, but it's good to see the kid being...well, a kid.

"What about you, Hayes?" Quinn asks, bringing me into the conversation, like she's sensing how I'm feeling. "Did you have fun today?"

"Yeah, Uncle Adam. Did you have fun today?"

I grin at her echo. "Well, it wasn't fort building, but I did get to skate, and I always find that fun."

Flora tips her head to the side. "What's it like?"

"Skating?"

She nods. It's the first time she's ever asked me about my career. She obviously knows what I do from me taking her to the rink all the time, but she's never been curious enough to ask more about it.

"Well, it's fuc—*fudging* magical," I say, stopping myself from cussing at the last second. I'm sure she's heard worse from living with her father, but still. "It feels like you're floating almost."

She screws her lips up. "Like when you're in the bathtub and you lie on your back?"

"Yes, exactly like that." I point at her. "Only this time, you're standing upright, and the wind is whipping against your face and it's *fun*. The best feeling in the world. It's my favorite thing."

Her eyes widen like she can't believe what she's hearing. "Can I try it?"

Now it's my turn for wide eyes. "You want to try skating?"

She nods. "I think it would be fun. And you do it…"

Pride swells through me. She wants to skate. Like me.

Skating is what kept me going when I was younger. It was the only escape I had from my parents and Aiden and all their bullshit. If I hadn't had the local rink where I spent absolutely all my free time, I'm not sure how my life would have ended up.

"Then we'll go skating," I promise, sure I can figure out a way to get her out there soon.

"Wait. Is it cold?" she asks, suddenly looking a little worried, like she's just realized we'll be on ice.

Quinn laughs. "Don't worry, I'm sure Uncle Adam will bundle you right up and you won't even realize you're on ice."

Adam.

She hasn't said my name before. It's…strange. And even stranger that I don't hate it. I always prefer to be called Hayes—have since I started playing hockey—but hearing it now…well, it's not the worst thing ever.

"Coming in hot!" Tex warns.

We move our glasses out of the way as he sets our plates in front of us.

"You folks need anything else, you holler," he says before leaving us to our dinner.

The second the scent of the chicken sandwich hits my nose, my stomach grumbles, and I realize just how hungry I am after my workouts today. I pick it up, taking a massive bite before it even registers that Quinn's not touching her food.

I swallow. "What's wrong?"

"They forgot her pickles. I'll be right back."

She rises from the bench seat, ready to charge after Tex in Flora's honor.

"Wait." I hold my hand up. "They didn't forget them." I point to the grilled cheese. "They're in there."

She wrinkles her nose. "They're…in the sandwich?"

Flora looks up, her teeth clamped around her grilled-cheese-and-pickle sandwich, looking completely innocent as she digs into the monstrosity.

I laugh at the disgust as Quinn watches her. "Yes, they're *in* the sandwich. Gross, isn't it?"

"Does that mean you fibbed earlier when you said you don't eat weird stuff?"

Flora giggles around her sandwich, shaking her head. She swallows down the huge bite of the horrid combination. "It's not weird. It's good."

"Whatever you say, kid." Quinn shrugs, reaching over her for the ketchup, then flipping open the top and squeezing a huge glob right into the big bowl of mayo on her plate. She picks up a fry, stirs the concoction up with it, and eats it.

Now *I'm* completely disgusted, and one look at how Flora's lips are turned down and her brows are furrowed tells me I'm not alone.

"What?" Quinn asks with a shrug. "It's not weird, it's good, remember?" She holds a fry out to Flora. "You want to try?"

"I thought I wasn't allowed any."

"I mean, you *did* make faces earlier when I told you I love ketchup and mayo with my fries. However, I'm willing to make an exception…but only once. Mostly because I know you're going to love it."

Flora doesn't look like she believes Quinn one bit, but she surprises me by reaching for the fry. "Fine."

She gingerly dips just the tip of it into the mayo-and-ketchup mixture and tentatively bites into it. At first, she seems unsure, but then her eyes brighten, and I know Quinn's just coaxed her over to the dark side.

"Do you like it?" Quinn asks, and the kid nods eagerly. She laughs. "See? I told you so."

She takes a handful of the fries off her plate and sets them on Flora's, putting the repulsive blend on the table between them.

A dipped fry is shoved my way. "You want to try?"

"I'd rather eat a trash-can-flavored donut with extra rotten banana slivers on it."

Quinn looks confused, but Flora? She howls with laughter, and I love every second of it. Unfortunately, that's how I spend the rest of my dinner—watching them enjoy their weird meals while I eat my very normal chicken sandwich and plain fries. They share looks, giggling like they have their own inside jokes already when they've only spent a day together, and I know one thing for sure—Flora needs Quinn. This is what she's been missing.

"May I use the restroom?" Flora asks after we're finished with our dinner.

"Of course." Quinn scooches from the bench, letting her out. "We'll be right here when you get back."

She watches Flora the whole way to the bathroom, not sitting down until she makes it safely inside. The diner is small, and there's an extremely slim chance anything could happen to her here, but I admire Quinn's protectiveness.

"So," she says as she settles back on the bench, "did I pass your test today? Am I hired?"

"Do you *want* to be hired?" I toss back.

Are you sure you're ready for this? That's what I'm really asking her.

"I had more fun today than I've had in a long time, and I really like Flora. So, if you're on board, I'm on board."

"Even if it means living with me?"

She rolls her eyes. "I think I can manage," she says indifferently, but I don't miss how her hands tremble as she picks up her Diet Coke, taking a long pull.

I hold my hand out to her. "Should we shake on it?"

She sets her drink down, wiping her hand on her thigh before extending it out my way. Our palms slide together, hers still a little damp from holding her glass, mine covering hers almost completely.

"Deal?"

"Deal," she echoes.

We shake.

And I pretend I don't like the feel of her hand against mine.

CHAPTER 8

QUINN

I am woefully underprepared. I've been slowly packing a few things over the last few days, but I still have a good portion of my apartment to go, and the movers are set to arrive shortly.

I'm never going to be ready in time. As I look around at the piles of junk I have stacked everywhere, I can't help but think, *Where the hell did I ever get the money to afford all this?* Then I look at my stack of maxed-out credit card bills and remember, *Oh, yeah. I didn't.*

I sigh, tossing yet another bill to the side. I've been good about not spending money this last week, and not just because I've had to be since I'm living on my last paycheck from The Dock, but because I know *something* has got to give when it comes to my spending habits. I'm too old to be screwing around like this. I need to get my life on track and fast.

Flora is the key to all that. I had so much fun with her on Monday and can't wait to do it again. I never thought I'd actually be excited to babysit, but I am. She's full of curiosity and has that old-soul type of vibe that just makes being around her a delight. Plus, I love to make her laugh, especially because she seems like she could use it so much.

Hayes on the other hand… Well, I'm looking less forward to having to spend time with him. I wonder if he's always been so grumpy and uptight or if that's new for him. I could have sworn my brother mentioned before that he's a troublemaker, but I just don't see it now.

We discussed a little more of my duties, including him making sure I'm CPR certified—I am, thanks to my summer stint as a lifeguard—and me living there full-time and taking care of Flora when he's on the road and when it's gameday. On the other days, I'll be allowed to do whatever I want with no obligation to the kid. It's like I'm her cool aunt coming to stay for a while, only it's for the next seven months, and that's *if* they don't make the playoffs.

Then I remember how much he's paying me, and I tell myself I can endure anything for seven months, even if it means living with a guy who clearly doesn't like me.

I grab a pair of shoes—one of entirely too many—

and examine them. They're black booties and can go with almost anything, but so can the other three pairs of nearly identical ones I already have in my keep pile. I toss them into the donation box before I have a chance to think about it anymore…then grab them right back out two minutes later because I just can't bear to part with them.

Small steps, right?

I repeat this process over and over, the donation pile staying eerily the same height while my other boxes fill up. I glance at the clock on the oven that's been taunting me since I rolled out of bed this morning. I only have an hour until the movers get here.

"Ugh, there's no way I'm going to get everything done."

There's just too much stuff to go through and only one of me. I need help.

A knock sounds at my door as if I've manifested someone on the other side. The only problem is I don't *know* anyone else except my mother, who is certainly still at the bakery at this point. She was overjoyed when I told her I accepted the job with Hayes, so maybe she decided to stop by anyway…

I toss aside the three purses I'm holding, then dodge piles of other stuff as I make my way to the door. I grab the knob, ready to pull it open, then pause.

I don't know who could be on the other side. It could be my landlord here to harass me for more of the rent I still owe. Or a kidnapper. Who knows.

"Who is it?" I call out.

"The fucking milkman. Who do you think it is?"

Hayes?

I yank open the door to find him leaning against the frame. The first thing I notice is that he's huge. Like the taking-up-the-entire-doorway kind of huge.

The second is the backward baseball cap that sits on his head with a Seattle Serpents S stamped on it. I've never seen him with his rust-colored hair pushed back. It makes his eyes stand out even more.

The third thing is the tattoo on his forearm, one I haven't noticed before because every time I've seen him, he's been wearing long sleeves. I never pegged him for an ink guy, but I don't hate it. At all.

"What are you doing here?"

He holds up a roll of tape as if that's supposed to explain everything. "Moving you, obviously."

"Obviously? I didn't realize that was obvious at all. How did you even get my address?"

"You gave it to me."

"I—"

Crap. I did. Hayes had me write all my info down so he could give it to his "people"—whoever the hell they are—and we could make this job official. I never thought he'd use it for any other reason.

"Are you going to let me in?" he asks. "Or did you plan on spending all afternoon glaring at me?"

"I thought you were hiring a moving company."

"He did," a new voice says, and Hayes steps out of the way to reveal a familiar-looking face. He steps forward, extending his hand my way. "Hello, ma'am. I'm Fox. It's nice to meet you."

I shake his hand, noting his bright white smile, perfectly straight teeth, and amber eyes.

"Fox. You're the goalie, right?" He nods. "That save you made with your skate last season was incredible."

Not that I'd ever tell my brother I sometimes watch Serpents games when I'm supposed to be rooting for his team instead.

His cheeks flush, and he shuffles his feet.

"*Howdy, ma'am. I'm Fox. By golly, it sure is awfully nice to meet ya,*" another guy mocks with a roll of his eyes.

"I didn't even say howdy." Fox shoves the second guy, who barely stumbles.

He pushes him back and steps up with a grin. "Hey, I'm Lucas Lawson, but my teammates call me Lawless Lawson. We're your moving crew."

I lift my brows. "Lawless Lawson? Seriously?"

Hayes and Fox snicker.

"Shut up," Lawson growls. "Lawson will do just fine."

I roll my lips together, repressing my laugh. I wave them into my apartment. "Well, if you're here to move me, we better get started."

They crowd into my tiny apartment—which now suddenly feels infinitely smaller—looking around at the mess I've made.

"Um, so, did a moving company already come through?" Fox asks, his eyes wide as he takes it all in.

There are piles of clothes and kitchen items and stacks of boxes, but that's about all the heavy lifting there is to do out in the living room.

"Nope," I say, following behind them, snatching up an old bra and tucking it behind my back. "I've sold all my furniture over the last few days to pay my back rent, so it's just all this stuff, plus my bedroom and the spare room, which is honestly a lot more of this."

The guys all exchange a look.

"What?" I ask, not liking it one bit.

"You sold your furniture?" Hayes asks.

"Yep. Couch, TV, TV stand. Those went super fast on Marketplace. The kitchen table and chairs were a little slower but eventually went, too. Even sold my bookshelves for twenty-five bucks each."

His brows slant together. "Does that mean you've just been inviting strangers into your home?"

I don't like the way he's talking to me, like I'm Flora being reprimanded.

I lift my chin, crossing my arms over my chest. "*You* just brought strangers into *my* home."

"I know those fuckheads."

"Hey!" Lawson says, looking truly offended.

Fox just shrugs.

"That's completely different than just handing out your address to random people over the internet," he continues as if Lawson never said a word.

I want to kick him out. Or in the balls. I haven't decided which.

"That's just reckless and stupid and—"

"Are you finished?" I interrupt.

"Excuse me?"

"Are. You. Finished?" I repeat, slower this time, just to make sure he understands me. "Because I sure am. I did what I did, and it's over now. So, if you're finished scolding me like a child, I'd like to get this place packed so we can get this reckless and stupid shitshow on the road, *boss.*"

The room is completely silent, not a single noise to be heard. Then Lawson bursts out laughing, his body doubling over as he clutches his stomach and howls.

Fox whistles lowly. "Pretty sure she just put you in your place." He claps Hayes on the shoulder twice, his grin wide. "Come on. Let's get packing."

Hayes inhales sharply like he's ready to go another round, but to my surprise, he drops it.

"Fine. Where do you want us to start?"

I point to my bedroom, which is all packed and ready to go. All right, fine, so this huge pile out here is *from* my bedroom, but still. "In there. Everything can go in the truck."

"Yes, ma'am." Fox tips an invisible cowboy hat as he walks by with Lawson—who is still laughing—trailing after him.

Hayes stands there a moment, not moving and still glaring at me. I raise a single brow, letting him know I'm ready to go toe-to-toe anytime he is. I have no problem telling off people I care nothing about. It's probably why The Dock didn't want to keep me around much longer. If customers got rowdy, I let them have it.

It's the people I *do* care for that I have a little more trouble with, like my siblings or my dad and his disappointed glances.

But not Hayes. I have no problem standing up for myself when it comes to Hayes.

He takes three steps, closing the distance between us. His eyes look nearly white this close, and he smells faintly of cedar and something sweet—maybe my mother's bakery. He's so imposingly tall I have to tip my head back to meet his heated stare.

"When you're living with me, just try to remember my house isn't open to the public, okay?"

Then he brushes by me, marching into my bedroom and leaving me gaping after him.

And I wonder if I've just made a big mistake agreeing to move in with him.

The guys spend the next few hours moving the rest of my big furniture, then start clearing out the boxes I'm finished with. I'm so behind that they spend more time standing around and goofing off than actually moving anything.

I feel so bad I order them a few pizzas, which I refuse to let Hayes pay for even though he tries. I don't care if it is the last of the money I made selling my furniture—I'm feeding them.

"All right. What's next?" Lawson asks, hands on his hips after finishing his fifth slice of pepperoni and mushroom.

I severely underestimated how much these guys could eat. Only two slices are left, and I haven't had even one.

My stomach growls at the thought, and I realize I haven't eaten yet today. Or dinner last night. I've been saving all my money to get me by until I get my first check from Hayes, and I ran out of ramen noodles yesterday at lunch. Hell, I haven't even had my usual butterscotch candies.

"Well, let's see," I say, looking around the apartment and ignoring my hunger. I'll worry about food later. I want to get this done so I don't waste more of their time. "I'm almost done with these piles, then all these boxes will be ready to go. After that, we just have my spare bedroom, but that's where I moved all my most precious stuff so it didn't get crushed."

"Are those all clothes?" Fox asks, and I try not to notice the judgment in his tone as I hold up a shirt, weighing if I want to keep it.

I toss it in the keep pile, then grab another.

"You know, my sister started an online store this way. She had a ton of clothes she never wore, so she sold them all and made some good cash. I mean, I'm not saying you have to, of course. Just a thought." The goalie rushes the last part out.

"Thanks, I'll—"

"Here." I look up from the blouse I'm holding— one that still has the tags—and am surprised to find Hayes standing over me. He's holding a napkin, a slice of pizza on top of it, and it's extended my way. "Eat."

"What?"

He shakes it at me. "Eat. Before these dicks finish it off before you get any."

"I only had"—Lawson counts the number of slices he's eaten on his hands—"six pieces!"

Damn. I was off by one.

"Are you sure?"

Hayes rolls his eyes. "I'm sure. I can hear your stomach growling over there. Eat."

I don't understand him. Just earlier, he was bitching at me for being careless, and now he's feeding me for the second time. I need this guy to decide whether he's going to be a jerk or not.

"Thanks," I mutter, accepting the pizza. It's cold by now, but I don't care. I'm too hungry to care. I bite into it and should be embarrassed by the noise that leaves me, but I'm not. It's the best thing I've had to eat in days. "Oh god. This is so good." I close my eyes on a moan, the pepperoni and mushroom flavor exploding over my tongue. It's not even close to my favorite kind of pizza, but right now, it tastes just like heaven.

When I drag my eyes back open, Fox and Lawson are already heading for my spare bedroom to get started in there.

Not Hayes though. No. He's staring right at me, his eyes narrowed just a bit and his nostrils flaring.

"What?" I sigh. "Is there a problem with the way I'm eating my pizza now?"

He doesn't say anything, just turns on his heel and marches out of the room.

Okay, weirdo.

I finish off my slice, then toss the napkin in the trash and sort through the rest of my clothes as the guys carry box after box from the spare bedroom. I used some of the money I earned from selling my furniture to rent a cheap storage unit for my things until I can figure out what else to do with them. I think it's going to be a lot fuller than I anticipated.

When I finally have the last of my wardrobe packed away—along with two massive heaps of things to be donated—I wander into the other bedroom to see how it's going.

"Holy crap," I say, taking in the nearly empty space. "You guys really cleared this place out."

"Yep. Almost finished," Lawson says, walking past me carrying two boxes.

"We'll be out of your hair in no time, ma'am." Fox's arms are just as loaded down as he makes his way from the bedroom.

"Would have been done even sooner if we didn't have to keep repacking boxes because you're not filling them enough." Hayes grabs a box labeled *Books*, then shakes it. "Like this. It's practically empty. We can add more."

The events of last night slam into me—me walking

around my apartment packing up all my most embarrassing items and stuffing them into boxes so the movers wouldn't see anything I didn't want them to. My heart is no longer in my chest. It's in my throat. It's in my ears. It's making my head throb as Hayes pulls back the cardboard flaps.

"No! Stop!"

I rush forward, falling to my knees just inches away from him, but it's too late. *I'm* too late. The box is open, and he's looking down into it.

Right at my sex toys.

Time stands still and so do we, neither of us moving or saying a word. I hold my breath, waiting for him to do something, *say* something—*anything*! But he doesn't.

He swallows once, then grabs a stack of *actual* books and sets them on top before quickly closing the box back up and rising to his feet. I stay there, on my knees, watching him go with all my special toys right in his hands. I can't quite decide what's worse—the fact that he didn't say anything or the fact that I definitely saw the outline of his cock.

And he was hard.

CHAPTER 9

HAYES

She has a box of sex toys.

A box!

Not one or two, but a whole fucking variety pack of them—one for each day of the week and then some.

I haven't been able to stop thinking about it the entire day—not when we closed the door on the rental truck, nor when we unloaded more boxes into her storage unit than at the donation center. Not even when Fox and Lawson helped me get her stuff moved into my house and then left me there alone with just her, as Flora is out with Hutch and Auden for the day. I haven't been able to stop thinking about it all, and I wish to fuck I could.

Especially the part where my dick got hard. It's not my fault, though. I saw them, and my mind immediately went to sex, something I haven't had in months, which isn't the norm for me. Truthfully, though, until today, I haven't given my newfound abstinence much thought. I've been far too busy trying to be a functional adult for Flora to even worry about the next time I'm getting laid. Given my history, I'm sure most people agree that isn't a bad thing.

Now that the thought has crossed my mind, it's right at the forefront, and it's all thanks to Quinn and her damn box of sex toys. I wouldn't mind taking them for a spin. Does she use them regularly? Where does she use them? In her bed, her hand tucked under the blankets and hidden like she's doing something naughty? Or does she spread her thighs without a care in the world? Is she loud, or does she moan softly? Does she—

The floor squeaks, and I spin around like I've been caught doing something I shouldn't be—and I guess I have. There my new roommate stands, her brown hair in a braid that hangs over her shoulder, wearing an oversized cream-colored sweater, her jeans dark and form-fitting. Those damn ridiculous earrings she loves so much dangle from her ears, hippos in tutus today. Flora would love them.

"Thank you."

"For what?"

"For helping me move. And for the bag of

butterscotch candies I found in my room. You didn't have to do that."

I shrug. "I owed you, remember?"

She smiles, and I hate how much I like it, especially when the dimple near the bottom of her lip pokes through.

"So I was wondering…" She tucks a loose strand of hair behind her ear. "Could you give me a hand with moving my dresser? It's not quite where I want it."

It's the first thing she's asked of me since I saw her sex toys, and I find it amusing how timid she is asking such a simple question.

"Sure. I just called in some Chinese. I hope that's okay. Hutch and Auden should be back with Flora around the time the food arrives. I promised them dinner for watching her today."

She nods. "That sounds good. I'm excited to see her."

I grin. "She's been talking nonstop—or at least as nonstop as Flora talks, meaning she's mentioned it more than once—about how she can't wait for you to live here with her. I think…I think you make her happier than she's ever been before."

Quinn frowns. "That's heartbreaking. She's seven. Her life should be nothing but happiness."

Sometimes, with my life now, I forget that not

everyone's had the same childhood. I can relate to
Flora and her shitty upbringing far more than I care to
admit. I was a lot like her at her age, quiet and
uncertain around other people. Then I grew up and
realized I could use those people like they've used me
all their lives—I could get lost in them, escape the dark
corners of my mind. So, that's what I did...and it bit
me in the ass more times than I can count.

I hope that's not what Flora is doing with Quinn
and whatever bond they're forming is genuine. Flora
needs that. And I might need it too.

That's later though, something way far down the
road when I'm at a more stable point in my life and
not barely hanging on.

"Lead the way," I tell Quinn, nodding toward the
hall.

She turns, her absurd earrings swaying with the
movement, and I follow her to her bedroom, trying
very hard to keep my eyes off her ass and my mind off
her sex toys.

Fuck. There I go thinking of them again.

She leads me to her dresser, standing on one side
and pointing to another.

"I'd like it over there instead." She points to the
wall beside the window. "It'll give me more natural
light while doing my makeup."

I want to tell her she doesn't *need* makeup, but what

do I know? She could be wearing it right now, but I wouldn't even be able to tell. I've seen the magic women can work with that stuff. Sometimes, when I think they're wearing nothing at all, it's a lie.

"Sure. Ready when you are."

I grab one end of the dresser, she is stationed at the other, and we lift it. I hold the bulk of it so she doesn't have to do much of the work. If she notices, she doesn't say anything as we maneuver it to the spot she wants. She stands in front of the mirror, leaning forward to fix something on her face, presumably testing the light, and my eyes drop straight to her ass.

It's wrong. So fucking wrong. She's my new nanny, for fuck's sake. But I can't help it. Not when it looks so good in her tight jeans.

She stands up straight, and I snap my eyes away, pretending I wasn't looking, but the second our eyes collide in the mirror, I know one thing for sure—she saw. Her nostrils flare, but that's the only reaction I get before she spins and points to her bed.

"I want you there."

"Excuse me?"

Her eyes widen. "I… Uh…" She clears her throat. "I meant I want to move the bed too, so could you go over there?"

Oh. That makes more sense.

I move to where she's pointing, and we adjust the

bed to how she likes it. Why she didn't boss Lawson and Fox around to do this is beyond me. That's what I hired them for. And by hired them, I mean blackmailed them into it, reminding them I had pictures of them doing nefarious things from our last trip before Lawson became a good boy for his girl, Rory, and stopped going places with us. Fox just didn't want anyone to see that he certainly felt like a woman dancing in the aisles during the Shania Twain show we went to.

"You good over there?" I ask after getting my side situated.

"Ugh. No. I think a screw came loose on the headboard."

"Here. Let me."

I round the bed, snatching up a screwdriver, and squeeze in beside her. I'm not overly handy with tools, but I can at least tighten a few things to get them to sit right. I crank the screw down, then tighten two others, giving her headboard a shake. It's not going anywhere.

"There," I say, rising to my feet.

But it's a mistake because Quinn is *right there*, watching my every move, and I run right into her.

"Oh shit. Sorry, I'll just—"

"No, let me—"

We move at the same time, both in a panic to escape the other. Our feet tangle together, and we go tumbling right onto the bed. Instinctively, I roll my hand under her head to help break her fall, which is exactly how I end up on top of her, completely trapped and peering down into wide hazel eyes.

I should move—I know I should—but I can't seem to find the strength to do so. She's soft beneath me, her body pressed tight against my own as I fit perfectly between her legs. Am I imagining it, or did she just rock her hips against me?

Her lips are parted just slightly, and her breaths are uneven. She darts her tongue out, running it along her plump, rosy lips, and I track the movement. Are her lips sweet? Or does the taste of her match the sass and salt in her words? Will her kisses be soft and tentative, or will they be hard and passionate?

"Hayes, I…"

I kiss her.

I fucking kiss Quinn Benson because I can and because I want to and because she brought a box of sex toys into my house and I can't *not* kiss her right now. She groans against me, her hands crashing into my hair as she pulls me closer, and I let my full weight fall against her. It's a perfect fit, my hard cock right between her legs. I can feel the heat coming off her and I can't get enough.

She hooks her leg around my waist, and I run my hand down her side, cupping her ample ass and pulling her tighter to me. She moans a little and I use it as my chance, pushing my tongue through her lips and into her mouth.

I'm a fucking goner.

She tastes sweet, like those damn butterscotch candies she loves so much, and like everything I thought she would. But as good as it feels…as good as *she* feels…I know it's wrong. We shouldn't be doing this. *I* shouldn't be doing this.

But I also can't seem to stop.

Distantly, I hear a sound. Something familiar that I can't place, but the worry of it fades when Quinn drags her nails over my scalp with a light caress, her hips driving up into mine, and I rut against her like a possessed man.

Stop, my head screams.

Not a fucking chance, my body says.

"Yo, Hayesy!"

I pause. *Was that…?*

"We're back!" Hutch calls as I faintly hear the click of the front door, then the unmistakable sound of Flora's footsteps.

That has me snapping into action. I scramble off Quinn, who looks just as mortified as I feel, and I hold my hands out like I'm trying to tame a wild animal when that wild animal is me.

"Shit. Fuck. *Shit.* I—I—*Fuck.*" I scrub my hand

over my face...over my lips...anything to brush away the evidence of what I've just done. "I'm sorry. I—"

"It's okay," Quinn says, sitting up, her breaths heavy and her voice wobbling with panic. "We just got lost in the moment and..."

That's all she says, also unable to find the words.

I nod, swallowing thickly. "That won't happen again."

I march out of the room before I do something ridiculous like kiss her again. That *won't* happen again. It can't.

Even if I really fucking want it to.

"Thanks again for watching her," I say to Hutch as we dig through the remainder of the Chinese takeout container, both of us looking for whatever scraps we can get.

I thought I had ordered enough, but it was clear when Quinn dug into it that I was gravely mistaken. I guess I shouldn't have been surprised given how loudly her stomach growled earlier and the way she ate that slice of pizza like it was the first meal she'd had in days. Looking back now, it could have been.

"Noft a pro em," my captain says, his mouth full of

garlic chicken and brown rice. He chews and swallows. "Sorry. Not a problem, man. She was fun."

I tip my head to the side. "Really?"

He laughs. "All right, maybe *fun* isn't the right word, but she was easy. Didn't throw a fit and wasn't rude, so that's a successful outing to me." He shrugs.

I look over at Flora, who is seated at the dining room table we've only used one other time. Quinn is on one side of her, Auden across. They're debating their favorite Disney princesses, every now and then looking to Flora to chime in, who mostly says she hasn't seen a movie or doesn't know who they're talking about. And here I thought watching Disney movies was a rite of passage. Not for Flora, it seems.

I turn back to Hutch. "You don't think that's... unusual?"

He considers me a moment, then shakes his head. "Is she a little quieter than most kids? Sure. But is it unusual? Given that she's been thrust into this new life out of the blue, I'd say no, not unusual. She's likely just a little scared and maybe a little sad about not having her father around anymore."

Oh, I highly fucking doubt that. I bet she breathed the biggest sigh of relief the second she was placed in the care of literally anyone else. There's no way she misses that hellhole. When I flew out to get her, I took a detour by his house. I only made it three steps inside before I had to walk out or I was going to do something I'd majorly regret, like find the motherfucker and wring his neck myself.

But Hutch is likely right about the rest, or at least I hope he is. If not, that means my brother screwed her up worse than I thought, and it's going to be really hard to kick his ass when he's behind bars.

"You know," Hutch starts, setting his Chinese to the side, and I get the feeling this is about to be a serious conversation if he's putting his food down. "I haven't talked to you one-on-one much this offseason."

Oh god. Here it comes.

"How are you doing with everything that's going on?"

Yup. Knew he was gonna say that.

I sigh, setting my own food to the side. "I'm fine."

"Good." He grins. "I'm impressed, you know."

I shift from one foot to the other. "What do you mean?"

"By you. How you're handling all this."

I shrug. "No big deal."

"But it is," he argues. "You've come a long way. You're a good guy, and I'm proud of you."

I bet he wouldn't be so proud if he knew that not even an hour ago, I had my new nanny pinned to the bed and was kissing the hell out of her.

"You've matured over the last few months.

Definitely not that same punk-ass kid who came here from the Carolina Comets and caused trouble. You're older and wiser, and now you've got this big responsibility, and you're handling it." He glances over the dining table at Auden. "Way better than I handled shit when I had to make big decisions, that's for damn sure." He shakes his head like he's shaking away the memory of how things fell apart with them for a little while, then he looks back at me. "So, yeah, I'm proud. That's all."

I swallow down the emotion that claws at my throat. I didn't realize I needed to hear all that until now. This has been hard with Flora, and it feels good to be recognized for the work I've put in.

I nod once. "Thanks, Captain. I appreciate that."

He rolls his eyes when I call him captain. "Don't start that shit."

"Sorry, Captain." I smirk, then dodge the dish towel he flings my way.

"So," he says, flicking his head toward Quinn. "How's that going so far?"

I trail my eyes to the table where the girls are still talking, not paying us any attention at all. Quinn is now resting both elbows on the table, one hand propping her chin up and the other playing with her hippos-in-tutus earrings as she gives Flora all her attention. She's looking at her like the kid is saying the most important thing in the world, and for all I know, she could be.

As if she can feel my stare, Quinn turns, and our eyes lock for the first time since our kiss. All throughout dinner, we didn't even so much as glance in the other's direction. But now...now I feel like I couldn't look anywhere else even if I tried. I see her swallow, see how her lips part and her breaths grow heavier. I see the way she wiggles in her chair just the slightest.

Then Flora sets her hand on her arm, and all the tension bursts like someone just stuck a needle into a balloon. She's the first to look away, and thank fuck too, because if she'd looked at me like that a second longer, I might have forgotten I'm not supposed to kiss her again.

"Good, I guess. She just got here," I say, dragging my eyes back to Hutch.

He's staring at me, his lips tipped up in the corners, and now *I'm* the one wiggling. *Why the fuck is he looking at me like that?*

"What?" I mutter.

He just laughs, shaking his head lightly. "Nothing, man. Nothing at all."

But his words don't *feel* like nothing. They feel like something. Even so, as badly as I want to know what, I'm too damn chicken to ask.

Hutch and I transition to talking about the

upcoming season as we polish off the rest of the Chinese and the clock ticks closer to Flora's bedtime. Somewhere in the middle of our conversation, Auden and Hutch lock eyes, and Hutch turns to me and says it's time for them to go. It's as simple as that—one look, and they know what the other is thinking.

"Thanks again for watching Flora today," I say sincerely as I walk them to the front door.

"Any time." Hutch pats my shoulder, giving me that same proud grin he did earlier.

I fidget under his stare, trying to ignore it and how damn good it makes me feel.

"She's a doll." Auden smiles, then wraps me in a hug before I can protest.

Hutch glares at me over her shoulder, and I make a show of squeezing Auden extra tight.

"And Quinn, too," she says softly for only me to hear. "I like her a lot. Don't do anything to scare her off, okay?"

Oh you mean like kiss her on her first day of living with me?

I nod, releasing her before my captain breaks my hands and I can't start the season.

"I'll try."

"Good." She sends a wave to Quinn and Flora, then loops her arm into Hutch's. "Puh-*lease* tell me we're stopping for ice cream on the way home?"

He sighs, but there's no annoyance in it. It's pure

delight, and it's funny to see how deeply my grumpy teammate, who once swore off love, has fallen for his girlfriend. I'm betting there are wedding bells in their future sooner than either of them thinks.

I close the door behind them, then turn and point to Flora.

"It's bedtime for you."

For the first time ever, she groans in protest, and I'm not even mad about it because she's acting like a kid, not an eighty-year-old trapped in a little body.

"But can't I just have five more minutes?" she begs.

Quinn rolls her lips together, hiding her smile. "How about you take a shower, then I'll read you a story instead of going straight to bed, deal?"

She nods and races off toward the bathroom.

"No running!" I call after her for the first time, and I only kind of mean the words as she skids to a quick walk instead.

Maybe this was what she needed all along: being around people more, going out more often. Maybe she's more like me in that aspect than I realize.

I turn back to Quinn, who has disappeared completely.

Wait. No, not completely. She's in the kitchen, stacking the empty food cartons and tossing them in the trash.

"I didn't hire you as a maid, you know that, right? I have a housekeeper already. I don't need two."

"Are you saying you were going to leave this mess for them to clean up instead of picking it up yourself?"

I scoff. "No."

Though there's a small chance I would have. Okay, so a *big* chance. A lot of things may have changed around here since Flora came to me, but my gumption to clean up after myself only extends so far. I'm not a pig by any means, but I have been known to put off cleaning up a bit until the housekeeper comes.

"Well, I'm still cleaning up. You bought dinner, so it only feels right."

"You know this gig comes with free meals, right? I'm not going to expect you to cook for Flora and me every meal. And I'm going to be lazy more often than not and just grab whatever's quick."

She frowns, which isn't at all what I expected when I said *free meals*.

"You're a terrible hockey player."

I huff out a laugh because there is *no way* she's standing in my kitchen insulting my playing. "Excuse me?"

She shrugs, reaching into the cabinet under the sink and producing a container of disinfectant wipes. "I'm just saying. Your game starts with your diet, and if you're eating like crap, you're playing like crap. If I were getting paid three point seven five million a year to play a game, I'd want to make sure I'm earning the paycheck and not just showing up to cheer my buddies on from the bench."

She quotes my AAV as she wipes down the counter like she's been reading too many hockey blogs. Thing is…she has a point. I've been getting some variation of this lecture from older guys for a while now. First, it was Cameron Lowell, my last captain on the Carolina Comets. Then it was Locke and Hutch and even Pritchard, the really old veteran who hardly talks to anyone. I guess it wouldn't hurt to maybe pay attention to what they're saying.

"Fine. But you're still not expected to cook for me, got it? You're here for Flora, and that's it."

She flicks her hazel eyes to mine for only a moment, and I'm suddenly transported back to her room and her bed. That definitely didn't seem like she was here for Flora only. I need to fix that, set the record straight, and assure her that there will be absolutely no other incidents like that between us—never, not once. She needs to know she can trust me on that.

"Quinn, about earlier. I—"

"Done, Just Quinn!"

I whirl around to find Flora standing barefoot with

her pajamas haphazardly pulled on and her body still sopping wet and dripping onto the floor.

"That was an awfully fast shower, little flower," Quinn says, tossing the disinfectant wipe into the trash, then wiping her hands on her shirt as she walks by me, avoiding all eye contact.

"I was in there forever!" Flora argues.

"That was three minutes—*tops*. Are you sure you cleaned everywhere?" Quinn lifts Flora's arms like she's checking for dirt, and given that Hutch and Auden took her out to Discovery Park today, she really might be. "Did you make sure to get the fleas out of your hair?"

"That was *not* a flea! I told you it was just a leaf."

"Uh-huh. Whatever you say, kid."

Flora huffs playfully, and I'm not sure how long it'll take me to get used to this new side of her, but I hope it takes a while because I'm enjoying it far too much.

"Will you braid my hair like yours?" she asks.

Braid her hair? She's never asked me to braid her hair.

"Of course I will," Quinn says, guiding her toward her room. "Come on. I can braid while you read, and then we'll switch. Sound good?"

Flora nods and starts going on and on about the book they're reading, but that's not what's drawn my attention. It's the look Quinn is giving me over her shoulder—full of questions and longing and worry.

That last one isn't necessary. I'm not going to fire her over what happened. I was as much to blame for it as she was. We made a mistake. We slipped. It won't happen again.

It can't.

I grab another wipe from under the sink to distract myself and run it over the counter again, then make my way to the dining table to clean up the scraps of whatever's been left behind and wipe that down, too. I straighten things in ways I've never straightened them before, and when everything is back in the same place my housekeeper left it, I flip off the lights and pad down the hall, unable to stay away any longer.

Flora's light is out, but the rotating nightlight I bought her is casting just enough glow around the room so I can see them tucked into her bed together. Flora's eyes are heavy and she's barely able to keep them open as she rests her head on Quinn's shoulder. There's a book propped up on her stomach, and she's reading so softly I can barely make out the words.

Then suddenly, Quinn lets out a loud "Rawr!" that causes Flora *and* me to jump.

Both girls giggle, and Quinn closes the book.

"All right. That's enough for tonight. Some of us have school early tomorrow." She runs her hand over

Flora's head, smiling down at her. "Good night, little flower."

Flora sighs. "Good night, Just Quinn."

Quinn rises from the bed, and I scramble away, tucking myself into my bedroom just as she closes Flora's door with a soft *snick*. I watch through the crack in mine as she leans against the wood, exhaling heavily like she's exhausted from the day, and I wouldn't be surprised if she was between moving and everything else.

But there's something else to the sigh, like she's relieved almost. I move to ask her if everything's okay, but she beats me to it.

"You did it, Quinn," she says to herself. "You survived day one, and you didn't die, you didn't mess up, and you're not on the verge of being homeless, so you did it. Now, don't fuck this up just because he slipped up and kissed you earlier and you want him to do it again. Got it?"

She nods, answering herself like a completely crazy person. But that's not the part that gets me. It's what she said.

She wants me to kiss her again.

And fuck if I don't want to too.

CHAPTER 10

SERPENTS SINGLES GROUP CHAT

Lawson: HAYESY. Why'd you run away after praccy today? I had questions!

Keller: Probably because he's tired of looking at your ugly mug.

Lawson: My mug is NOT ugly. Rory thinks I'm hot.

Keller: Your mom thinks I'm hot.

Locke: Oh god.

Fox: Here we go.

Lawson: Actually, just this morning, my mom told me she's looking forward to this season but maintains that you, Kells, should have been traded over the summer.

Keller: Weird. Because she told me this morning that she wished she had swallowed.

Locke: OH FUCK.

Fox: Damn. He WENT there.

Hayes: Shit, I think even I might have to dip out of this one.

Hutch: Dude.

Keller: Holy shit. I think I might have actually gotten Lawson to shut the fuck up.

Lawson: Oh, don't worry. I'm still here. Just trying to figure out which of your legs I should break. Which one are you more partial to, left or right?

Keller: Please. Like you could ever get close enough to hurt me. I'm too fast for you.

Lawson: Yeah, right. We all know I'm the fastest one.

Keller: Bullshit.

Lawson: Want to bet? Race tomorrow?

Fox: I feel like I'm back in elementary school right now, two idiots seeing who is the fastest on the playground.

Hutch: You definitely have the idiots part right.

Locke: I'm betting Keller wins.

Lawson: WHITLOCKE! HOW DARE YOU!

Lawson: And to think I looked up to you.

Locke: You did not.

Locke: Did you?

Lawson: Well, now you'll never know.

Lawson: We're racing tomorrow, Kells, and I'm going to wipe the ice with you.

Keller: Fucking bet.

Lawson: Hayes? You still there?

Lawson: Hayesy?

Lawson: Here, Hayesy Hayesy! Here, boy!

Hayes: I'm not one of your dogs.

Hayes: What do you want?

Lawson: Um, did you not scroll up? I had a question and you bolted after praccy.

Hayes: Because I was tired of looking at your ugly mug.

Lawson: So you did scroll up, then. Good.

Lawson: How's it going with the new nanny? Has she ripped into you again? Because, man, that was a HOOT.

Hayes: Shut up.

Fox: It really was funny...

Hayes: Shut. Up.

Lawson: Well, is she working out?

Locke: I'm curious too.

Hutch: I'm curious AND pissed that I missed the kid getting his ass chewed.

Lawson: It was glorious. Next time, I'll take a video, and I'm positive there will be a next time.

Keller: I know someone else who deserves having their ass chewed.

Lawson: Can we not talk about your weird butt-biting kink right now? We're focusing on Hayesy.

Lawson: So...?

Hayes: She's working out. Flora loves her.

Lawson: And you?

Hayes: Do I love her?

Lawson: No, you shit-for-brains. How do YOU feel about her?

Hayes: I don't know. She's fine, I guess. Been busy with hockey. Haven't been paying her much attention.

Hutch: Hmm.

Hayes: What's that supposed to mean?

Hutch: Nothing.

Hayes: That didn't seem like nothing, so come on. Just say whatever you want to say.

Hutch: It really was nothing.

Hayes: Whatever.

Lawson: Someone's testy.

Keller: Probably needs to get laid.

Lawson: Is that why you're always grumpy, Kells? Because you need to get laid?

Keller: I got laid this morning. When your mom was at my house.

Fox: Damn, Lawsy. You walked right into that one.

Locke: Even I don't feel bad for you on that.

Lawson: You know, one of these days, you're going to meet my mother and you're going to feel terrible for ever saying such awful things about her. She's a lovely lady.

Hayes: Brave of you to let him meet her after everything he's said about her.

Keller: Aw, it's so sweet you're a momma's boy, Lawsy. Warms my fucking heart.

Lawson: Proud of it, too.

Fox: I also love my mother.

Hutch: Mine's the best.

Locke: My mom just sent me a box of homemade oatmeal cookies, so I'm pretty sure MY mom is the best.

Lawson: See, Kells? It's cool to love moms.

Keller: I love moms plenty. I just loved yours last night.

Lawson: That's it. I'm leaving the group chat.

Keller: FINALLY!

Lawson: Who am I kidding? I love you fuckers too much.

Lawson: Group hug?

Hutch: Fuck no.

Locke: Not happening.

Hayes: No fucking way.

Fox: I'll hug you, Lawsy.

Lawson: Knew I could count on you, Foxy.

Lawson: What? No comment, Kells?

Keller: Was just trying to find the most eloquent way to say I'd rather drink acid than ever touch you, but I think that about covers it.

Lawson: You love me. Just admit it already.

Keller: Absolutely not.

Hutch: I don't know. I saw you laugh at one of his jokes at praccy earlier.

Keller: Correction: You saw me laugh at HIM, not his joke. Big difference.

Hayes: That is a big difference.

Lawson: You're taking HIS side, Hayes? WTF?

Hayes: No.

Hayes: Well, sort of.

Lawson: And to think I loved you the most.

Hayes: You did not.

Lawson: You're right. I didn't. I love Fox the most.

Fox: Aw, thanks, man! I love you too!

Hutch: Now I'm curious. Who do you love second most?

Lawson: It goes: Foxy, Hayesy, then Lockey and Hutchy are tied.

Locke: We're tied? Why?

Hutch: How am I not higher? We're dating twins, for fuck's sake!

Lawson: *shrugs* Is what it is.

Fox: You left off Keller.

Lawson: But did I?

Keller: Don't worry. The feeling is mutual.

Hayes: Can't believe I'm second to Fox. That's bullshit.

Fox: I'm still so honored.

Locke: I'm a little offended I haven't beaten Hutch out in some way. There's no way we're tied.

Lawson: Too bad. You are.

Locke: I demand a recount!

Hayes: Me too!

Fox: I'm personally good with our ranking.

Locke: Shut up, Foxy.

Fox: Aw, come on. Let's all play nice now.

Keller: When do we ever play nice?

Lawson: IDK but we should start because you're awfully mean to me, Kells.

Hutch: He's just mean because he loves you.

Keller: TAKE THAT BACK RIGHT NOW!

Locke: Aw, that's cute, Kells. You love Lawson.

Keller: Do fucking not.

Hayes: You do too. Just admit it.

Keller: Never.

Fox: I don't know. I think you might.

Keller: I hate you all.

Lawson: I don't. I'm actually enjoying this quite a lot. It's nice not being the one who gets picked on for a change.

Hutch: Can it, Lawson.

Locke: Yeah, shut up.

Hayes: Fuck off, Lawsy.

Fox: Pipe down!

Lawson: Aw, man. You too, Fox?

Fox: You're right. I'm sorry.

Keller: Fox, you wimp!

Fox: Sorry!

Lawson: Keller, stop being mean or we're kicking you out of the group.

Keller: FINALLY!

Lawson: I'm just kidding. We love you too much.

Hayes: We love you, Kells.

Hutch: Love you, man.

Locke: Love you.

Fox: Love ya, bud.

Keller: Son of a bitch. Look what you started, Lawsy!

Lawson: I LOVE YOU, TOO, KELLER!

CHAPTER 11

QUINN

"Look, Just Quinn! Watch!"

"Wow! That's awesome!" I say for the tenth time in as many minutes.

I don't know how parents sit around and watch their kids jump off the same piece of playground equipment thirty times in a row and act amazed each time. Well, to be fair, I don't know how parents do this at all. I've only been with Flora for two weeks and I am beat. I wake up exhausted and go to bed even more worn out. And she's not even as rambunctious as other children her age. Compared to them, she's a walk in the park.

As tired as I am, I wouldn't trade it. I've been enjoying my time with her far more than I've ever enjoyed any other job, and it's even had me looking into courses to see what it would take to do something like this for a living. Then, of course, all my past failures come barreling into the forefront of my mind, and I click out of the browser before I let myself dream too much.

Flora jumps off the top again, then races to the stairs to do it again.

"How is she not tired yet?" I mutter.

"Because kids have an infinite amount of energy," a woman says as she takes the empty spot next to me. "Mind if I sit here?"

"Not at all." I scoot over to give her more room on the small bench I've been occupying for the last thirty minutes.

It's Monday, and I promised Flora we could go to the park for an hour after school, then grab froyo on the way home to celebrate surviving preseason together. She was thrilled with the idea and told me on the walk here that she didn't even learn anything in class today because she was too focused on watching the clock. I probably should have told her to pay attention in class, but her excitement was so contagious I didn't even care.

"Is this your first time here? Haven't seen you around before," my new seatmate says, her gorgeous emerald and gold snake earrings jostling as she gets situated.

I nod. "That obvious?"

She pinches her thumb and forefinger together. "Maybe a little."

I laugh, holding my hand out to her. "I'm Quinn. I just started nannying that one." I nod to Flora, who is *again* jumping off the platform by the slide.

"Gina, mom to that one over there." She points to a little girl who is on the swings and kicking her legs like her little life depends on it.

"She's adorable."

"*Rotten* is what she is," Gina says with a smile. "Is this your first nannying job?"

"It is."

"And how's that going for you? Ready to pull your hair out yet?"

Now I'm the one to pinch my thumb and forefinger together. "Maybe a little."

She laughs. "I can't say it gets any easier, but you do get used to it. Waverly is my fourth, youngest, and *final* baby. She's a breeze compared to my other children."

"Four children? Gosh, I must sound like such a wimp complaining about one."

"Not at all. No caretaker is exempt from how tough it can be. Unless, of course, you're nannying for that man because *good god*."

I peek over my shoulder in the direction Gina is looking, my eyes going right to the man I've barely seen for the last week while he was on the road.

Hayes.

His hands are tucked into his jean pockets, his hair is perfectly messy, and his beard is still in need of a trim. Even so, he looks like he just walked off the set of a photoshoot instead of leaving the rink where I know he's been all day, the Seattle Serpents t-shirt he's wearing proof.

Preseason was a success—as were my first overnights alone with Flora—and now Hayes is back for a few days before the regular season kicks off with a three-game homestand. While I'm sure Flora will be happy he'll be around more, I'm honestly not sure how I feel about it, especially after *The Kiss*.

It's been on a nonstop loop for the last two weeks every time I close my eyes, and I can't shake it. Can't stop thinking about how desperate I was for his touch. How he kissed me with such ferocity I swear my lips were still swollen the next day. The way his body felt against mine, heavy and warm like the perfect blanket on a cold winter night, like he was everything I didn't know I was missing all these years.

Then I remember the look in his eyes. The mortification. The remorse. The utter disappointment. As much as I wanted it, it was wrong. We shouldn't have done it. And I should have come to my senses a lot sooner than I did, certainly long before I wrapped my leg around his waist and dry-humped him.

I don't know Hutch and Auden all that well, but I could have kissed *them* for coming home when they did and putting a stop to it because I have no doubt our clothes would most certainly have come off if they hadn't interrupted. I cannot repeat the mistake of sleeping with my boss. I need this job far too much to let something like my unchained libido get in the way. So what if Hayes is easily the hottest man I've ever seen? I cannot and will not climb him like a tree…even if I really, really want to.

He must feel my stare on him, because when he looks up, our eyes collide, and I swear I see his brows cinch together more. I'm relieved by it. It's better than what I've been getting since *The Kiss*, which has been him fleeing from every room I enter and ensuring we are never, ever together alone. At least if he's scowling at me, he's back to not liking me. I can live with that.

"Oh, boy. That *is* the man you're nannying for," Gina says, her voice all breathy now, and I don't entirely blame her. "You're right. I don't feel bad for you at all."

I chuckle as Hayes approaches, his tall frame casting a shadow over us.

"What are you doing here?" I ask.

Is he here to check up on me? To see if I'm taking care of Flora okay? To make sure I'm doing my job?

He shrugs. "Called it good on practice a bit early, and I saw your text. Figured I'd stop by."

He looks over at Gina, then does something I'm not expecting—he smiles. And not just a small, *Hey there* sort of smile. It's a *real* smile—a big one. The kind I bet he's used many times on many women before. One he has a hell of a track record with.

"Hey," he says smoothly, still grinning. "I'm Hayes. Nice to meet you..."

"Gina," she offers with a smile of her own. "You're not Hayes as in Adam Hayes, are you?"

"Depends on who's asking." He winks.

He fucking winks! He's flirting with her. He's being playful. He's being...well, fun.

What the hell? Am I in some sort of alternate universe? The Hayes I know doesn't do that. He just sulks. Am I... Am I the reason he's like that?

Gina throws her head back with a laugh. "Oh, you're slick. I like that. My husband probably wouldn't, but I do. He's a big fan, by the way."

"Yeah? Here." He reaches behind him, producing a hat he must have had stashed in his back pocket. "Take this, then."

"You...what?" Her jaw drops as she takes it from his outstretched hand. "My husband is going to faint.

Hang on, I think I have a pen somewhere if you wouldn't mind signing it."

"Not at all."

As she digs around in her bag, Hayes looks out to the playground, searching for Flora, I presume. I can tell the moment he spots her, his megawatt grin back in an instant. He's not here to check up on me. He's simply here for Flora.

"Oh, found one!" Gina exclaims, shoving a pen Hayes's way.

"Great." He takes it and scribbles his name across the bill of the hat, then hands them both back to Gina. "You guys got tickets to the home opener on Saturday?"

She shakes her head. "We have four children. We can't afford that."

"Well, here, let me give you this number." He reaches behind him again, this time producing his wallet, then pulls out a card and hands it to her. "Call this guy and tell him I said to give you as many tickets as you need for the game, and we'll make it happen."

"Holy shit." She grabs her chest. "You're about to give me a heart attack."

Hayes laughs. "Don't do that. Then you won't be able to see us win on Saturday."

He winks again, and I swear Gina swoons.

"Mom! I have to pee!" A little girl who looks like a

mini Gina comes rushing over. "Hurry! I'm gonna pee my big-girl panties, and if I do that, I won't get ice cream, and I *really* want ice cream!"

Gina rises to her feet with a huff. "Duty calls." She looks at Hayes. "Thank you so much for your kindness. It…" Her eyes shine with emotion. "Well, it means a lot. These last few months…they've been so difficult, and this kind of thing never happens to us." She turns her attention to me. "You lucky girl, you."

I laugh. "It was great meeting you, Gina. Maybe we'll see you around sometime."

"I'm here nearly every day," she says as her daughter grabs her hand and drags her toward the bathrooms. She rolls her eyes, then gives us a wave before rushing along so there are no accidents.

Hayes takes the spot she's abandoned, and I bet passersby are getting quite a laugh seeing the two of us together with how giant he looks on the small bench.

"That was really nice of you," I say after a few quiet moments.

He shrugs like it's no big deal when it clearly is. He could have ignored her or lied about who he is or any number of things, but instead, he not only gave her a signed hat but also her whole family tickets. I don't understand how this man who walked over with his eyebrows basically kissing they were pulled so tight is the same man who just did all that. The same man watching Flora play like he's watching the most cinematic masterpiece he's ever seen.

"Do you guys come here a lot?" he asks, his attention still on his niece.

"First time. It's a celebration for surviving preseason."

His lips twitch. "For you or her?"

"Yes."

His chest rumbles with light laughter. "She seems happy. More like a kid."

I nod. "She does. She's still quiet and shy, but I think she's getting there. The first five minutes we were here she wanted to read her book instead of play. I finally coaxed her to go try it with a promise of a movie later tonight, and now I'm not sure how I'll ever peel her away."

"And you?" he asks, turning to me for the first time since he sat down. "You're doing okay? With…well, everything, I mean?"

I try to hide my surprise at him asking about me. "I'm good. It would be a straight lie if I said I was handling this with zero issues and wasn't having approximately five and a half mini panic attacks a day, but I'm managing."

He laughs. "Five and a half? Those are rookie numbers. I was having about five and a half every hour when she first got here. Shit, I still have about ten a day." He runs his hand through his hair, leaning forward and resting his elbows on his knees. "I'm not sure I'll ever get used to this."

"Can I ask—"

He stiffens before I even get the question out, and I instantly start backtracking.

"I'm sorry. I shouldn't have tried to pry. I—"

"It's okay. I guess you should probably know if you're going to be sticking around."

He sits back with a sigh, his eyes still tracking his niece as she runs around the playground. He doesn't speak for several tense moments, and when he does, it's not at all the story I was expecting to hear.

"My older brother decided dealing drugs was more fun than being a father. He got busted for running a ring in addition to a whole slew of other charges like assault and gun possession, and now he's serving a life sentence for it. I got a call in the middle of the night about her. Aiden and I hadn't spoken in years aside from his random drug-infused calls where he'd beg for money and I'd tell him to fuck off." He scoffs. "I had no clue she even existed until that phone call."

He…*what?*

I might not get along with my siblings all the time, but I can't imagine a world where I just didn't talk to them. Or one where I didn't know my nieces and nephews even existed. And for so many years? I can't fathom it.

"I guess her mom skipped out, and when child services tried finding her, they found out she died a few years ago," he continues. "My parents... Well, honestly, I have no idea what happened to them. I left for college, and I never looked back. They haven't been in the picture for a long, long time. I guess Aiden was all she had. I don't know exactly what kind of life she was living before, but whatever it was, it wasn't good. I might not know shit when it comes to kids, but I know for certain she's better off with me than she ever was with that dumbass."

He's clearly upset with his brother, and rightfully so. But there's also a twinge of pain and regret in his voice, and I know there are older wounds there he's not opening.

He rubs a hand over his beard. "Anyway, that's the short version of a very long story. So if you're wondering why Flora and I act like strangers sometimes, it's because we are."

"You're not strangers, Hayes. You're her family. That means something."

"In my experience, family doesn't mean shit."

"Family isn't always about the *actual* family we're born into. It's about the people we choose to let into our lives, the people we choose to love. And you're clearly choosing to love Flora, so, yeah, it does still mean something."

He swallows thickly, then nods once but doesn't say anything more, though I know there *is* more. There has to be. Nobody makes a statement like *Family doesn't mean shit* without a story to tell. I want to know his story more than I've ever wanted to know anything before, but it's not my business to ask.

"Uncle Adam!"

We both swing our heads to the tiny voice and find Flora running full speed toward us. Her long dark hair —which I assume she got from her mother or father— flows behind her, the ponytail I put it in before I sent her off to play long since destroyed. She races right up to him, skidding to a stop before running into his knees.

"I didn't know you were coming," she says between choppy breaths.

"Yep. I got off work early today, so I figured I'd swing by and crash your girls' afternoon. That okay?"

She nods several times. "You can come get frozen yogurt with us."

He looks at me, one eyebrow cocked. "Dessert before dinner, huh?"

I lift a shoulder. "I told you—we're celebrating."

His lips twitch. "Seems like a good enough reason

for me." He turns back to Flora. "Let me guess, chocolate with *extra* sprinkles?"

"*And* a cherry," she says with a grin.

"Wow. Big plans, huh? Well, then come on." He rises from the bench, taking her hand in his, and I follow behind them. "Let's go get some froyo, then dinner, since I guess we're doing things backward tonight."

"Can we have grilled cheese for dinner?"

He looks over at me, probably because he's hardly been home lately and likely has no idea what we do and don't have in the fridge. I mimic holding a shopping cart and grabbing things off the shelf like that old dance move.

He tips his head with a grin. *What?* he mouths.

I roll my eyes. *Shopping,* I say back.

He nods, finally understanding, then says to Flora, "We'll have to swing by the grocery store, but I can make that happen."

"Sweet," the kid says, and I have to roll my lips together to keep from laughing.

I have no idea where she picked that up, but I love it.

We meander over to the local froyo shop, where Flora piles about a pound of sprinkles—no exaggeration—onto chocolate goodness. I opt for butterscotch and far fewer sprinkles, while Hayes surprises me with his pick—watermelon topped with coconut. I wrinkle my nose at the blend.

"What?" he asks when he notices as we walk slowly to the grocery store, enjoying our treats.

"It's just...watermelon? Really? Out of all the flavors, you get that one?"

"I like watermelon."

"I *hate* watermelon. And coconut, for that matter."

"Yet you like butterscotch?" he says like it's the most disgusting flavor ever. "You must lead a sad, sad life."

"I don't like watermelon either," Flora announces.

"See?" I say as if that makes my opinion completely valid, even though I know for a fact she just had a watermelon popsicle two days ago.

Hayes shakes his head. "Can't believe you're turning my own niece against me."

"Can't help that I'm cooler than you."

"Yeah, Uncle Adam, Just Quinn is cooler than you."

"Hey! Watch it, or I'll become *extra* uncool and forget to put pickles in your grilled cheese."

She gasps. "That's... That's... That's not nice!" she sputters at his audacity.

We laugh at her, and warmth spreads through me. For the first time since *The Kiss*, things feel good.

Normal. *Natural.* And a lot like something I could get far too used to if I let myself.

"What is wrong with you?"

"Not a damn thing." Hayes grabs the order separator, moving it down the belt and behind my stuff for the third time.

I stomp my foot, well aware that I probably look more like a seven-year-old than the actual seven-year-old standing next to me, but I don't care.

"Stop moving it."

"No," he answers simply.

I grab the separator again, but before I can get far, Hayes snatches it out of the air, stopping me. I yank on it with a grunt. He yanks back. And I go right along with it.

Suddenly, Hayes is *right there*, his nose barely ghosting over the tip of mine. Having him this close reminds me of the last time he was this close, when he was on top of me, kissing me senseless, when I rocked my hips against him like some wanton girl unable to control herself.

"Knock it off," he growls, and it does nothing to

clear the images from my mind. "This is included in your job."

"We never discussed that. We—"

"Well, I'm changing the fucking rules," he argues. "So put your damn groceries with mine and stop arguing, or I swear, I'll—"

"What, Hayes? What will you do?"

He grins wolfishly, his light eyes flashing with something I can't quite put my finger on.

"Oh, Quinn," he says, his voice low and throaty. "I doubt you want me to answer that question in public, *especially* with little ears around."

He flicks his eyes down to Flora, who is watching us intently, which means she's also watching me make a complete ass of myself because I'm too stubborn to let her uncle pay for my groceries. He shouldn't be the one paying for my stuff given how much he's paying me to take care of his niece. I did some research, and he's overpaying me by a lot, especially with how little experience I have doing this. With fifty grand sitting in my bank account, the least I can do is pay for my own groceries. If not for the sake of my pride, simply so I don't go and do something reckless like spend it on clothes or shoes or handbags I really don't need given the overloaded storage shed I'm now paying for.

"Fine," I say, releasing the order separator, still

glowering at him. "But we're not done with this conversation."

He just laughs at my response, then proceeds to pay for the entire order, all the while flirting with the woman behind the register who keeps shooting daggers my way whenever he's not paying attention. After yet another fight, he *oh so graciously* allows me to help him carry the groceries back to the house. We follow behind Flora as she carries nothing but her jar of pickles, an extra pep to her step that wasn't there earlier.

"This is a terrible place to put this," I mutter as I slide a jar of pasta sauce onto a shelf that's way too high.

Hayes sighs, the paper bag crinkling as he pulls out more groceries. "And where do you suggest I put it?"

"Um, not so high that I need a step stool." I spin to face him. "Ooh! Can I rearrange your kitchen?"

He scowls. "No."

"Booo!"

"Booo!" Flora echoes from her spot at the kitchen table, where she's been coloring since we got home.

I laugh. "At least she's on my side."

"Still bullshi—poop"—Hayes catches himself at the last minute—"that you've turned my niece against me."

"She didn't. I still like you, Uncle Adam."

"Yeah, she still likes you, Uncle Adam," I confirm, and I don't miss the way his eyes darken when I tease him.

"I just like Just Quinn more."

She says it so casually I can't help but laugh loudly.

"What are you laughing at?" Hayes glowers at me, but I can see a twinkle in his eyes that wasn't there when I first met him.

I suspect this ordeal with Flora has changed each of them in ways they never anticipated, and the versions I'm starting to see are much closer to who they truly are.

I finish unpacking the groceries while Hayes takes charge at the stove, spreading butter over way too many slices of bread for just three people, then topping them with far too much cheese before tossing them onto a skillet. He loads one up with pickles, which makes me grin, even though it's disgusting.

When finished, he slides three plates onto the kitchen table—one with pickles, one plain, and one weighed down with three sandwiches. I follow behind him, dumping a handful of chips onto each plate before taking what's become my seat over the last few weeks. We chat over our meal, mostly Flora and me ganging up on Hayes, and then he slips off to do whatever he does while I get the kid ready for bed.

"And that, little flower, is why you don't need the

prince to rescue you. You're capable of rescuing yourself just fine. Got it?" I tell her as I close the book I've been reading for the last half hour.

She nods sleepily. "Got it, Just Quinn."

I lean over, nuzzling my nose against her forehead. "Good night."

"Night," she mumbles back as I crawl out of the bed and flip off her bedside lamp.

I tiptoe from the room, closing her door gently. The house is dark and quiet, the faint sound of water the only thing breaking the silence as I pass his room.

I pause.

Hayes is in the shower.

My mind reels with images of what he must look like under the spray, what shape his body must be in after all the training he puts it through for hockey. I bet his ass is perfectly sculpted, and it probably looks incredible as the water droplets slide over it.

God, Quinn, get ahold of yourself. He's your boss, for crying out loud!

I shake away the thoughts, pushing them to the dark corners of my mind that I pretend don't exist, then hurry through the house just as the water shuts off. Hayes finds me ten minutes later, in the kitchen with a mug of tea between my hands while I act like I wasn't just picturing him naked.

"Just got off the phone with my guy," Hayes says as

he pads into the room, looking entirely too good in a pair of black sleep pants that leave little to the imagination and a plain gray t-shirt that makes his eyes pop. "That lady at the park today—"

"Gina," I provide, taking a drink from my tea.

"—she claimed the tickets. I guess we'll be seeing them in the stands Saturday night."

"*We'll* be seeing them?"

"Yes. You and Flora are coming to my game, right?"

"I...I didn't know we were invited."

His brows are like magnets, always pulling together, inching inward once again. "Of course you're invited. Why wouldn't you be?"

I lift a shoulder. "I don't know. I just thought..."

I don't finish my sentence because I don't know what I thought. I figured he'd maybe want Flora there, but I didn't realize that would automatically mean I would have to go too. I'm not opposed to it. I love hockey, and I've watched Brody play my entire life. But being in the stands for him specifically feels... Well, I don't know exactly how it feels, but just thinking of it makes my lower belly warm.

"It'll, uh, be a first for me." He runs a hand through his still-damp hair. "I've never had anyone in the stands for me before."

"*Ever?*" The question comes out so incredulously,

and I hear it right away. "Sorry. I just… We go to all of Brody's games whenever he comes to town. We've even flown out of state for a few. We…"

I don't finish the sentence because I'm unsure what else to say. I can't imagine that nobody has ever shown up to support him throughout his career.

"The only person who ever cared about my hockey career passed away a few years ago before I got called up to the NHL, so…" Hayes shrugs like it's no big deal, but it's clearly something that bothers him. It's obvious in how his shoulders slink inward and how he drops his head to his chest.

"We'll be there," I promise, and he lifts his head. "We'll be the ones cheering you on."

Hayes doesn't say anything. He doesn't have to. His eyes say it all, and right now, they're telling me he's grateful. I think I'd promise him anything if it meant he'd look at me like that again.

CHAPTER 12

HAYES

"Dude, can you fucking believe this?" Lawson marvels beside me, his eyes wide as he takes in the crowd.

Usually, during warmups, fans are still milling about the arena, most of the seats empty while everyone gets their snacks, souvenirs, and whatever else they need.

But not tonight. Tonight, it's hard to decipher just how many seats are still empty, if any. They're feeling it, and I'm glad. We're fucking feeling it too.

"I know." I drag my eyes through the crowd, taking it all in myself.

And fine, if I'm being honest, I'm looking for my own little cheering team—Quinn and Flora. I never noticed how much it weighed on me that I never had people in the stands just for me until I gave those tickets to that lady from the park. I hadn't given it much thought before then because it never really mattered. I was alone. Who the hell was I going to invite anyway? A one-night stand or flavor of the week? Not a chance.

That's not the case anymore. I have Flora now.

And I guess Quinn, too, though that's a lot more complicated. I spent a lot of time avoiding her after our kiss, doing everything in my power to make sure we were never alone for more than a few seconds. I didn't want to make the same mistake I did her first night. It was difficult at first, running away every time she was near, but the more distance I put between us, the clearer things became: she's Flora's nanny, and that's it. Nothing else.

It was easier after that. Sure, I almost slipped in the grocery store when she was being a brat about paying for groceries, but I didn't, and that's progress. Maybe I am growing up.

I slide my eyes to where I told Quinn to bring Flora for warmups, but the space is still empty even though we've been on the ice for five minutes now.

Where the hell are they? Did they get lost? Are they stuck in traffic? Were they in an accident? Is Flora okay?

Lawson grabs my shoulder, jostling me and pulling me from my panic spiral.

They're fine, I tell myself. *They're probably just shopping or getting snacks.*

"I'm just so fucking jazzed," he says. "I can't believe I—Wednesday!" He zooms across the ice without another word, not stopping until he's at the boards. He drops to his knees and starts stretching. It would look totally normal and not at all out of place if he wasn't looking over his shoulder the whole time at his girlfriend with a shit-eating grin on his face. Rory stands there, rolling her eyes at him. Her twin sister, Auden, is beside her, patting her shoulder like she's sorry Rory is dating the guy. I'm sorry for her too. I shake my head at his antics and continue my perusal.

Come on, Quinn, where are you?

I scan the rows, just in case they're in their seats instead of up at the glass, but I still come up empty. I—

The air is sucked from my lungs. I figured Quinn would wear something Serpents related to the game, but I certainly wasn't expecting my breath to get caught in my throat at the sight of her in it.

It's fucking stupid is what it is. I've seen thousands of fans in jerseys before. This shouldn't affect me one bit, and I can't even put my finger on *why* it's affecting me. Is it Quinn specifically or is it just because I *know* her?

I tear my eyes from her before my mind really starts to wander and look to Flora, who is also wearing a Serpents jersey that's just a little too big for her. It's so damn adorable. They skip down the stairs. Well, it's more like Flora pulls Quinn down them. They stop once they hit the glass, Flora's little nose pressed against it as her eyes scan the ice. Quinn stands above her, doing the same.

They're looking for me.

Fuck, why do I love that they're looking for me?

I skate toward them, not missing it when Flora finally spots me and her blue eyes light up. She bangs on the glass with delight, and I can't help the pride that swells in my chest. Just like I can't help my gaze drifting to Quinn and her dark green, gold, and black Serpents jersey. There's no number on the sleeve. *It's blank...*and relief floods through me at the realization that she's not wearing some random number or name on her back. It shouldn't matter to me.

No—it *doesn't* matter to me. I'm just her boss. A boss who knows her lips taste sweet like butterscotch, but still her boss. She doesn't need to be wearing my number.

I push the thought aside and wave to Flora, who is beaming up at me with stars in her eyes.

"Uncle Adam! Look!" she yells, then spins around.

Quinn gathers her hair so I can read the jersey, but she doesn't need to. I know what it says.

Uncle Adam.

18.

I blink once. Twice. Three times and then four

times. Fucking anything to get the sting of the tears to go away. I don't know why it's doing me in. I don't know why *any* of this is doing me in. Why my chest feels tight and it's hard to breathe and my throat feels like I've been drinking sand all day. I've never had this kind of support before, and fuck, it's getting to me.

I skate away before I do something ridiculous like start crying, then I snatch up a puck with the end of my stick and bounce it up and down a few times before carrying it back to the glass. I point to Flora in a silent, *Do you want this?*

She nods, and I flip it over the glass. Quinn catches it easily, then hands it to Flora, who hugs it tightly like I've just given her a stuffed animal or something.

I laugh. I can't believe how far she's come in the last few weeks. Even though I was resistant to Quinn at first, I'm starting to think hiring her might have been one of the best things to ever happen to Flora, even if it does mean I'm having to work overtime to keep myself in check when it comes to her. To not succumb to my urges to touch her. Or kiss her again. Or look at her ass in those tiny sleep shorts she walks around in late at night when she thinks everyone else is asleep, though I can see her through the crack in my door.

I tap the glass with my stick, sending them a wave, and move on to my drills. I shoot pucks at Fox, then Dash, our other tendy, then run through my usual stretches before heading off the ice and back to the locker room.

"You boys fucking ready?" Lawson yells once we're all back in the circular room. "We're fucking winning this thing! No bars held or whatever the fuck the saying is."

"Holds barred," Keller provides with an exasperated eye roll. "Asswipe."

I look around the room, catching the eye of a few of the guys, almost all of them smirking because they know this is just what Lawson and Keller do—give each other endless shit.

"Aw, come on," Lawson says with a grin. "Don't be a Grumpy Gus just because you know you're riding the pine tonight, Kells."

"Fourth line, yet I'm still out there making better plays than you are."

"Not a chance."

"Bet I'll score before you do this season."

Lawson smirks. "I score more than you every night. Unless you count your two girlfriends getting *handsy* with you, that is." He lifts his palms into the air for show, as if we don't all understand what he's getting at.

Keller rises from his cubby, already marching toward him. "I swear to fuck, Lawsy, I—"

"All right, all right, settle down," Coach Smith says, calming us like the children we are certainly acting like.

Keller retreats to his stall with a scowl, and Lawson plops down in his, still smiling because I guess he has a death wish or something.

Coach Smith stands at the top of the room, his hands on his hips as he quietly commands the attention of the room, and we give it to him. This time last year, we were sitting in this room with a different coach who was lackluster at best, and we had no confidence in this team, not really. This year is completely different. We're determined to take it all the way. We want that Cup, and we want it bad.

"First game of the season, boys," he says. "It might not seem like a big deal because we're staring down eighty-one more games after this, but the truth is, this game can set the tone for the rest of the season. I'm not saying we have to get out there and win. We all know that'd be amazing. I'm talking about the way you play tonight, win or lose. I'm talking about the plays you make or don't make. The way you back your teammates up. The grit you have. Your determination. How much you give the game. *That's* what I'm talking about. So are you ready?" He looks each of us in the eye. "Are you ready to get out there and play a game you can be proud of when you walk back off that ice? Can you do this? Because I sure as fuck believe you can."

It's a simple speech but effective because damn if

my heart doesn't start to hammer in my chest with the anticipation of getting out there and proving to him that he's made the right decision to believe in us. I believe in us too.

"Let's get out there, then. Let's show that sellout crowd what we're made of. Yeah?"

"Heard!" the room says before clapping twice.

"Good. Hutchy, read it!"

Hutch stands and reads off the starting lineup.

"You ready?" Fox asks beside me once he's done.

"As I'm ever going to be," I tell him.

"You gonna stay out of the box this year?"

I laugh. "Going to give it hell."

"Good, because we're getting the Cup this year. I can feel it. Something about tonight feels different. I just know it."

He's right. Something about tonight does feel different.

And I think a lot of it has to do with a certain two girls in the stands tonight.

"Hustle, hustle!" Keller yells from the bench. "Move, Hayes! Wheels!"

Not wanting to let my teammate down, I pump my

legs harder and catch up with the Vegas player, bodychecking him into the boards. We're down two goals halfway through the third. We have a lot of hockey left to play still, but right now, it doesn't feel like it. Our ship is sinking fast, and we need a lifeline soon, or we're going home with zero points.

"Attaboy!" Keller shouts as I knock the puck away from our opponents.

"Motherfucker," the Vegas player mutters.

I laugh.

"Think that's fucking funny?" he snarls.

I laugh harder, and he crosschecks my chest. Now I'm definitely *not* laughing. I crosscheck him back, and I see the ref's arm go up.

Good. Give us both penalties. I don't care.

He blows the whistle, jabbing his finger in my direction.

"18, Seattle!" the ref yells, and I wait for him to make a call on the Vegas player too, but he never does.

"What the fuck!" I scream. "You've gotta be shitting me! He got me first!"

"Don't care, didn't see it. Box!" the ref responds, pointing to the penalty box I am all too familiar with.

"We were right in front of you! How did you not see it? What a fucking joke!" I holler back as I'm escorted to the open door, not giving a crap if the mic picks it up or not.

It's a bullshit call, and judging by my teammates shouting from the bench, I'm not alone in my feelings. I slam my stick down, fuming. Why is it I'm always the one getting the shit end of the deal? I didn't do anything that asshole didn't do first.

They call for a TV timeout, and I let my eyes wander to the stands, past the opposing fans taunting me beside me, to where Flora and Quinn are, only to find Flora standing, her little thumb pointed down as she boos the ref.

I laugh. Quinn catches my eye and shrugs, and I shake my head with a grin.

Play resumes, and I'm forced to watch as my teammates battle off a power play. They're doing well, blocking shots left and right and keeping them from getting into position. Coach Smith throws Lawson out there with Locke and Hutch at the end of the kill, and I know exactly what he's looking for.

"Come on, come on," I mutter as I stand, watching the last seconds tick by.

"Go, go, go," the penalty box attendant says when my time is up.

I race out of the box, the puck landing right on my stick, and I pump my legs, driving the net hard. I see my opening the second the Vegas goalie goes down just a few seconds too early. I drag the stick back and shoot.

The puck goes off the pipe and in.

"Fuck yes!" Lawson says, running me into the boards as he hugs me. "That's what we need, baby!"

"Way to redeem yourself," Hutch says, smacking my helmet.

But I don't care about their praise. My eyes go right to the stands, where I find Flora jumping up and down on her chair, clapping wildly as she grins bigger than I've seen her grin before. Quinn stands beside her, fingers in her mouth as she whistles, her hazel eyes shining with pride. Seeing them happy is infinitely better than anything these assholes on the ice are saying.

I push them off me. "Got work to do still."

I skate by the bench, bumping fists, then get settled back into position. We battle hard for the next several minutes, getting a few good looks but no lucky bounces. We're so fucking close, and I can feel it. We just need one thing to go our way, and we have a chance at winning this.

The fourth line hits the ice to give the top guys a break before the final two minutes, during which we'll undoubtedly pull Fox if it comes to that. Keller fights for his position in the front of the net, being the pest we all know he loves to be, and Jobe takes the shot.

The next thing I know, the place is louder than I've ever heard before, and the puck is sitting in the back of the net. Keller tipped it, and we're fucking tied.

"Fuck yes!" Lawson grabs my shoulders, shaking me hard as he bounces on his skates.

The whole bench is cheering and yelling, and we're feeling it now. Even Fox is celebrating on the other end of the ice.

"Told you I'd score before you," Keller says to Lawson as he skates by, and Lawsy doesn't even have a response for him. He's too damn jazzed about the goal to care about the chirp.

"Hey, hey, settle down," Coach Smith yells behind us. "We still have time left. Let's get reset and go again. Top, let's go."

I jump the boards with Lawson, Locke, and Hutch behind me, and we take our positions, all business now. I win the draw, sending the puck back, and Locke takes it, dragging it back to get set. He passes it to Hutch, who passes it back to him. I get into position, smacking my stick against the ice, letting him know I have an opening. Smartly, he goes to Lawson, who has an even better one.

Lawson zooms up the ice with the puck and into the zone, and we all chase after him. He rims it around the boards to me, and I shoot it back to him. He tries on the goalie's weak side, but the goalie gets over too fast. It doesn't matter. He leaves Lawsy a juicy rebound, and he capitalizes on it.

The goal horn goes off with just seconds to spare, and we win our first game of the season.

"Yeah, fucking suck it, Kells!" Lawson yells as we crowd around him.

"Yeah, yeah. I still scored first!" the perpetual grump hollers back as he skates onto the ice to celebrate, but even I can see the hint of a smile at the corner of his lips.

Me? All I can focus on are the two girls in the crowd. They look happier than anyone else in this arena, and damn if that doesn't feel good.

I finally walk into the house at nearly midnight, having had to do far too many post-game pressers, if you ask me. It's quiet and dark save for the soft under-cabinet lights in the kitchen. I have no doubt Flora is already in bed, and Quinn likely is too.

I toe off the dress shoes I hate wearing and head straight to the kitchen. I pull out an electrolyte drink from the fridge and down half of it in one go while I work to get my heart rate down, still running high from the adrenaline from the game.

I'm always like this afterward. It usually takes me a few hours to calm down properly so I can relax and get some rest. It's a blessing because it gives me time to go over the game and see where I can improve, but it's a curse for the exact same reason.

Tonight is even worse with how heightened my emotions were having Quinn and Flora there. The look on the kid's face when I scored, Quinn looking at me like she wanted to rip my clothes off right there...I don't know which one affected me more.

I finish the drink and toss it in the recycling before shutting off the lights and making my way to my room. I have my hand on the door, ready to turn in for the night when I hear a soft noise coming from just down the hall.

I sneak close to Flora's room and press my ear against the door. Maybe she's getting up for pickles again? Or maybe she's sneaking more chapters of her book? But there's nothing.

Hmm. It must be coming from Quinn's room, then. Curious, I inch closer, and it's clear that the sound is definitely coming from her room. I can't make out what it is. It's like a soft buzz, almost like a phone against a bedside table. Or like a—

Oh fuck.

No. There's no way it's what I think it is. Is there?

I hear it, and it's unmistakable.

A moan. *Her* moan. It's the sweetest sound I've ever heard, and I immediately want to hear it again. I shuffle closer. Apparently *too* close because my foot hits the door and it slowly creaks open.

Fuck!

I scramble away, pressing my back against the wall next to the door, holding my breath as I wait for the buzzing to stop and Quinn to burst out of her room and lay into me as I deserve.

But it never happens. The buzzing continues, and I swear I hear Quinn moan again. My cock, already stirring against my slacks, stiffens at the sound, and *fuck me*, I want to see. I want to see her so badly I can't stand it. Just a tiny peek. A glimpse. That's all I want. I—

"Oh, Hayes. Yes, right there," she whispers, and it's my official undoing.

I don't know what possesses me to do it. Maybe it's the lingering rush from the game, or maybe it's just because I really fucking want to. I push the door open, the light spilling across her face.

She doesn't freak out. She doesn't stop.

No. Quinn stares right at me, her lips parting as her chest heaves, her hand still under the blanket, the toy still buzzing, the sound much louder now that I'm closer. I step inside the dark room and close the door behind me with a soft *click*. I wait. For her to tell me to get the fuck out. To scream. To give any indication at all that I'm not welcome here.

She does nothing.

My eyes adjust to the dark, and I use the moonlight spilling in through the window to guide me closer, not stopping until I'm at the edge of the bed and standing over her. I pause again, waiting once more for her to object, but still, she doesn't.

She swallows harshly as she watches me, and I get it. I feel the same way. Like I gulped down that electrolyte drink hours ago instead of minutes. I fist the sheet, tugging it down to reveal just what it is she's doing under the blanket, and *holy fuck* is it a beautiful sight. She's wearing nothing but her Serpents jersey, her pink cunt shrouded by black curls on full display, and a pink toy is pressed between her spread legs.

Now it's *me* who swallows roughly, watching as she drags the toy in soft circles, the moonbeam catching her wetness with every stroke as she stares up at me with hooded eyes.

It's fucking gorgeous. *She's* fucking gorgeous.

I can't help myself when I reach out, my fingers coasting over her soft thighs. Her breath stutters at the contact, her skin instantly breaking out into goose bumps. I trace my fingertips over them, her movements never ceasing. I palm my aching cock with my other hand, trying to quell the pressure that's building. I've never been so fucking close to coming just by watching someone, but I swear I could do this all day, standing here as Quinn plays with her pretty pussy.

I could. But I really don't want to. I want to touch her more. I *need* to touch her more.

I drag my fingertips closer to where the toy is pressed against her, and her breaths pick up. Her chest now resembles that of someone who has just run a marathon.

"Do it," she whispers hoarsely into the dark room. "Touch me, Hayes. *Please.*"

The last word is my ruin.

Knee on the bed, I lean over her, and it feels eerily like the last time we were in her room together. I hover over her, my lips just inches from hers, only this time it's different, especially when I slide my hand between her legs, covering her hand with mine and taking control of the buzzing toy, her slickness already coating my fingers as she spreads her legs even wider. She groans deliciously when I move it to just the right spot, her head lolling back, her eyes closing.

"Don't you dare close your eyes, Quinn. Look at me when I make you come," I command, moving it away from the spot she loves just because I can.

She whimpers softly but snaps her hazy gaze to me, her lips parted, and her breaths shallow. Even though I know this is so wrong for so many reasons, she looks fucking gorgeous like this, completely out of control and at my mercy. I want more of it. I want more of her.

"Hayes…" she moans. "I'm so close. I'm…"

But she doesn't finish, and I understand why. It's too much for me too. My cock feels so fucking heavy I wish I could pull it out and paint her with my cum.

I can't. I shouldn't. Hell, I shouldn't even be doing *this*.

But I am. We are. And I want nothing more than to hear her call my name as she falls apart.

"Let go, Quinn," I tell her, moving the toy back to that spot she loves so much. "Come for me."

She nods, sinking her teeth into her lower lip, her eyes never once leaving mine as she relaxes, and it's not even ten seconds before the levee breaks. Her back arches up, her legs shaking so violently I can feel the bed quake.

But that's not what gets me.

It's the single word she whispers as she comes.

"*Adam.*"

It takes every ounce of willpower I have not to come in my pants like some sex-deprived teenager. Instead, I focus all my attention on her as she comes down from her high, her body melting into the mattress as I drag the toy away from her greedy cunt and flip it off, tossing it aside.

The room is quiet save for Quinn's choppy breaths,

and the reality of what just happened starts to crawl into the corners of the silence, finding a home and rearing its ugly head. I just helped Quinn masturbate. I just got her off. She just said my name as she came. I want to do it again. And more than that…I think she'd let me.

"Hayes, I—"

But I don't let her finish. I press my lips to hers in a hard, harsh kiss, nothing like the kind of kiss I *want* to give her. It's over far too soon, and when I wrench my mouth from hers, her eyes are wide, and she's panting as she tries to catch her breath.

"Next time you come to my game, you wear my number, understood?"

She nods.

I rise from the bed and march from the room, darting back down the hall to the safety of my own bedroom. I march straight to my bathroom and strip off my suit, not even bothering to toss it into the hamper before I step into the shower, my cock in my hand before I've even stepped under the hot water. It takes three strokes before I'm coming in a rush, my seed spilling all over the stall wall, and when I do, there's only one thing I say.

"*Quinn.*"

CHAPTER 13

QUINN

I knew he was home.

I was so keyed up after the game, I couldn't sleep. I thought a quick orgasm could help take the edge off and I'd be out like a baby, but when I heard the front door open, then his feet moving across the hardwood, I didn't stop. I don't think I could have even if I'd wanted to. The idea of getting caught was far too thrilling for me to resist.

I listened as he got closer and closer, never once even considering turning off the toy. I thought he might stop and listen, but I never expected him to push my door open, or come into the room. The door must not have latched all the way, and I've honestly never been more grateful for that mistake in my life because it was like once it was open, he couldn't stay away.

Frankly, I didn't want him to. No, I *begged* him to

come closer. To touch me. He did, and it was fucking magical. Hands down the best orgasm of my life.

Next time you come to my game, you wear my number, understood?

His words float through my mind for the hundredth time since he whispered them. They were so hot. So...*possessive*. Like he was staking his claim. The funny part is, I didn't even realize I was wearing the jersey until he said something. I just left it on because it was comfortable and breezy, and honestly, I was too lazy to change. I guess Hayes noticed, though.

Then he stormed out of my room and left me unable to sleep, the exact opposite thing I was hoping the orgasm would accomplish. I didn't fall asleep until about three AM, and I'm feeling it today.

"Just Quinn?"

"Hmm?" I ask, looking down at Flora as we walk down the sidewalk to my mother's bakery. She was up early this morning asking about chocolate donuts, and I couldn't say no to her.

I was, however, surprised when Hayes decided to come along, especially given he still hasn't so much as looked at me all morning. But I can't think about that, not when Flora's observing me with her dark brows pinched together and eyes full of concern.

"Sorry, little flower. I'm just tired today. What did you ask?"

"I was wondering if we could go to the park again today, but if you're tired, we can just go home."

I smile. She's too damn sweet. I glance over at Hayes to see if he's witnessing this, but he's too busy staring at the sidewalk, avoiding any and all eye contact with me.

Seriously? I don't understand why he can't act like an adult about this.

"We can go to the park. In fact, let's make Sunday mornings official park days, huh? We can call it Sunday Funday at the Park with Just Quinn and Flora the Little Flower."

She wrinkles her nose. "That's a long name. Let's just call it Park Day."

I laugh. "Deal. Want to watch a movie tonight, too? I can make popcorn, and maybe if you're lucky, I'll even show you how good it is when you dump M&M's into it."

"M&M's and popcorn? I don't know…"

"Hey, you loved the mayo and ketchup on your fries, didn't you?" She nods. "Then trust me on this."

"Fine, but if it's bad, I'm never trusting you again."

I chuckle as Hayes pulls open the lilac door to B's Bakes. Oh, look, I guess he hasn't forgotten all his manners. He just hates me.

"Flora!" my mother calls as we walk in.

"Hi, Mom. I'm here too."

She waves me off, not caring, all her attention on Flora as she practically runs to the donut case. I cannot believe how far she's come in the last few weeks. Sure, she's still shy around people she doesn't know, but she's starting to flourish around the ones she does. I love seeing her like this, happy and like an actual *kid*. I hope it only gets better from here.

"You want your chocolate donut with sprinkles?" my mother asks her.

She nods. "*Extra* sprinkles. And a chocolate milk in a mug, please."

"You got it!"

My mother happily punches the order into the screen and turns her attention to me and Hayes, her eyes dancing between us. I know the second she recognizes the awkwardness there, her smile slipping a little. She doesn't miss the stiffness in his shoulders either, the way his lips are turned down in a frown, and she definitely doesn't miss how he's standing as far away from me as possible.

She pulls her lips back up, but where it was genuine with Flora, it's now forced.

"Your usual, Hayes?"

He nods, not *using his words* as he's instructed Flora to do so many times.

My mother purses her lips. "Sure."

She turns her gaze on me, so many questions in her

eyes. Ones I really don't want to answer in front of Flora.

I tap her head. "Hey, little flower. Why don't you and your uncle go grab our table, hmm? I'll get this."

It's telling that Hayes doesn't even insist on paying. He just grabs Flora's shoulder and steers her toward the table by the window. I watch them go, then blow out a deep breath before facing my mother again.

Her purple-coated lips are pressed tightly together. "I know for a fact that man should be smiling right now. The Serpents just won their first game last night. He has no business looking so...so...well, grumpy. Is everything okay?"

I shrug. "I don't know. He's just in a mood today."

But I do know. I *really* know.

"So you're telling me he just woke up on the wrong side of the bed or something? Nothing else big is going on? Everything's okay? Because you're not wearing any ridiculous earrings today, and you *always* do."

I know what she's really asking: *Is everything okay with you two?*

My mother likes Hayes, but she loves me, and I love her for being so concerned for me right now.

I nod, swallowing down the heaviness that's settled into my throat. "Yep. All good."

"Hmm," she says, her lips pulled into a flat line.

She doesn't fully believe me, and honestly, I

wouldn't believe me either. It's clear something is wrong with Hayes, but I'm not about to tell my mother it's because we couldn't keep our hands to ourselves last night. She'll kill me if she finds out I've likely already ruined this.

"Well, if you need to talk or anything, you know you can call me, right?"

I smile. "I know, Mom. I appreciate it. Now, can I get some breakfast? I'm starving."

She rolls her eyes. "Oh, Quinn, never change, kid. Never change."

She's wrong though. I do need to change. I cannot keep repeating the same mistakes, which means no matter how badly I want it to happen, Hayes and I can't be a thing. I have to start making good decisions, even if it means giving up something I really want.

And what I really want is Hayes, even if he is my boss.

"Are you finished?"

"Yes." Flora pats her belly. "Thank you for dinner, Just Quinn."

She says it like she's just eaten the best meal of her life instead of a can of soup I cracked open and a grilled cheese sandwich…for the third night this week. Man, I really need to learn to make something else for her.

"You're welcome, kid. Now, go take a shower. You have school in the morning, and we need to start getting you ready for bed."

"Ugh. Again?"

"Yes, *again*. And you better get used to it because you're going to have school for"—I quickly count the years in my head—"at least nine more years."

"Ten," Hayes corrects. "Ten more years. She's in second grade, so it's ten."

It's six o'clock in the evening, and it's the first thing Hayes has said to me all day. He and Flora chatted about his game during dinner. She asked a bunch of questions about the rules, why he had to sit in timeout, and whether he had to go to the principal's office after the game because he got in trouble. In all that, he didn't say a single word directly to me.

Until now.

"Oh," I say. "Sorry, Flora, looks like it's ten."

"That's, like, *a whole decade*."

"That is, in fact, a whole decade. Now, go. Shower, then you can get one hour of reading before bed."

"I'm going, I'm going." She rises from her chair with a grumble, then trudges slowly down the hall, her footfalls extra heavy with every step.

I smile, but it slips from my face when I realize it's the first time Hayes and I have been alone since last night. Which means we need to talk about what happened, and I *really* don't want to talk about what happened.

I rinse our bowls and plates, then load them into the dishwasher before going for Hayes's dirty dishes. I reach for his empty plate, and his hand circles my wrist, stopping me.

I'm transported right back to last night and the way his hands felt on me. How gentle he was, such a contrast to how he normally is. How featherlight his fingers were as he teased me, never once taking his eyes off me. How absolutely fucking magical it was to come with him holding the toy to my clit.

But his touch only lasts a moment, like he too is remembering everything that has transpired between us.

"I got it," he says, releasing me and grabbing the plate instead.

I frown down at him. "It's no big deal. I'm already up."

"I said, *I got it.*"

"Fine." I let the plate go and it clatters loudly on the table, Hayes not expecting me to drop it, I guess. I turn back to the kitchen and flip on the hot water before grabbing the dirty soup pot from the stove.

He scoffs, his chair scraping against the floor. "Are you seriously mad at me for not letting you clean up after me?"

I look up at him. "Are you seriously acting like that's all this is?"

"Well, yeah, what else would it be?"

"Gee, Hayes, I don't know," I say sarcastically, scrubbing the pot with more force than is warranted. "Something to do with last night."

"Last night…" He shakes his head. "It was…"

"What?" I ask, letting the pot fall into the sink with a rattle. "What was it?"

"A mistake!" Hayes yells. "A big fucking mistake!"

"Oh," I say, because I don't know what else *to* say.

A big fucking mistake? Is that what he really thinks? Sure, we slipped up again, but *a big fucking mistake* is a bit much, isn't it? How could it have been when it felt so damn good?

"It *can't* happen again, Quinn," he says more quietly this time. "You understand that, right?"

I don't like how he's talking to me, like this is all *my* fault, and *he* wasn't a willing participant in the whole thing. Like he didn't go into his bathroom afterward and fuck his fist while he called out my name.

I heard him. I got up to get a drink of water because my mouth was so dry after coming so hard, and I heard him. He's as guilty as I am, so I don't know why he's placing the blame on me right now, but I do know it pisses me off. I'm not the only one who was in my bedroom last night. I'm not the only one who crossed the line. We both did, and he needs to admit it was his fault too.

"You're right, Hayes. It was a mistake. *A big fucking mistake*, as a matter of fact. And it won't happen again. I can promise you that."

I leave the dirty pot in the sink, walking away before I start crying because I refuse to let him see me cry. Not after last night. Not after everything.

He doesn't say anything else, doesn't try to come after me. I go through my nightly routine with Flora, reading her book aloud to her, even though my heart isn't really in it. When I'm finished, I step into the hall to find Hayes has closed his door and turned in for the night.

I'm not sure if I'm relieved or pissed, and I can't help but wonder if I've already fucked up the best job of my life.

The vibe in the house isn't any better than it was yesterday as I get Flora ready for school. Hayes sits quietly through breakfast, back to not looking at me and barely even speaking to his niece.

Honestly, Flora and I aren't any better. We're both dragging ass today. She's hardly awake as I braid her hair, and I'm so tired myself that I have to do it three times to get it right. I guess I shouldn't be surprised given I spent most of the night awake, tossing and turning and going over every single moment I've had with Hayes in my head.

Did I leave the door unlatched on purpose? Did I purposefully pick my noisiest toy, knowing he was coming home soon? Did I overreact to him ignoring me? Should I have kicked him out when he walked into my room?

The questions are nonstop, so I try to distract myself with a show. The second the couple kisses, I turn it off. I turn to a book, but the characters are banging within the first chapter, so I toss that aside too. I reach for my laptop and watch random videos on YouTube, anything to distract me, but it still doesn't work. All I can do is think about Hayes and potentially losing my job.

For the first time ever, I actually care about what I'm doing. I like Flora so much, and the thought of being ripped away from her just because Hayes and I can't control ourselves makes me sick. Then again, maybe it would be for the best if Hayes fired me. It's clear I'm not good at making decisions. I have no business molding the mind of a young kid when I can hardly keep myself in check.

I hear the front door swing open around ten thirty, but I stay in my room and away from Hayes. I try to convince myself I'm hiding because I'm so engrossed in what I'm doing, but the truth is I'm scared to leave my room. I don't want to face him after our *discussion* about what happened, after he blamed me—the wild and unpredictable one—for what happened between us.

But the longer I stay tucked away, the more frustrated I become. Until last night, I was never afraid to leave my room, never felt the need to hide. I don't want to live like this, and I also don't want to stay here with him—not after last night.

"Screw this. I'm leaving," I mutter to myself.

I don't know where I'm going. Maybe to my storage unit so I can start going through all the clothes I have stashed in there. I haven't missed them at all over the last three weeks, so it's clear I can live without them. There's no sense in keeping them around if I'm not wearing them. I should sell them and make some cash. I might need it soon anyway.

I push my laptop to the side, then swap my sweats for yoga pants and slide my crossbody bag over my shoulder before pulling open my door. I silently pray he's not out in the common area and won't see me leave.

Of course that's not my luck.

"Where are you going?" Hayes asks from the kitchen as I pass by and beeline for the door.

I pause, looking at him, and *ugh!* It's so unfair! Why does he have to look so good right now? Why does his t-shirt have to cling to his muscles and show off his tattoos? Why do his jeans have to sit so low on his hips? Why does his hair have to lie in that perfectly messy way? And why does he have to look so good barefoot?

"Out," I say, keeping it simple, hoping he drops it.

He doesn't. He pushes away from the counter, setting his bowl aside. "Out where?"

"What is this? Twenty questions? I'm just going out."

"Why?"

I glare at him. "You're not my father. I don't have to answer that."

"No," he says, padding closer. I don't *want* him closer. I want him far away because having him close is too dangerous. "But I am your boss, and this is my house. I have a right to know what's going on in it."

I was waiting for him to throw that in my face, and I scoff at his words. "I was under the impression that when Flora is at school, I'm allowed to do whatever I want as long as I'm on time to pick her up. So, I'm going out. That's the end of the discussion, *boss*."

His eyes narrow as I toss the moniker back to him. "You don't even have a car."

Crap. He's right. My poor Bug is still in the shop, and I've been driving his fancy-schmancy SUV to take Flora anywhere we can't walk.

Whatever. I can Uber. I don't want his help.

"I'll walk."

"No," he says. "I'll take you."

I jerk my head back, the whiplash of this conversation too much. "No."

"No?" He lifts his brows. "Why, Quinny, you're not sneaking off to the toy store now, are you? Buying something new to play with?"

If I wasn't so blown away by his audacity, I might actually be embarrassed by his question. But I'm not.

"Screw you, Hayes," I seethe, my teeth clenched tight.

He laughs. *Laughs!*

All it does is piss me off more. I roll my eyes with a huff and storm toward the front door.

"Wait!" he calls out after me.

I don't. I keep walking, ignoring the jerk.

"Stop!" he calls, this time closer.

I ignore him again, picking up my pace, trying to put as much distance between us as possible.

"Dammit, Quinn!" I can hear his heavy footsteps on the hardwood floor. He's right behind me, so close I can feel his body heat. "Would you just fucking wait?"

"Why!" I yell, spinning around and throwing my hands in the air. He skids to a stop, just barely missing crashing into me. "Why should I, huh? So you can tell me what a mistake it was again?"

"No! It's just…" He sighs. "I…I—"

"What, Hayes? What? What could you possibly say to me right now—"

Only I don't finish my sentence. I can't.

Adam Hayes is kissing me—*again*—and it's just as magical as it was the first and second time. It's soft and sweet yet hard and demanding. His hands crash into my hair, holding me close like he'll never get to kiss me again. I'd let him kiss me any time if he promised to kiss me like this.

I clutch his shirt, pulling him even closer because I'm not sure I'll ever get enough, and he groans as his big body crashes against mine, pushing me against the door with a heavy thud. My head bounces off the wood, but I don't care. I can't care. Not when he feels as good as he does.

He traces my lips with his tongue, begging for entry, and I don't dare deny him. My head is fuzzy, and I feel dizzy as our tongues tangle together, like I'm going to pass out, but I don't want to pass out. I want to savor this moment for as long as I can, savor the taste of him. It's something sweet, and I realize what he was eating—ice cream.

It's butterscotch. *My favorite.*

His kiss turns softer and sweeter, less impatient and more languid, and I'm so glad I'm pressed against the door because I melt into him, craving this softer side of him as much as I crave the harder side. Speaking of hard...he is. His cock presses against my belly, long and heavy, and I want so badly to reach my hand between us and feel him. He got to touch me. It's only fair I get to touch him, right?

So I try to, only to have my attempt thwarted when he grabs my wrists and holds them against the door above my head in one hand. I'd be impressed if I wasn't so annoyed by it. I groan, but he just chuckles, clearly the one in charge here. He continues kissing me, running his free hand down my throat and over my arm, down my side and back up again, like he's memorizing every inch of me. I get it. I want to memorize every inch of him, too.

I don't know who pulls away first, but suddenly we're a mess of stuttered breaths as we gasp for air, my back still pressed against the door and Hayes crowding me, caging me in like he's afraid to let me go for fear I might run.

And I just might because *What the hell?* We just

kissed. Again. We just crossed the line. Again. We are so, so screwed.

I run my tongue over my bottom lip, peering up into his silver eyes, unsure what to do.

"What was that for?" I ask.

"I had to get you to shut up somehow."

I buck at him with my hips, trying to wiggle free, but he doesn't let me.

"Stop. That's not what I meant. I just meant—"

"What?" I snap. "What did you mean?"

"I… Well, I guess I did mean that. It's just…"

I sigh. "You're going to need to make up your mind here, Hayes. This hot and cold doesn't work for me. You can't keep kissing and touching me and then act like I'm the only one at fault here. We're both adults. We—"

He cuts my words off with his mouth once more. I want to resist. To pull away. To stop him.

But I can't find it in me to do it. I want to kiss him more than I don't want to.

He moves his lips against mine expertly, his grip on my wrists softening just a bit, but not enough for me to get free. I both love it and hate it because I want to touch him so badly, like the way he's touching me, tracing his fingertips over my side, across the band of the yoga pants I'm wearing like he's trying to decide if he should try to take them off or not.

Do it, Hayes, my mind screams. *Touch me.*

But he doesn't listen. Instead, he pulls away again, and I groan. He laughs darkly, and I glare at him.

"Shut up."

"You first." He grins, then runs his fingers over my waistband again, this time pulling it away and snapping it back into place, and I love the bite of its sting.

He peers down into my eyes, his silver stare hard and serious. "Look. We both know this is a bad idea."

"A big fucking mistake, right?"

He nods. "It is. The biggest…"

"But?"

He shakes his head. "No but. That part is true and even you can't deny it."

He's right. I can't. What we're doing is wrong on so many levels. I should do the right thing and tell him to stop, but I can't quite make the words come out.

"I want this, though," he says on a whisper, almost like he's afraid to say the words any louder. "I want *you.* I'm tired of pretending I don't."

I want you too.

"Then take me, Hayes." I lean forward and ghost my lips over his as I rub my body against him like some desperate girl, and I guess I am. "Take me, because right now, I'm at your mercy. I'm all yours."

He closes his eyes as I kiss one corner of his lips,

then the other. "It's wrong. You're here for Flora. Not for me."

"It can be both. I can be here for you both."

What the hell am I even saying? *Stop this, Quinn! Be better than this. Don't repeat your past mistakes.*

But I don't listen to me. I don't listen to what I *should* do. I listen to what I want.

"That's not… This isn't what I intended when I hired you."

"I know that." I kiss down his chin and neck, and he groans when my lips trace the column of his throat, the noise so loud it vibrates against my lips. "But it's what I'm offering."

"Quinn…" he whispers.

"Adam," I respond, and I know it's his downfall.

Suddenly he's not trying to resist me anymore. No, he's tugging me closer, hauling me against him, his lips crashing into mine with such force I'm not sure how I won't be bruised later. I don't care. My mind is in other places as he slides his hand into my yoga pants and right down past my underwear, cupping my pussy with his warm hand.

"Fuck, you're already so wet," he mutters, his fingers slipping between my folds.

I nod, even though he's not asking a question.

"Feel so fucking good," he says as he slips a single digit inside me, and I cry out in relief.

He laughs, but this time I'm not even upset about it. I can't find it in me, not when he's dragging his finger in and out of me and it feels so, so good.

"I want to fuck you against this door, Quinn. I want it to be so loud and so hard that people walking by know exactly what's going on. Would you like that?"

I nod. I'd like that *very* much.

"Me too. So much."

"Then do it already."

Another laugh.

"Patience, honey," he says.

Honey.

It's the first time he's called me that, and I don't hate it. If anything, I like it entirely too much. I want to hear him say it again. I'm about to ask him to, but he yanks his hand from my pants, and this time, when I cry out, it's not relief—it's pure frustration.

"What the fuck, Hayes? I—"

But I don't get the chance to finish. He's yanking my yoga pants down my legs, then scooping me into his arms. I allow it, curling my legs around his waist as he carries me to the couch, too impatient to take us anywhere else. He drops down, and I straddle his lap, his cock straining between us.

"Fuck," he mutters when I roll my hips against him, loving the way he feels sliding against me.

It's not enough. I need more. I grab the hem of his

shirt, tugging it up, and Hayes gets the picture. He grabs the shirt himself, sliding it over his head and tossing it I don't know or care where. I'm too distracted counting the ridges on his stomach, too busy running my hands over each and every dip, then dragging them up through the light hair that covers his chest.

He lets me explore him. Lets me lean forward and press my lips against his collarbone. Allows me to kiss the base of his throat, to run my teeth along his skin, to trace every freckle he has with my tongue. Then start all over again.

Quinn, you need to stop. Be responsible for once in your life.

I ignore the voice in the back of my mind and scoot down to get more of him, but he drags me back up, pressing his mouth against mine in a possessive kiss. His hands dive into my hair, tugging me so close I don't know where he ends and I begin, and I don't give a shit. None of it matters when he's kissing me like he is.

He drags his hands down my back, breaking our kiss to pull my shirt over my head, tossing it across the room like he did his own. I expect him to reach for me again, but he doesn't. He just sits there, catching his breath and staring at me as I sit in his lap.

I wonder what he sees. Swollen lips from his kisses? My hair a wreck from his hands? My chest red from getting so worked up?

"Fuck, you're beautiful, Quinny," he whispers, reaching forward to trace the cup of my simple black bra. "So fucking beautiful. I can't wait to fuck you."

My breath stutters in my chest. He says it so simply. So directly.

I can't wait either.

"But first, I want to taste you." He grabs my hips, jerking me to him. "I've been dying to taste you."

He pulls the cup of my bra down, closing his mouth around my already hard nipple, flicking his tongue in a delicious rhythm that shouldn't be getting me so close to the edge but is.

Or maybe it's just Hayes. I don't know.

Like he knows I'm thinking of him, he peeks his silver eyes up at me and grins, my nipple caught between his teeth. I wish I had a camera right now so I could take a picture of this and keep it forever. He lets me free with an audible *pop*, then moves on to my other nipple, spending as much time kissing it as he did the other. It feels so, so good, yet it's not nearly enough.

"Hayes." I groan, dragging my nails over his head. "I want…"

"What?" He trails his lips from my breast up to my throat, sucking on a sensitive spot just at the base. "What do you want?"

"More. I want more. I want *you*."

"Then take me." He repeats my words back to me. "Take me."

I drop my hands between us, straight to the button on his jeans, and finally—*finally*—Hayes doesn't stop me. I drag the zipper down, and he arches up, helping me shove them down his legs, taking his boxer briefs right along with them. I get my first glimpse at naked Hayes.

He's magnificent. And huge. *Too* huge.

He chuckles deeply. "Don't worry, honey. I'll fit."

I wrap my hand around him, loving how heavy he feels, and then curl my wrist up. He tosses his head back with a loud groan.

"*Fuuuuuck.*" He drags the word out. "I'm so not going to last."

I jerk him again, and he makes another strangled sound. I continue playing with him, all the while his breaths getting more and more choked like he's literally struggling to breathe. Suddenly, his hand comes out of nowhere, wrapping around my wrist and stifling my movements.

"Enough," he barks.

"But I—"

My words are cut off as he slams his mouth against mine in a rough yet brief kiss. He presses his forehead against mine, his eyes darkening by the second, a crazed look in his eyes I haven't seen before.

"If you want to get me off, then ride my cock, honey."

I'm not stupid enough to ignore his request. I use his shoulders to push myself up, holding my underwear to the side and sliding over him.

He was wrong, I think as I sink lower.

"I can't." I shake my head when he's not even halfway in. "You're too big."

"Breathe." Hayes pulls me toward him, pressing his forehead against mine. "Just breathe."

I exhale, taking another half inch.

"That's my girl. Just like that," he praises, and warmth spreads through me at his words. "You're doing so good. Taking me so well."

He rubs my back, easing into me with such gentleness, and before I know it, he's right—he will fit. And he feels good. Almost too good. Almost like—

"Oh god." Panic claws up my throat. "Condom. We didn't…"

"I'm good," he says. "I just got tested at my last physical."

"Me too. I mean, I didn't have a physical, but I was tested recently."

After Marco, actually, but I don't tell him that. He doesn't need to know I slept with my last boss too.

"Then I'm good if you are."

I nod. I'm good. *So* good. Especially when he rolls

his hips into me. I moan, head rolling back, eyes falling closed.

"Hey, no." He tugs on my hair, just hard enough for it to throb a little, and I peel my eyes back open. "Look at me when I'm inside you, Quinn. I want to see you when I make you scream my name. Understood?"

I nod, and he rocks into me once more.

"Good. Now, put your hands behind your back and ride me like you mean it, honey."

CHAPTER 14

HAYES

It's funny that I preached patience when I clearly had none, not even able to pull her bra off all the way before I had to have my mouth on her.

But now, seeing her like this, her tits hanging out as she rides my cock into oblivion, I can't seem to care. Fuck, she's beautiful. Her hair is a tangled mess from my hands, her cheeks are flushed from exertion, and there are red marks from my beard across her chest. So fucking impatient for my cock she didn't even take her underwear off.

I love it, even though I shouldn't. This is so wrong. She's my nanny. I shouldn't be fucking her in the living room in the middle of the day. Hell, I shouldn't be fucking her at all. I should be keeping my hands off her. We should be putting so much distance between us we have to shout at each other to be heard.

But I can't stop. I don't *want* to stop. I don't want to be responsible anymore. I just want to have fun, and right now, this is *really* fucking fun.

Hands behind her back, Quinn bounces on my lap, her movements frantic yet rhythmic as her pussy squeezes me tight. She was worried about me not fitting, but I'm only worried about never being the same. How could I be after this? After knowing how good she feels? How her greedy cunt takes me so easily? How am I supposed to go back to polite conversation over donuts and bagels? How am I supposed to go back to talking about school schedules and all that other mundane shit? How will I ever be able to focus knowing this is what she feels like?

I palm her tit, rolling her rosy nipple between my fingers before inching upward, curling my fingers around her throat. She doesn't lean away. No, she leans into it, wanting it. I apply a bit of pressure, and she moans, the sound vibrating through my hand.

"That feels so good. I'm so close, Hayes." Her eyes are barely open, so lost in the lust. "Please tell me you're close."

"I'm close," I promise, barely able to hold back.

I've been masturbating far too much since we first kissed, but it's still never been enough to stave off my want for her. The fact that I'm holding back so much right now tells me it was never going to be.

"I need…" she pleads, and I know just what she's begging for.

I press my free thumb against her clit, and she lets out a low moan, sinking into my touch.

"Yes, yes, yes," she chants. "More."

I oblige, drawing short circles over her sensitive button as she rides me faster, harder, my hand tightening around her throat. I'm not sure which of us actually lets go first. Maybe it's her cunt squeezing me so tightly that causes the chain reaction, or maybe I'm just that unable to control myself. Her entire body shakes as she comes, and I follow right along with her.

"*Adam!*" she screams, just as I promised I'd make her do, and I stare into her hazel eyes as I surge up into her, wringing out every last drop of her orgasm that I can.

She slumps forward, collapsing against me. As we struggle to catch our breaths, all I can think is *It's not enough.* I want more. I *need* more.

I lift us off the couch in one swift motion, and she doesn't even argue as I carry her through the house and into her bedroom. I lay her back on the bed and crawl over her, sliding back inside her warmth, my cock still hard and ready to go again.

"Yes," she moans as I rock into her. "More."

I give her more, give her everything I have, fucking her slowly at first, then hard and fast. She eats it up, begging for me to touch and kiss her, so I do. I press my lips to hers, then down her chin, over her neck, and suck on her sweet nipples. I touch her everywhere I can because I don't know if this will be the last time. It certainly should be.

Only when I've had my fill do I let go, spilling into her again as she comes for a second time. As I slide out of her and crawl up beside her in bed, tucking her against me, all I can think is, *It's still not enough.*

I wake a short time later, and it takes me a moment to realize where I am. That familiar scent of butterscotch hits me, and I know.

Quinn.

I circle my arm around her waist, pulling her back tighter against me, and she sighs when I drag my hand down, holding her pussy. But I don't take it any further. We just lie there as I hold her, my mind reeling from what happened earlier.

One minute I was annoyed with her for being so damn stubborn and walking to God knows where, then the next, I was kissing her. I couldn't have stopped myself if I tried. She was yelling at me, her hazel eyes so full of fire, looking so fucking cute with her lips pinched together, and I couldn't help myself—I had to taste her again.

Like she knows I'm thinking about her, she wiggles back against me, dragging her ass over my already hard cock.

"Are you sore?" I ask when she does it again.

I don't know why I'm asking. I've never cared with previous partners. I've always just taken what I wanted, when I wanted it, and they offered it willingly.

She shakes her head. "No. I'm good."

"Good."

In one swift movement, I roll her to her back, sliding over her and fitting myself between her legs like it's where I belong. Her eyes are bright with mischief as I settle against her.

"Hi."

"Hi back," I say, then I kiss her just because I can.

A quick kiss turns into something more heated, far faster than I expected, and soon, I'm sliding my cock against her soaked slit, wanting another round.

"Fuck, you feel so good."

"You too," she murmurs, dragging my lips back to hers.

But I wrench my mouth free before she can get too carried away, and she whimpers. Her sounds of displeasure soon turn to joy as I kiss my way down her body, shouldering my way between her thighs.

"Is this okay?" I ask.

Why? Why do I care?

She nods.

"Good. Now, eyes on me, honey."

She pushes up on her elbows, watching as I slide my tongue over her clit, her hips bucking off the bed. I get it. I do. She tastes so fucking good, and I don't even care that I came inside her twice and can taste the saltiness of myself on my tongue. It's not enough to deter me, especially not when she's looking at me like she is—like she'll die if I don't taste her again.

I drag my tongue back over her clit, and she sinks her teeth into her bottom lip. She begins to close her eyes, then she snaps them open wide like she's just remembered my instructions.

I chuckle against her. "Good girl. Keep them open."

She nods her head vehemently as I lick at her more, touching every inch of her I can find before I suck her clit into my mouth with a force that has her crying out.

"Attagirl. Scream for me, Quinny. Tell me who this pussy belongs to."

"You!" Her eyes flutter closed against her will. "You, Adam. My pussy belongs to you."

"You're damn right it does."

I curl two fingers into her, and she's nothing but a

heap of sighs and moans as she bucks against me, coming all over my tongue and my hand.

And yet, it's still not enough.

I crawl back up her body, taking her mouth in a heated kiss. This time it's me who sighs as I sink into her, her pussy gripping me like it's welcoming me back home.

Being inside her like this does feel like home. It feels like everything I never knew I wanted, which is ridiculous because she drives me crazy half the time, her smart mouth and her eye rolls and her inability to take no for an answer. I don't even like her, yet I fuck her slow, then fast, then slow again, and she clings to me all the while, sighing in my ear and begging for more. I don't stop when she shatters around me again, nor when I fill her with my cum again.

When the last of my orgasm is squeezed out of me, only then do I slow my pace until I'm just lying on top of her, our lips barely brushing together, the taste of butterscotch and her on my tongue.

"You're kind of heavy," she mutters, shoving against me lightly.

I laugh, rolling off and tugging her to my side because I can't seem to *not* touch her. "That's rude."

"Not sorry. Now I can breathe."

She slides her fingers through the hair on my chest, her ear pressed against my heart, and there's no way she doesn't hear how hard it's thumping right now. I could say it's from the nonstop sex or an aftereffect of my orgasm, but it would be a lie.

It's her. It's Quinn. It's being this close to her.

I have no fucking clue how to feel about that.

"Hey, Hayes?" she asks after several quiet minutes.

"Yeah?"

"What are we going to do?"

"What do you mean?"

She leans up on her elbow, shooting daggers my way. "What do you mean *what do you mean*? I mean, what are we going to do about *this*?" She wags her finger between us. "Where do we go from here?"

"I…"

I don't say anything because I don't have a good answer for her. The right answer would be to chalk this up to getting it out of our systems and walk away, or for me to fire her. I don't want to do either of those things.

I want more of this. More of her.

But I also know it's wrong. I'm supposed to be turning my life around, improving myself, setting an example for my niece. I'm not supposed to be fucking her nanny.

"Where do *you* want to go from here?" I flip the question to her.

She nibbles on her bottom lip, thinking about it for

a moment. "Well, I certainly enjoyed what just happened."

"Me too."

"What if we just…do this?" she asks.

"Do what?"

"You know, fool around."

I raise my brows. "I'd call what we did more than just *fooling around*."

She rolls her eyes. "You know what I mean. *Fucking.*" The word goes straight to my dick, which has no business being half-hard again. "What if we just keep doing it? A friends-with-benefits sort of thing."

"But we're not friends. I'm your boss, and you're my employee."

It's funny because a few months ago, I wouldn't have cared one bit about power dynamics. I would have taken what I wanted from her and forgotten about her when I was done. Now though…now it feels like regressing, and for the first time in my life, I don't want to regress.

Even so, I'm not sure this one afternoon together was enough either.

"I'm not going to report you to HR, if that's what you're worried about. Wait, do we even have HR?"

"Honey, I *am* HR."

She smiles. "Say that again."

"I am HR."

"No. The other part."

I think back to what I just said. "Honey?"

She nods, the tops of her cheeks turning pink. "I like that."

"You do, huh?" Another nod. "Well, that's interesting...*honey*."

She giggles. "Okay, stop. We're trying to have a serious conversation here."

"I'm sorry, *honey*. I'll stop."

"Hayes..."

"Yes, *honey*?"

"See? That's why this is perfect. You're so annoying. I could never fall for you."

I laugh, but there's just a hint of unease that settles into my chest, and I don't know what it means.

"So, friends-with-benefits type thing, then, huh?" I ask.

"Yep. Just sex."

"Just sex." I nod.

"Flora could never find out."

"No. Of course not. We keep her out of this entirely."

The last thing I want is for her to get too attached to Quinn or the idea of us together because that's certainly *not* happening. We're just having fun. That's all.

"And when we've both had our fill, we walk away.

No harm, no foul," she says. I'm not sure if she's trying to convince me, herself, or both.

"The perfect plan," I echo.

But as Quinn tucks herself against me again and snuggles close, it doesn't *feel* like the perfect plan. In fact, it feels like I'm making a huge mistake.

Even so, I can't find it in me to stop.

"Fuck!" Keller throws his glove down the hall, and our poor equipment manager has to duck to miss being hit by it.

We lost in overtime. Sure, it's only our second game of the season and we still got a point, but we all know every point matters, especially when we should have had no problem beating the team we played tonight.

I can't help but feel guilty, having taken two penalties, allowing Winnipeg the chance to test their power play against us and score on it both times. If I had just stayed out of the box, we could have won and walked away with both points. But no. I couldn't stay out of trouble. Again.

"Hey, Kells, you dropped your glove," Lawson says, picking it up and chucking it back at him, smacking him right in the back of the head with it. Leave it to

Lawson to screw with Keller even when he's moments away from exploding.

I get where Keller is coming from though. We should have been better out there. *I* should have been better out there, but I wasn't, and I know exactly why. My mind was stuck halfway between watching my teammates battle for pucks and remembering what it felt like between Quinn's thighs this afternoon. We rolled around in her bed for hours, touching each other until she absolutely had to go pick up Flora. Though I hated the idea of washing the scent of her away, I hopped in the shower when she was gone, and by the time I got out, they were back and things were just as Quinn had promised—normal. There were no lingering looks, no secret touches. We went about our usual routine. There was no way anybody would have been able to tell what we were doing all afternoon.

But I knew.

Every look at her was a reminder of how soft her skin was. Every laugh or sigh was a reminder of how she sounded under me. And every time she looked at me, all I could think of was how she looked when she came, my cock buried deep inside her.

I carried those reminders with me on the drive to the arena, all throughout warmups, and not once did I shake the images as I stepped onto the ice even though

I should have been paying attention to the game. She distracted me, and she wasn't even here.

"I'm sorry," Fox says as we pile into the locker room, our heads hanging low. "Fuck, I should have made those saves. This is all my fault."

"It's on me," I say, taking the blame. "You were great, Foxy."

"I wasn't. I sucked. I—"

"Would you sad sacks knock it the fuck off?" Hutch stops at the top of the room, hands on his hips as he commands our attention. "It wasn't any one person's fault. We're a team, remember? Always we, never I. We play out there together. Losing that extra point was a team effort."

"More like *non*-effort," Lawson grumbles, then cowers back into his stall when Hutch shoots him a nasty look.

"Stop beating yourselves up. Yeah, we should have kicked their asses all day long, but we still skated away with a point, and that's better than none. Now we regroup and play better the next game. Heard?"

There are a few mumbled *Heard*s through the room, but they're barely audible.

"I said, *fucking heard?*" our captain yells.

"Heard!" we repeat back, clapping twice.

"Good. Now, rest up tonight. We're hitting the ice first thing tomorrow."

He stomps over to his stall and begins removing his pads just as Coach Smith walks into the room.

"Well, I was going to come in here with a speech, but it looks like Hutchinson had a peek at my notes because he just said everything I was going to." Coach nods at Hutch, mutual respect and understanding in the simple gesture. "Eight AM tomorrow. Tell your wives, husbands, partners and whoever else you need to tell that it's going to be a long one. We're running PP and PK until *I'm* satisfied, got it?" We all nod. "Hayes?"

I snap my head up. "Yeah, Coach?"

"Meet me in my office whenever you're done."

I swallow down the bile that's trying to work its way free. "Yes, Coach."

He leaves without another word, and the room is unusually quiet as we all strip off our gear and hit the showers. I don't rush through my post-game routine, but I don't dawdle either, knowing Coach wants to talk to me. I have no doubt it's about the piss-poor excuse of a game I just played.

Fuck, it's only the second game of the season and I'm already being called into the office. This is the exact opposite of what I wanted this year.

"Think a few of us are going to hit up Top Shelf. Want us to save you a seat?" Fox asks.

I shake my head. "Nah. Gotta get home to the kid."

He shakes his head. "Don't think I'm ever going to get used to hearing that."

I don't think I'll ever get used to saying it.

When there are just a few stragglers left, I make my way to Coach Smith's office. I figure if he's going to yell at me, might as well have as minimal an audience as I can get.

"Hayes," he says as I step through the doorway. "Have a seat."

He tosses his pen onto his desk, sitting back in his chair as I take the one opposite him. He runs a hand through his black and gray beard before placing it over his stomach, interlocking it with the other. The position screams relaxed, but it doesn't make my shoulders any less tense. He notices.

"You can relax. I'm not here to chew you out for those penalties you took."

My shoulders sink just an inch.

"We all have shit games. It happens. Of course, if this becomes a pattern like it was back in North Carolina, then we have a problem."

He levels me with those all-knowing brown eyes of his.

I shake my head. "No pattern, Coach."

"Good." He nods. "Now, how are things at home? How's it going with your niece? She adjusting okay?"

I smile just thinking of her. She was asking so many questions before I left.

"Why are you wearing funeral clothes?"

"Why can't Just Quinn and I come to the game?"

"Do I really have to go to school tomorrow?"

"Flora's good," I tell him. "She's really coming out of her shell."

"And you've got your nanny situation all settled?"

My nanny.

My nanny who I know tastes like butterscotch.

My nanny who I know sounds like the most beautiful symphony ever penned when she comes.

My nanny who I spent the entire afternoon fucking.

I shift in my chair. "Yeah, I got it figured out."

"That's good. I'm glad to hear it. I won't lie, while I was eager to get my first NHL coaching job, I was a little worried when I saw your name on the roster. Don't think I've forgotten all the shit you pulled with the Comets."

I grimace. "Yeah, sorry about that. I'm...I'm not that guy anymore."

Or at least I *hope* I'm not that guy anymore, despite what I'm doing with Quinn.

"No, you're not. You're a good guy, Hayes. You

have a bright future ahead of you and now you have that little girl to take care of. You need to set a good example for her, so if you don't keep on the straight and narrow for you, do it for her. Make good choices for her."

Make good choices for her. It sounds so simple, so easy. Yet I've already majorly fucked it up by screwing the first person in her life she's actually opened up to. I'm such a piece of shit.

"I will," I promise, hoping he can't tell it's a lie.

"Good. You're bringing the kid to the family skate, right?"

It's something new Coach Smith is starting this year. He wants us to bring our families to the rink so we can all get to know one another. Even the guys who don't have anyone like Keller, Fox, and Locke have to come too. Even they have to "bring that homeless guy who lives down by the arena," Coach said. So, I guess we're all going.

"Yep. We'll be there."

I should probably mention this to Quinn at some point. I meant to tell her yesterday, but I was too busy avoiding her. Then the plan was to tell her today, but I was too busy *not* avoiding her and forgot.

"Feel free to invite your nanny too. The more the merrier."

Bring Quinn around the guys? That sounds...

dangerous. Although her brother is a hockey player, so I'm sure she's used to their bullshit. Plus, their families will be here, which should mean they'll all be on their best behavior. At least they better be.

"I'll ask her about it."

"Good. Now get out of here." He flicks his chin toward the door. "You boys have a long, long day tomorrow."

"Good night, Coach."

"Night, kid."

I practically run from his office, eager to get away from his sage words that make me feel like shit.

Make good choices for her.

I think of it the whole way home. Through every traffic light and turn, it's on my mind. Even when I pull into the driveway, the house dark, I'm still thinking of it. When I walk inside and have my usual post-game drink, it's right there at the forefront. And when I walk past my room and straight into Quinn's, those words are practically on repeat.

Make good choices for her.

But I don't.

And I have nobody to blame for it but myself.

CHAPTER 15

QUINN

"We're so pleased with the progress she's made," Mrs. Aguilar, Flora's teacher, says as the kid waves goodbye to her friends. "She was so shy when Mr. Hayes first brought her in, but now look at her—she has friends."

I wasn't around when Flora first started school, but I remember how reserved she was even around me when I first met her. That little girl seems so far away now compared to the one in front of me.

I smile. "It's amazing, isn't it?"

"It is! I can't help but notice that she began blossoming around the time Mr. Hayes brought you on board. I think he made a wise decision in doing so."

My hackles rise. Is she saying Hayes is a bad parental figure? That he was somehow messing things up with Flora?

"Not that he's a bad guardian or anything," she

says, sensing my anger. "He was doing great on his own. But I think your presence has helped...bridge that gap between them, you know?"

I nod. I do know. I've witnessed it myself. They no longer sit in silence during meals or stare at each other awkwardly. They talk. They interact. Flora even helped Hayes with his tie before his game yesterday. They're like a little family now instead of strangers, and it warms my heart to see.

"Anyway," Mrs. Aguilar says, "just thought I'd let you know we think Flora is doing great and to keep up the good work."

"Thank you. I appreciate that," I tell her as Flora runs up to me, skidding to a stop beside us. "And I'm sure Mr. Hayes does too. I'll be sure to let him know."

We wave goodbye to Flora's teacher, then start our journey back to the house. I normally drive to pick her up, but it's a nice day out today, and I could use the walk to clear my head, especially after yesterday.

I did not anticipate falling into bed with Adam Hayes, nor did I think it would happen a second time. Or a third. Or the fourth. And I certainly did *not* expect the fifth when he came home from his game and snuck into my room at nearly midnight.

I can't say I'm complaining about that last one. Hell, I can't say I'd complain about *any* of them. Not when they felt so, so good.

I should probably be more disappointed in myself for sleeping with my boss *again*, but I can't find it in me to be. We're just having fun. It's not a big deal and we're two consenting adults. Where's the problem in that? As long as Flora isn't affected by it and I can still do my job, it shouldn't be such a big deal.

So then why do I keep getting this heavy feeling in my stomach when I think about it? Sure, I was the one who suggested it to Hayes in the first place, but even as I did, the words left a sour taste in my mouth. I ignored them last night because it was easier to when I was snuggled against his warm, hard body, but now? Now it feels less and less like a good idea.

Yet...I don't want to stop. I don't want to stop at all. Yesterday felt way too good, and I know for a fact I haven't had my fill of him yet. I've barely even scratched the surface. There's no way I could walk away now, even if I know I should.

I shake those thoughts away, tucking them into the back of my mind for me to spiral over later, and focus on the little girl by my side.

"So, how was your day?" I ask as we wait at the crosswalk.

"Good. Mrs. Aguilar wore a dress that had kittens on it."

"I saw that. I think she'd love my yarn-ball

earrings. Get it?" I nudge her. "Because cats love to play with yarn."

She shrugs. "I've never played with a cat before."

"Ever?"

"I wanted one really bad because my friend from my old school couldn't stop talking about hers, but my daddy said I couldn't have a pet because I was bad and didn't deserve it."

I frown. "That's not true. You know that, right?"

She just shrugs again, and it makes my heart ache. Her dad already sounded like a piece of work, but now I don't like him even more. I'm not saying every kid deserves a pet because there are some right little shits out there, but Flora isn't one of those kids. She's good, and her dad's a jackass for saying otherwise.

"I have an idea," I say, tugging on her hand and moving us to the opposite side of the crosswalk.

"But we live that way." She points in the direction of Hayes's house.

"I know, but trust me, okay?"

"Okay."

I should probably be worried she's going along with this so easily and not more curious, but I'm too excited about my idea.

"You're going to love this. I promise."

"All right, Just Quinn. But if I don't…"

"If you don't, *I* promise to eat a grilled-cheese-and-pickle sandwich for dinner tonight."

She beams. "You got yourself a deal."

"Mmm. This totally normal and pickle-free grilled cheese is *so* yummy."

Flora giggles, and I toss her a wink. I won the little bet of ours by a mile. The second I dragged Flora into the pet rescue, her eyes lit up, and she ran to their cages, sticking her fingers through the bars and cooing at the creatures.

She then begged and begged and begged to take one home—something I should have seen coming—but luckily for me, they were all already adopted, and I dodged that bullet. Before we left, I took a card from the owner, promising I'd be back after I spoke with Flora's uncle. Now I just have to convince Hayes it's a good idea.

He looks between us, his eyes narrowed in suspicion, and I just shrug.

"What?"

He points his fork—the one he's using for some weird protein-pasta thing he's eating—between the two of us. "You two are being weirder than usual."

Flora giggles loudly again, and I shoot her a look that says, *Calm down, you're gonna make him more suspicious.* Of course, that sends her into an even bigger fit of giggles, and soon I'm laughing along too, Hayes the only one completely confused by what's going on.

When I get Flora settled down, Hayes is sitting back in his chair, big arms folded over his chest. He looks so good like this, his hair still wet from his shower, muscles barely contained inside the Serpents tee he's wearing. He even trimmed his beard a little, making him look a bit less crazy, though I will miss the feel of it between my legs.

We've kept things totally normal between us today. Granted, he spent most of his day at the rink to make up for the Serpents losing in overtime last night, but still. We've been good. It's almost like we didn't break any rules.

Then he runs his tongue over his bottom lip, and I remember the feel of it as he licked at my pussy. *Oh yeah, we did break the rules. We broke them big-time.*

"What am I missing?" he asks, and I got so distracted by staring at him I almost forgot what we were even talking about. So much for things being totally normal.

I shake away all thoughts of our sexcapades and fold my hands together on top of the table like I'm ready for a serious conversation, and I guess I sort of am.

"Flora has something she would like to ask you, and I think it would be great if you kept an open mind."

He eyes me warily before slowly sliding his gaze to Flora. "What do you want to ask me?"

She sits up straight in her chair, tipping her chin high and clearing her throat. "I would like a cat."

Hayes barks out an abrupt laugh. "No."

"But I—"

"Absolutely not."

"I—"

"I said *no*," he says, more sternly this time with a finality that has her little shoulders sagging and the corners of her lips turning down.

She drops her chin to her chest and nods.

"Okay," she whispers, and my heart fucking breaks for her.

"Go get ready for bed," he tells her.

She scurries from the table without another word. I half expect her to slam her door closed with frustration, but that's not Flora's style. It *is*, however, my style, and if I don't get a good explanation from Hayes, I'm about two seconds from marching out of here and slamming my own door closed.

"Stop looking at me like that," he mutters, shoving out of his chair and taking his plate to the sink.

I don't even have it in me to be impressed he's cleaning up after himself. I'm too busy being pissed. How dare he talk to her like that. How dare he shut her down so coldly. How fucking dare he make her feel like her father did!

"You didn't even hear her out," I say to his back.

"Because I don't need to. We're not getting a cat."

"Why not?"

He sighs. "Because I said so."

"That's not a reason."

He drops his plate into the sink, making a loud clang, then spins to face me. "Because I don't need another thing to take care of, okay? I don't need another responsibility, another thing to completely screw up."

Is that what he thinks he's doing?

"You're not screwing up, Hayes. You're doing the best you can with what you've been given. But those words don't mean shit coming from me. You're not going to listen to me until you believe it, and I'm telling you right now, you better start believing it soon. Right now, you have a hurt little girl in the other room, and the only reason she's hurt is because you're scared."

I rise from my chair and go to check on Flora, leaving Hayes behind to clean up the mess.

He's the one who made it anyway.

It's nearly midnight when my door creaks open, and I'm not entirely surprised by it. I haven't spoken to Hayes since I walked out of the kitchen. Flora hasn't either. I put her to bed, only reading a few pages of her book before calling it a night. We were both too upset to continue. After, I shut myself in my room, resisting the urge to run back out to Hayes and give him a piece of my mind for upsetting Flora the way he did. It's one thing to have a conversation with her and tell her no, but it's another to handle it the way he did, especially since Flora doesn't understand that *she's* not the problem, he is.

I lie still as Hayes sneaks into my room, the door snicking shut softly behind him. He doesn't walk in right away. He just stands there, like he's waiting for me to kick him out.

I should. I really, really should. But I don't.

I sit up in bed and flip on my bedside lamp, and a yellow haze illuminates the room. Hayes is standing with his back pressed against my door, his head bent low just like Flora's was earlier at the table. It's funny how much they look alike sometimes.

He sighs, then lifts his head, and I hate that even in this hideous light, he still somehow manages to look so damn good in a simple gray t-shirt and flannel sleep pants.

"Are you still mad?" he asks quietly.

I nod. "Yes."

"Do you want me to leave?"

I shake my head. "No."

And I hate that too.

He stalks toward me, sitting on the edge of the mattress. "Look, you were right. I was a jerk to her earlier, and she didn't deserve it. It's just…" He rubs a hand over his beard, then sighs. "This is hard enough, you know? Adding a pet… It'll just be even more I have to worry about. Is she feeding it? Is she taking care of it? Is she making sure it doesn't escape? And don't even get me started on the inevitable vet visits with my schedule. It's a lot."

He looks stressed just thinking about it, and the urge to make him feel better overwhelms me. I crawl out from under my blanket and wrap myself around him until I'm sitting in his lap. He slips his arms around my waist as I wind mine around his neck, forcing him to look at me.

"Flora wouldn't be doing it alone, Hayes. I'd be helping her."

He shakes his head. "That's not fair to you. You

shouldn't have to take on more responsibility because I can't."

"What if I want to?"

"Then you're crazy."

"I mean, I am sleeping with my boss, so maybe."

He groans. "That's another thing I'm doing wrong."

"What?"

"You. This. Us. We aren't supposed to be doing this."

I shrug. "We're just having fun." I pause, then say, "Can I ask you something?"

"Sure."

"You're the youngest, right?"

"Unfortunately."

"Hey, there's nothing wrong with being the youngest." I narrow my eyes at him, and he cracks a smile—just barely, but still. "But there are two roles for the youngest—they're the wild child who can't be tamed. That's me, by the way."

Now he's really smiling. "You don't say."

"It's true. Crazy, I know." I wink at him. "Then there are the youngest who are forgotten. Their parents already raised other kids, so they're sort of forced to raise themselves. These kids become fixers, especially because they've always relied on themselves for everything. So they think every little problem should fall on their shoulders. I have a feeling you're a fixer."

"I'm not, though. I'm not, but I'm trying to be. I'm the wild child."

I shake my head. "No. You *became* the wild child. You weren't always, were you?"

He darts his eyes away, and I know I'm right.

"I actually got straight As in school. Full-ride scholarship. Can you believe that? I was at the top of my class. My parents didn't give a shit, obviously, but I did. If I had good grades, I could play hockey, and I *really* wanted to play hockey. Not just because it was my ticket out of that shithole town and shit life, but because I loved it. It was the only thing I had to get me through. I *had* to be good, or I'd wind up like them or Aiden, and that was the last thing I wanted."

He talks about the game the same way my brother does—like he would be lost without it. In Hayes's case, I think that might be true.

"Hockey saved you."

He nods. "Hockey saved me."

I have so many questions I want to ask him, so many things about him I don't know. But I can't think of them now, not when he's slipping his hand into my underwear, palming my ass. I know he's doing it on purpose. He's distracting me. He's avoiding talking about anything real. And I'm willing to allow it, especially with how good it feels as he kneads my cheeks, spreading them apart and letting his fingers dip into the crevice just enough to tease me.

"You know," he says, kissing my collarbone. "I don't think I ever noticed this mirror on the back of your door…"

"It's been there since I moved in."

It's such a stupid statement, but that's what I am right now—completely stupid. I can't be blamed. He's dragging his lips over my neck and up my jaw, nipping at me as his cock grows harder and harder by the second.

"It's giving me ideas."

"What kind of ideas?"

"Ideas where you finger your pretty little cunt, and I get to watch." He releases me, falling back on his palms that felt so good against me, and I feel so naked without his touch. "Turn around, Quinn."

I scramble to do what he says, flipping around in his lap until I'm facing the mirror. I straddle him backward, gasping when he spreads his legs, widening my thighs. I'm wet. It's so fucking obvious, the dark stain on my cotton underwear easy to see even in the dim light. I should be embarrassed, but I'm not. I can't be bothered. The look Hayes is giving me—like he's hungry and I'm the only one who can satisfy his need —doesn't allow room for it.

He grabs the hem of my shirt, pulling it over my head and dropping it to the floor so I'm sitting in his lap in nothing but my soaked panties.

"I want to see you," he says in my ear, and I barely hear him over my own heartbeat. He wraps his hand around my stomach, and goose bumps break out over my skin as he slides it up, cupping my breast in one hand and pinching my nipple. "Show me."

I nod, sliding my hand between my legs to the edge of my gray panties and pulling them to the side, revealing myself. He's seen me plenty before, but with the way his eyes widen and his nostrils flare, you'd think it was his first time.

"Fuck," he groans in my ear, and it's so damn hot I can hardly stand it. "Touch it. Touch it and tell me what you feel."

I slip a finger over my clit, and though the touch is soft, I still shudder, already so on edge. I circle the sensitive spot a few times, teasing myself before diving lower and slipping one finger inside.

I sigh, resting back against him. It's not as good as his touch, but it's better than nothing, especially right now.

"What do you feel, Quinn?"

"Warm."

"What else?" he prompts, practically panting in my ear, his eyes locked on what my finger is doing.

"Wet."

"And?"

"Tight." I sink my teeth into my bottom lip. "I'm so fucking tight, Hayes."

"Don't I fucking know it, honey."

He growls, low and throaty, like he's barely able to hold himself back right now, and I know the feeling. I add another finger, loving how his eyes spark when I begin thrusting them into my pussy, my fingers shining with my arousal.

Hayes watches me the whole time as I bring myself closer and closer to the brink, teasing with the palm of my hand over my clit every so often while he continues running his fingertips over my nipple. His attention doesn't waver from what I'm doing between my legs, and it's somehow too much and not enough all at the same time.

I want more. I want him.

I wiggle in his lap, and he chuckles.

"Do you want more?"

I nod. "Please."

"Then ask. Use your words, Quinny."

I hate begging. Absolutely hate it. But I'll do it if it means just a little bit of relief in this moment.

"Touch me, Hayes. Make me come. Make me scream your name."

He grins. "Happily."

He swats my hand, replacing my fingers with his, and I instantly feel so much fuller than I just was.

"Oh god," I moan, wanting so badly to close my eyes, but I know if I do, he'll stop, and more than anything, I don't want him to stop. I rock against him, not caring how eager it makes me seem, and he slides even deeper.

But it's still not enough. I want more.

"Hayes…"

I don't have to say anything else. He already knows. He slips a third finger into me, and now it's almost *too* much. I drop my head back, slamming my eyes closed against the sting of the stretch, and he grabs my chin, jerking it back down.

"Look at yourself," he says, his voice scratchy with need. "Look at the way your cunt stretches around my fingers. You're dripping for me. So fucking wet. All for me."

"For you," I say.

My eyes drop to where his fingers are lost inside me. His tattooed arm flexes as he pumps in and out, his thumb barely brushing against my clit. God, I look like a fucking mess. Sweat is slicked down the back of my neck, my hair is everywhere, and I'm the only one who is naked, Hayes still fully dressed.

"Do you want to come?"

"Please."

"Can you be quiet?"

I shake my head. "No."

"I didn't think so. But you're going to have to be, honey. Understood?" I nod. "Good. Now cover your mouth while you come on my hand."

I've never slapped my hand over my mouth so quickly before, and Hayes barely waits until it's there before he's surging into me, fucking me hard and fast with his fingers, his thumb on my clit as I ride the wave.

"Oh fuck," I say into my hand. "I'm coming. I'm—"

My orgasm slams into me, my legs shaking with the force of it, and I've never been so thankful for Hayes's instructions as I scream into my hand, unable to hold it back any longer. He fucks me through the onslaught, never once letting up, and I don't care that my pussy is sore from being stretched or that my legs are aching from being spread so wide.

I can't care.

Hayes slips his fingers from me and into his mouth, licking off my orgasm from each digit one by one, like it's his favorite meal and he wouldn't dare leave a drop of it behind. It's so carnal. So crude.

And I love every second.

I turn my head to his, capturing his mouth with mine, tasting myself on his tongue. He kisses me hungrily, like he's still not satiated. I'm not either. I wrench my mouth from his and crawl off his lap onto my knees between his thighs. I hook my fingers in the waistband of his flannel pants and tug them down.

"What are you doing?" he asks even as he lifts himself, allowing me to undress him.

I take his heavy cock in my hand, pumping it a few times before sliding my tongue from the base of his shaft to the tip, then back down again. I tease him over and over, sucking the head of him but not taking it any further, enjoying being the one in charge far, far too much.

He looks down at me with hooded eyes. "Tease."

I grin around the tip of him.

"As much as I'm enjoying this, I really want to fuck your throat."

He's so big and can barely fit there. There's no way I'm going to be able to deep throat him. Yet, my pussy throbs at the idea.

"Would you let me?" He runs his fingers over my jaw as I continue to tease. "Would you let me spill my cum down your throat, Quinny? Would you let me use you until you're so raw you're hoarse tomorrow?"

I nod.

"Use your words," he reminds me.

"Please, Adam. Use me."

"Good." He rises to his feet, gripping the base of

his cock as I stare up at him with want. "Then hold your hair back and put your tongue out."

I do as he asks, then wait. He slaps his heavy cock against my tongue a few times, then slides it against me, testing the friction.

"Fuck. So warm. So soft."

He slides in more, stretching my mouth around him the way he stretched me around his fingers. He gives me an inch at a time, letting me breathe through it until he bumps the back of my throat, and I gag a little. I feel him twitch at the sound.

He settles there, letting me get used to the feeling of him before backing away, and I gasp air in. He does it again, over and over until I'm taking him easier. Longer. Deeper.

But he's holding back. I can tell, and not just because his legs are shaking. It's the way his shoulders are tense and the sweat that's forming along his hairline. He wants to let go so bad, and I want him to, too. I hum around him the next time he slides in deep, letting him know I'm ready, and he gets the picture.

"Going to fuck you now," he mumbles, and it's the only warning I get before he completely gives in, surging into me and slamming against the back of my throat.

He was right—I am going to be hoarse tomorrow, but I welcome it if it means I get to feel him like this right now. I keep my promise, letting him use me until he's spurting into the back of my throat, a low groan leaving him as he fills me. I swallow him down the best I can, but it's too much, some of his cum dribbling down my chin.

Hayes pulls me up by my hair, then slides his tongue along the salty line before slamming his mouth over mine. He spins me around, pressing a hand to the middle of my back before I fold over and he surges into me from behind. I let out a loud yelp at the sudden intrusion.

"Shh!" he says, curling his body around mine and covering my mouth as he slides into me again. "Be a good girl and keep quiet, Quinny."

I nod, moaning as he fucks into me hard and impossibly deep. I'm tired and sore and I can barely keep myself up, but it's still somehow the best I've ever felt. I'm as quiet as I can be, and Hayes follows behind me shortly after, the room going from the sounds of our slapping bodies to nothing but our harsh breaths as he maneuvers us onto the bed, then collapses beside me. I lie there, struggling to catch my breath and unable to move, unable to think. I've died and this is the afterlife, I'm sure of it.

"Why?"

The sudden noise startles me, and I lift my head, turning to look at Hayes.

"What?"

He rolls his head, his silver eyes bright. "Why does Flora want a cat?"

I smile. "Because she's a kid and all kids want a pet. Didn't you?"

"Yeah, but I dropped it as soon as I was told I wasn't allowed to have one."

"She was told that too, by your brother. He said she was *bad* and *didn't deserve* one."

His dark brows slash together. "I fucking hate him."

I nod. "I think I do too."

He turns his stare back to the ceiling, going quiet once more. I watch him watch the blades of the ceiling fan turn and turn and turn again until my eyes are heavy with sleep, and I close them, ready to fall under its spell.

I don't know how long passes until Hayes says, "She can have the damn cat."

I fall asleep with a smile on my face.

CHAPTER 16

SERPENTS SINGLES GROUP CHAT

Lawson: Did anyone pack any extra underwear? I need to borrow some.

Locke: What in the actual fuck, Lawson?

Lawson: Well, did you?

Hayes: You are absolutely NOT asking that right now.

Fox: Look, I'm friendly and all, but that's too far even for me.

Hutch: I hate this group chat.

Keller: Fucking same.

Lawson: NONE OF THESE ARE REAL ANSWERS!

Lawson: I need underwear.

Hayes: Then go buy some!

Lawson: Dude, have you SEEN the prices of underwear these days? Those things are expensive!

Hutch: You make millions of dollars, dude.

Lawson: Easy for you to say. You're dating a billionaire.

Hutch: Who happens to be your girlfriend's sister. Does Rory know you're so chill about the idea of wearing other people's underwear?

Lawson: She'd totally understand.

Locke: But would she?

Fox: I'm guessing no. Because again...too far, Lawson. Too far.

Lawson: Whatever. You guys are the worst. Acting like I wouldn't wash them or something. I'm not rude. I have manners.

Keller: Should have packed better. You knew we were on the road for nine days.

Lawson: It's so many days though.

Keller: Would you rather be at home?

Lawson: I'm sorry. Have you SEEN my girlfriend?

Lawson: Wait. Don't answer that.

Lawson: But yes, I'd much rather be at home.

Lawson: But like...later this week. I want to beat the Comets and Columbus first.

Hutch: Please tell me someone has Greer's number so we can screenshot this conversation and show him how idiotic his brother is.

Hayes: I do!

Hayes: Sending it now, Captain.

Lawson: NO!

Lawson: I'M SORRY, OKAY?

Lawson: I. AM. SORRY!

Lawson: Greer is like SO mean. He's grumpier than Keller.

Keller: And that's saying something because I've met me.

Hutch: I don't know. I feel like they'd have some good competition with one another.

Fox: As if you have any room to talk.

Lawson: Oh, snap. Foxy getting sassy.

Fox: Sorry, Captain, but you know it's true.

Hutch: That's fair. Even Auden says I'm grumpy.

Lawson: She calls him Mr. Grumbles.

Locke: Awww.

Keller: Too fucking cute, Hutchy.

Fox: So sweet, Mr. Grumbles.

Hayes: Better than that stupid nickname Lawson came up with for himself. Lawless Lawson? Get real.

Locke: Can we just talk about the fact that he gave HIMSELF a nickname? So dumb.

Keller: The dumbest boy in all the land.

Lawson: Um, this dumb boy can still read, and he's incredibly offended!

Hutch: Not as offended as we are that you asked to borrow our underwear.

Lawson: I WAS GOING TO WASH THEM!

Hayes: Still gross.

Lawson: Your face is gross.

Lawson: Can we talk about something else? Like literally anything?

Fox: Sure. How's it going with your new nanny, Hayes?

Keller: Yeah, when do the rest of us get to meet her? I want to see her chew you out in person.

Lawson: Ah. Still such a highlight of my offseason.

Fox: Mine too.

Locke: I'm getting increasingly jealous that I didn't get to see this.

Hutch: I don't know what you guys are talking about. She was super nice when I met her.

Hutch: Auden can't stop talking about her earrings.

Hayes: I fucking hate those stupid things.

Lawson: I don't know. I thought they sounded cool.

Fox: They did.

Keller: Even I want to see them. And see if her ass is as nice as you say it is.

Hayes: Keller, I fucking swear...

Keller: What? We were all thinking it.

Fox: I wasn't.

Lawson: Me either.

Hutch: Nope.

Locke: Literally only you, man.

Keller: Come on. WTF? I'm not the bad guy here! That's Lawson's job.

Lawson: Excuse me, I'm a good boy now.

Keller: Fine then. It's Hayesy's job.

Hutch: Not anymore. He's, like, responsible and stuff. So is Locke. And Fox is...well, he's Fox. Ever the gentleman.

Fox: Howdy.

Locke: Sorry, Kells. Looks like you're the bad guy now.

Keller: This is bullshit.

Keller: Totally unfair.

Keller: Hayes, go back to being a shitbag.

Hayes: Sorry, man, no can do. I've turned over a new leaf.

Keller: Then turn it back over.

Hayes: Not happening.

Lawson: Haha, Kells, you suck the most now.

Keller: Not as much as your mother sucks.

Hutch: Booo!

Locke: Booo!

Hayes: Booo!

Fox: Booo!

Lawson: What's it like to be the most hated, Kells?

Keller: Never felt better.

Lawson: Liar.

Keller: Fuck you, Lawsy.

Lawson: Love you too, buddy.

CHAPTER 17

HAYES

I love being on the road. Exploring new cities and meeting new people is one of my favorite parts of playing hockey. Right now, I should be loving it even more with the eight-game heater we're currently on, but on this long, nine-day trip, all I want is to be back home with Flora.

And fine, if I'm being honest, Quinn too.

It's not even entirely because I miss the smell of butterscotch or the way she tastes or the way she sounds when I'm inside her. I miss the ten thousand throw pillows she's put on my couch and the punny dish towels she's hung around the kitchen. I miss her snark and her eye rolls, and I even miss those ridiculous earrings she wears all the time. When I called to FaceTime with Flora last night, she had on a pair that were kittens wearing space suits. It reminded me I need to ask Lawson about adopting a cat for Flora.

"Yo, Lawsy," I ask during the second intermission. "Can I get Rory's number?"

The room goes from a bunch of loud-as-fuck hockey players all chatting at once to complete silence in two seconds flat.

Lawson lifts his head from his stall opposite me, then cocks it to the side. "I swear, Hayes, if you're about to make some uncouth comment about my woman, I will murder you, witnesses and all. I'm not opposed to spending a few years behind bars if it means defending my girl."

Honestly, the thought of making a sex joke about Rory didn't even cross my mind, and that's saying something for me.

I hold my hands up. "Nah, man. Totally innocent. I, uh, I want to adopt a cat, actually."

"What? All sad and lonely by yourself, so you're becoming a cat man now?" Keller asks.

"Guarantee even with that kid, I still get more pussy than you."

There's my old self.

"Your new nanny already putting out?"

I rise from my stall before I can stop myself, marching toward Keller, who is smirking like a cocky prick.

"Hey, whoa, easy," Fox says, standing up too. "Let's chill."

Locke joins in, both of them looking ready to hold me back if they need to, but they aren't the ones I'm paying attention to. It's Hutch. His head is tipped to the side, his eyes sharp as he studies me.

In hindsight, maybe I *shouldn't* have gotten out of my stall and tried to attack Keller. It makes me look awfully guilty, and though I am, that's the last thing I want to seem like. I tear my eyes away from him, turning my attention back to Keller, who is still fucking grinning.

"Leave Quinn out of this."

He shrugs. "Whatever, man."

He goes back to lacing up his skates like what just happened was nothing. For him, it probably was. I swear he gets off on getting riled up before games. He lives for the thrill of the spar. Usually Lawson is his partner, but I guess tonight it's me.

It's all my own fault too. I'm fucking anxious and all keyed up, ready to go home. It's been a long nine days, and I'm ready to be back in Quinn's bed.

No. Wait. *My* bed. I'm ready to be back in *my* bed.

Okay, fine, Quinn's too. But that's not the point. I just want to be home.

I blow out a breath, then return to my stall. Locke and Fox only sit down when I do. They don't have anything to worry about. I'm not going to jump Keller. Hell, just a few months ago, I would have said the same thing if the roles were reversed.

Man, what the fuck is up with me lately? Maybe Hutch is right. Maybe I am growing up.

Speaking of my captain...

He's still staring at me. Still studying me. Waiting for me to slip up again. But I don't. I stay on my best behavior the rest of the night, and we even win, beating Columbus 5–2, and that's *with* me taking three penalties.

Guess I can't change all my spots.

"Trick or treat!"

"Whoa!" I jump back, pretending to be scared of the little girl dressed in a black shirt and pants and a pink tutu that looks like it's been dipped in mud. Her face has been painted green with little black lines made to look like whiskers that match the ears on her head. "And just what are you supposed to be?"

She huffs, rolling her eyes. "I told you, Uncle Adam. I'm a zombie cat." She lifts her furry gloved hands like claws. "Rawr!"

If I thought the cat talk would die down after I told

Flora no, I was wrong. She's just found more subtle ways to bring it up. I've been pretending to be annoyed by it even though I've secretly been in talks with Rory —Lawson did finally give me her number—about adopting one. What Flora doesn't know is that one of her treats tonight is going to be delivered here in the form of the tiniest black kitten, and I can't fucking wait.

"My bad. I totally forgot you're obsessed with cats now." I pat her head, careful not to mess with her cat ears. "Are you ready to go get some free candy from strangers?"

"I thought I wasn't supposed to take candy from strangers?"

"You're not."

"Then why do I get to do it tonight?"

Fuck. She has me there.

"Because… Because…" I rack my brain, trying to come up with a good reason, but I have nothing.

"Because your uncle Adam will be there to fight off any bad guys, *plus* we'll be checking your candy to make sure nobody has poisoned it."

"Poison?! Now I have to worry about poison too?!"

But I can't worry about Flora's questions. Not right now. Not when Quinn is walking into the kitchen wearing the most skintight one-piece I've ever seen in person. She's decked out in black head to toe, looking like she just stepped out of a superhero movie or something. In addition to the black spandex suit and tall black boots, she's wearing a black wig and black sparkly ears. She's even painted whiskers on her face and colored the tip of her nose pink.

It's hot. *She's* hot.

And fuck, I can't wait to peel it all off her tonight.

Well, maybe not the boots. Or the ears. We'll see.

"You don't have to worry about poison," she says as she messes with her ears. "Do you have your bucket?"

"Oh!"

Flora rushes to her room, presumably for her candy bucket, and it leaves me and Quinn alone for the first time since I got back from the road. I wanted to sneak into her room so badly last night, but it was late when we landed in Seattle and even later by the time I made it home. I didn't want to worry about waking her up.

Seeing her now, I'm regretting it.

Don't get a boner, Hayes. Not when you're about to take your niece trick-or-treating for the first time.

"There. All better." She drops her hands to her hips and grins at me. "What?"

I can't help myself—I close the small distance between us, capturing her lips in a heated kiss, coasting my hand up the back of her neck and holding her tight. She melts into me, and I press her to the counter, crowding every inch of my body against hers.

Fuck, I missed this.

I missed kissing her and touching her and smelling her and everything else that comes with her. I try not to read too much into that as I reluctantly pull my mouth from hers.

"What was that for?" she asks through harsh breaths.

"Have you seen your costume?"

She grins. "Why, Mr. Hayes, are you telling me you like my cat ears?"

"And those stupid yarn-ball earrings," I say, nuzzling her neck, loving it when they smack against my forehead. "You look hot, honey."

She giggles. "Thank you."

"I'm going to fuck you in those boots later." I slide my hand over her hip, tugging her close so she can feel how serious I am about this. I'm hard as hell right now. So much for not getting a boner.

"I was hoping you'd say that," she says.

"Why, Miss Quinn, did you wear them just for me?"

"Maybe I did. Maybe I didn't. Maybe I—"

"I'm ready!"

Quinn shoves at me and I fall backward, my back ramming right into the kitchen island. I grunt at the impact, hoping that's not going to hurt tomorrow for the game, and try to play it cool as Flora comes to a stop just at the edge of the kitchen.

"What's going on?"

"Your uncle was helping me with my earring. How do they look?" Quinn tucks her hair behind her ear, showing them off for the kid.

"Good. Are we ready?"

I laugh at her impatience, but I don't blame her for it. When Quinn told me she had never been trick-or-treating before, I was pissed but not surprised. Of course my brother didn't bother taking her. He's a self-centered jackass who didn't do shit with his daughter and only cared about whatever drug he could get in his system next.

"We're ready."

"Then where's your costume, Uncle Adam?"

"Oh! I almost forgot!" Quinn runs by us and back down the hall to her bedroom. She emerges a few moments later carrying another pair of ears.

"What is this?" I ask, taking them from her outstretched hand.

"Ears."

"Ears?"

She nods. "We're all wearing matching costumes tonight."

"Quinn…"

She widens her eyes, jerking her head toward Flora, and I sigh, giving in because *of course* I give in.

"Fine. I'll wear them." I slip them over my head, hating every second of it. "Happy?"

The two girls look at each other and burst out laughing.

"What's so funny?"

"Nothing. You just forgot to turn them on."

She reaches over and presses a button on the right ear, and it's so fucking bright I can see their pink shadow from here. There's no doubt in my mind I look stupid. Completely fucking ridiculous. I'm wearing light-up cat ears for fuck's sake.

But if it meant Flora and Quinn would smile at me like they are now, I'd wear them every day.

I think I might be in trouble.

"Flora! Someone's at the door for you!"

"For me?" she calls through the house, but I don't hear her feet hit the floor.

She's been sitting at the kitchen table since we got home, pulling piece after piece of candy from her bag, separating it by type, then handing it over to Quinn to inspect for poison, because apparently she's *very* concerned about it.

"Yep! I think you're going to be *meowy* happy about it."

"Did you just say *meowy*?"

Her feet hit the floor, and Lawson stands before me, bouncing on his heels. I swear he's more excited about this than I am.

"Dude, she's gonna freak." He rubs his hands together. "And Daisy is so going to kill me for coming home smelling like a cat."

"She will not. She's used to it from me," says his girlfriend, Rory, as she sticks her hand into the pumpkin-shaped candy bucket to pet the sleeping kitten that's tucked away inside. "Besides, who could be mad at this sweet face?"

"We are *not* getting another cat, Wednesday. Don't even think about it."

"Excuse me, you have *three* dogs. I have one pet— one!"

"Okay, wow. You're just going to forget you're the mother of my children, huh? Forget we're *co-parents*? Noted."

I roll my eyes at them and their bizarre conversation, then turn just as Flora marches into the living room. Quinn trails behind her with a smile.

"I was counting my chocolates," Flora announces

proudly. Then she spies Rory and Lawson on the other side of the door, and all her bravado vanishes. Her shoulders roll inward, and she shrinks down an inch, her steps slowing to a crawl.

"This is one of my teammates," I tell her, motioning her forward. "They brought something over for you."

"For…me?" she asks, hesitation clear in her voice.

I nod. "Yep. Come check it out."

She inches closer, then practically attaches herself to my leg as she peeks up at Lawson and Rory. Lawson drops to his haunches to match her height.

"Hey, kid. I've heard a lot about you. Name's Lucas."

"Hi, Lucas," she whispers.

He hitches his thumb over his shoulder. "This here is Rory, but you can call her Wednesday if you want."

"That's a day of the week, not a name."

Rory laughs, dropping down beside Lawson. "He's silly. Sometimes I ignore him. You can too." She holds her hand out. "It's lovely to meet you, Flora." They shake hands. "I'm a veterinarian. Do you know what that is?"

"An animal doctor."

"That's right." Rory grins. "And as an animal doctor, sometimes people bring me pets they don't want anymore or can't take care of."

"That's what happened to me," my niece whispers, and I grip the doorknob so tight my knuckles turn white.

Fuck my brother and his stupid fucking face. I'm glad he's in jail so he can't mess this little girl up more than he already has. He doesn't deserve her. He never fucking did.

Rory's eyes well up with tears, but she blinks them away as quickly as they came. "Well, then I guess you and this little creature have something in common."

She holds the pumpkin bucket out, and Flora cautiously—oh so cautiously—steps forward and takes a look inside.

One.

Two.

Three.

That's how many seconds it takes before she lets out the loudest shriek I've ever heard.

"A kitten!" she yells. "You got me a kitten!" She looks up at me. "You got me a kitten?"

I nod. "I got you a kitten."

"But I thought you said…"

"I know what I said," I say, dropping down to her level, "and I was wrong to not hear you out. So I thought about it"—I look over at Quinn, who isn't as composed as Rory and is definitely wiping away tears, before I turn back to Flora—"and I decided you're ready for one. You *deserve* one because you're the best kid I know."

It's lightning fast, so quick I don't even see it coming. Flora flings her arms around my neck, and she squeezes me so tight I can barely breathe, but I don't care.

She's hugging me.

Flora is hugging me.

She's never hugged me before, and I never realized how badly I needed it. Emotion climbs up my throat, robbing me of the ability to say anything as I squeeze her back just as tight, letting go far before I'm ready.

"Thank you, Uncle Adam."

"You're welcome, kid." I sniffle, hoping like hell Lawson isn't going to make fun of me for it later. "You want to hold her?"

"It's a her?"

Rory laughs. "Yes, she's a girl. I can teach you how to hold her properly if you'd like."

"Yes, yes, yes!"

I wave Lawson and Rory into the house, and they take Flora over to the couch. Rory talks to her about what to expect and how best to hold the kitten before pulling the black ball of fuzz from the Halloween bucket, coaching Flora as she takes hold of the little creature. She smiles down at it, happier than I've ever seen her before, and that includes the time we let her get *three* different flavors of ice cream.

"Hi, Pickles. It's nice to meet you."

"Pickles? Is that her name?" Rory asks.

Flora nods.

"Why Pickles?"

"Because I love her like I love pickles, and I love pickles *a lot*."

I laugh. It's perfectly Flora.

"Hey, man," Lawson says, walking over my way. "This is great. She loves it."

"She does."

"Just don't let her get too carried away, you know? Next thing you know, she'll be asking for another cat, and you'll have to say no because you're the man of the house, dammit. You can put your foot down whenever you want. And—"

"I'm getting another cat, Lawson," Rory says without even looking away from Flora.

"Yes, yes you are, Wednesday. Whatever you want." He turns back to me with an eye roll. "Women."

Only there's nothing but absolute love and admiration in his voice when he says it. The guy has fallen hopelessly in love, and it's hilarious to watch him get humbled by it.

"By the way, love the ears," he says, clapping me on the shoulder before returning to Rory's side, his hand going right to her waist like he can't help but touch her.

I don't care that he just made fun of my ears, which I didn't even realize I'm still wearing. I'm too busy watching Flora fall in love with the cat. She cuddles the kitten gently, running her finger over her nose and tickling her belly. She plays with her, wiggling a toy around for Pickles to chase. They bond, and it's so damn sweet I find myself having to look away a few times, my eyes stinging.

Quinn steps up beside me, butterscotch tickling at my nose.

"You're a good uncle, Hayes," she says quietly. "The best one I know."

As badly as I needed Flora's hug, I think I needed those words even more.

CHAPTER 18

QUINN

"Are you sure this is okay?"

Hayes lets out an exasperated sigh. "Yes."

I bet he is irritated. This isn't the first time I've asked the question. Or the second. Or even the third.

"But I'm not family. I'm just the nanny."

Just the nanny, I say like he didn't eat my pussy this morning before the sun even rose. I haven't been *just the nanny* for quite some time now, and with the look Hayes is currently giving me, he's thinking the same too. But going to a family skate day? That feels out of line, even for me.

"You're family, Quinn. Just deal with it."

I nod, following behind him through the parking lot as we walk into the arena. Halfway across, Flora holds her hand out for me, and I smile, catching up with them and grabbing it. She grins up at me.

Maybe Hayes is right because I certainly feel like family right now.

The last two weeks have flown by, and I swear Flora is becoming more and more like a kid every day. She's obsessed with Pickles and is doing so well with all the tasks that come with having a pet. And Hayes... Well, he's spent every night he can in my room, and I have no complaints about it. I should, but I don't. We've been having far too much fun for me to worry about any potential fallout.

We make our way into the rink, and it's so strange to see the building so quiet. The few times I've been here have been during games when it's bustling and filled to the brim with people.

"Hey, Gino," Hayes says, nodding at the security guy standing off to the side as he leads us through the building.

We get a short tour as we make our way down to ice level, where many players are already out skating around with their families.

"Hayes!" an older man with gray streaks in his dark hair calls out, waving us over.

A gorgeous redhead who must be at least ten years younger than him stands at his side, beaming up at him with nothing but love in her eyes.

"Hey, Coach." Hayes shakes the older man's hand. "Thanks for having us."

"Of course, of course." He drops his eyes down to Flora, who is now hiding halfway behind my legs. "Hi, Flora. Good to see you again."

She smiles shyly, her cheeks turning pink. "Hi, Coach Smith."

She's clearly smitten with him, and all I can think is, *Same, girl. Same.* I've never really been into older guys, but I could certainly get into this man. He turns his attention to me, and I can't help but stand up a little straighter. I've met a few of Hayes's teammates, but this is different, and I'm admittedly a little nervous about today.

Will they be able to tell we're sleeping together? That he sneaks into my room every night and whispers dirty, dirty things into my ear? That he calls me *honey* and fucks me until I scream? I sure as hell hope not. I don't need their judgment. I get enough of that from my family, thank you.

"Which must make you Quinn. Heard a lot about you. All good, of course." He tugs the redhead to his side. "This is my Emilia."

Not *This is Emilia.* No. *My* Emilia. I want to be somebody's *my.*

I sneak a glance over at Hayes and am surprised to find he's already watching me. I can't quite decipher the look in his eyes, which are a shade or two darker than normal.

I swallow, then turn back to the coach and his partner, waving at them. "It's lovely to meet you both."

"We have skates here you can use." Emilia points to a rack holding several different pairs. "Or if you brought your own, that's fine too. We also have snacks and drinks over there." She points across the way. "We just ask that you don't bring them onto the ice. Other than that, have fun!"

We thank them and move to the rows of skates. Hayes explains the sizing and picks out the best ones he can find, then directs us to one of the benches they have set out. Hayes gets his skates on, then works on Flora's while I lace up my own, having been out skating with Brody several times. I'm no expert like Hayes is, but I know enough.

"You ready, kid?" Hayes asks Flora once she's all laced up and ready to go.

She looks out to the ice, her lips turned down. "I don't know…"

She's scared. I try to look at it from her perspective —this big arena with bright lights and loud music and people she doesn't know. Not to mention she's never done this before. I would probably be scared too if I were her.

"Your uncle and I will be right there with you the whole time, okay? We'll even hold your hands if you need us to."

"You promise?"

I tuck my lips together to hide my smile and nod. "I promise. Right, Hayes?"

He nods. "Yep. We'll be right there. Promise."

"Then okay," she says, rising from the bench. "Let's go."

I look over at Hayes, who has pride shining in his eyes as she shoves her shoulders back and shimmies out toward the ice. She slips when she takes her first step, but Hayes is there to catch her, and she gives him a wobbly smile.

"See? Told you I got you. You okay?"

She nods. "I'm good."

She tries again, making it a few feet this time before stumbling. I skate slowly beside them as we make it halfway across the ice, Flora getting braver by the second.

"You're doing great, kid," Hayes tells her. "I'm proud of you."

"Th-Thanks," she says, still a little shaky.

We do this for about ten more minutes before she asks to try by herself.

"Are you sure?" Hayes asks, frowning slightly, and I love that he's so worried for her.

She bobs her head up and down, her tongue poking out the side of her mouth as she concentrates on skating. "I'm ready."

"Then go for it. I'll stay nearby in case you need me."

She takes off, her little legs moving as fast as she can get them to. She's not smooth by any means, but she's doing it. Hayes hangs back with me, watching her closely.

"She's horrible," he says, and I laugh.

"We can't all be professional skaters, you know."

He moves toward me, and for a second, I think he's going to wrap his arm around my waist and tug me to him, but he stops, almost like he catches himself, and I exhale sharply. I glance around, making sure nobody just saw that, but instead of being relieved they're not paying attention, I'm hit with jealousy because that's what they're all doing—touching. Laughing. Playing with one another.

The only person I want to touch me can't.

"Dude, is that the kid?" asks a mammoth of a man as he skates up to us. He's scowling like he's angry, but I have a feeling that just might be how his face is. "She's as bad a skater as Lawson."

"Hey! I'm not bad!" the man in question insists, skating to an abrupt stop and throwing snow up on the other grumpy-looking guy. "Stop being a dick, Keller."

"Stop saying *dick*. There are kids around," Keller throws back.

I laugh, and all eyes turn to me.

"Ah." Keller grins roguishly. "You must be *the nanny*."

I'm not sure I love the way he says it or how Hayes's shoulders stiffen when he does.

"Kells…" he warns.

"What?" The guy shrugs. "She is, isn't she?"

"I am." I stick my hand out. "But I usually prefer to go by Quinn."

He slips his hand in mine, and the only thing I can think is *It's not Hayes*. It's not bad, but it's not the same either.

"Nice to meet you, *Quinn*."

"You too."

Hayes steps forward, his shoulder brushing against mine, and I drop Keller's hand instantly.

"Who did you bring?"

Keller points to the corner where an old man stands talking to Coach Smith. "My neighbor Harry. He's a big hockey guy. Probably having the time of his life right now."

"Holy shit. Did you, like, do something *nice* for somebody?" Lawson gapes at his teammate.

"Shut up," Keller grumbles, and I have a feeling this is highly unusual for him.

"I think it's awfully nice you brought him along," Fox says, skating up to the group. "Ma'am." He tips his hat at me with a shy grin.

"*Awfully nice*," Lawson mocks. "See? I told you you say shit like that, country boy."

"Be nice, Lucas." Rory stops next to Lawson, her arm looped through Auden's. I've never seen them together before, and even though I know they're twins, I still didn't expect them to look so much alike.

"Hey, Quinn." Auden smiles at me. "You having fun listening to these idiots bicker?"

"They're...something."

Hayes looks down at me. "I'm sorry. I should have warned you."

"Brody Benson is my brother, remember?"

"Holy shit," Hutch says, wrapping his arms around Auden's middle and tugging her back against him, and I try not to let myself be envious of the simple action. "You're Benson's little sister? From Tennessee? No way."

I shrug. "That'd be me."

"That guy is amazing. Sucks to play against him because he's so fast, but damn is he fun to watch."

I smile, loving how they talk him up. Brody, of course, would let their praise go right to his head, but he's just like that. Always loves having his ego stroked.

"Dude, look at Flora, Hayes." Lawson points across the ice. "She's fitting right in with Locke and his ten thousand nieces and nephews."

We all look over and yep, Flora is having the time

of her life, skating around with Locke and a whole horde of kids.

"Man really took *family day* to heart," Keller remarks with his arms crossed over his chest.

"You're just sad your mom didn't want to be your date, huh?"

"Actually, I was more upset your mom turned me down. She was busy—"

"Don't finish that sentence, Keller!"

Lawson charges after him, but he skates away. Hutch and Fox take off after them.

"Dammit," Coach Smith says. "Boys!"

Then he joins in on the kerfuffle. It's chaos, but that's the beauty of hockey. It's wild and rough and certainly never boring.

Hayes looks down at me. "I should probably go help. You good?"

I wave him off. "I'll stay with the girls. Go rescue Keller. He might need it."

"Oh my god. Don't let Lawson hear you say that. He'll never shut up if he knows you like him." Rory rolls her bright green eyes.

"I don't understand how you put up with him half the time," her twin says with a shake of her head.

"Honestly, me either. But he's Lawson, so…" Rory smiles as she watches his teammates try to wrestle

Lawson off Keller, completely smitten with the exhausting man.

That same bitter taste from before climbs its way back up my throat. They're so free with their feelings and looks and touches, and I want that too. I look over at Hayes, who has given up on helping keep Lawson and Keller separated and is now over with Flora, teaching her how to skate backward.

He's changed so much since I first met him. He's not so on edge all the time, relaxing into his guardian role. He's become patient and gentle. Watching them, you'd never think they're uncle and niece. They're more like father and daughter, and it warms my heart to know he's loving Flora like she was always meant to be loved. She deserves it, and he does too.

"How is Flora doing with Pickles?" Rory asks as we begin a slow lap around the 200-foot rink. "Everyone adjusting okay?"

"They're both great," I tell her. "The cat even sits on the edge of the tub with her while she showers. They're infatuated with one another."

"I love that. My cat, Hades, is the same way. And of course, Lawson takes Daisy everywhere, even places he's not supposed to."

"Still cannot believe he snuck her into a movie theater," Auden says.

Rory just shrugs like she expects nothing less, and I'm sure she doesn't at this point.

"So, how are you liking working for Hayes?" Auden asks. "It's been what, two months now?"

I nod. "Yeah. It's going great, actually. I wasn't sure at first because I've barely babysat, but Flora is like the easiest kid ever."

"Wait. If you hadn't nannied before, how'd you get into this whole thing with Hayes?"

"Actually, it was my mother's doing. She knew Hayes because he's a regular at her bakery, and when she found out he needed a nanny, she sort of volunteered me. I happened to be between jobs at the time, then one thing led to another, and...well, here we are." I shrug.

"Wow. That's amazing. You like it, then?"

"I do. It's the best job I've ever had."

The words tumble out of me before I even realize what I'm saying, and the craziest part is that they're completely true. This *is* the best job I've ever had, and I don't just mean because of the money and the sweet, sweet benefits. I genuinely like nannying. I like playing with Flora and I like teaching her. Those little moments when everything clicks for her... I don't know. They make me happy, make me feel like I've accomplished something. This truly has been the best job for me, and I've had *a lot* of jobs.

"Have you thought about taking that and doing something else with it? Maybe teaching?"

"Auden," Rory scolds out of the side of her mouth. "Geez."

"What? I was just curious. She's got that spark in her eye, the same one you get when you talk about animals or when Hutch talks about hockey or me when I talk about building something—passion."

Is that what she sees? Truthfully, I hadn't given the job much thought beyond what I've been doing. Yes, I like spending time with Flora, but becoming a teacher? I don't know. Could I even do something like that? It's a big responsibility, and we all know how irresponsible I am.

But the thought doesn't scare me as much as I thought it would. In fact, it sounds like fun. Like something I might actually be able to do.

"I don't know. We'll see," I say noncommittally, but the idea still spins in the back of my mind.

We do a few laps around the rink, then when I see Flora is still busy with Locke and Hayes has his eye on her, I skate off to find a bathroom. Auden's words stick with me the whole time.

Is there really passion in my voice when I talk about taking care of Flora? Is teaching really an option for me? It would require me to go back to college for a third time, something I'm sure would please my parents but would give my siblings more ammunition if I fail. Is that something I want to really do? Could I even do it while still being a nanny?

I like to think I'm handling it all quite well between Flora's school schedule, Hayes's hockey schedule, and now taking care of Pickles too. Heck, I've even managed to clean out half of my storage unit over the last few weeks, and I haven't even spent any of the money I've made from selling it all. Would adding a few courses really be that hard?

I finish up my business in the bathroom and pull open the door only to step right into a brick wall that smells distinctly of cedar.

Hayes.

He catches me as I stumble, moving us back into a darkened corner and crowding me against a wall.

"Fancy meeting you here."

It's all he says before he takes my lips in his, kissing me hard until I'm gasping for air. When he pulls back, my knees are shaking, my breaths just as unsteady.

"Well, hello to you too." I smile up at him, and it's a long way given he didn't take his skates off and now stands even taller than usual. *Why is that so damn hot?*

"Sorry. I couldn't resist. Haven't gotten a chance to do that yet today."

I want to remind him we usually *don't* do that until he slips into my room under the darkness of night, but

I can't be bothered. Not when I want to kiss him again so badly.

I do, pushing up to my tiptoes and sliding our lips together in a soft, slow kiss. His tongue moves into my mouth, slick against mine as he explores, making me moan and writhe against him. Somewhere in the back of my mind I know this is a bad idea since we're so exposed, but then he presses his hard cock against me, and I lose all ability to think properly.

"You feel so fucking good," he murmurs into my neck. "Wish I could fuck you right here."

"Me too."

"Last night wasn't enough."

"It wasn't," I agree as he nips at my neck and I run my nails over his scalp, loving how soft his auburn locks are between my fingers.

"I can't wait to get you naked again."

"I can't wait either."

"Can we leave the lamp on tonight? I want to take you in front of the mirror. I want you to see how good you look when you're stretched around my cock."

"We can do anything you want," I promise him, meaning every word.

"Anything, hmm?" He slips his hand into the back of my jeans. "Even have a go at that sweet, sweet ass of yours?"

I hum with pleasure. I've never done any ass play,

always been too scared. But with Hayes? I trust him so much I'd be willing to try just about anything.

"Did you wear this on purpose?" he asks, fingering the hem of the Serpents jersey I'm wearing, the one with the number 18 on the back. "Just to tease me?"

I lift a shoulder. "Maybe."

"Fuck, you don't even know how hard I am seeing you in this."

I giggle. "Considering your cock is poking me in the stomach right now, I'd say I have a good idea."

"It's going to kill me staying away from you the rest of the afternoon, you know that, right?"

The feeling's mutual.

But I don't voice that out loud. It makes me think of all the times I've had to resist reaching out for him. All the times I've had to stop myself from kissing him when he's extra gentle with Flora. All the times I've had to walk away because I almost say something that resembles me liking him.

It's getting to be too many to count.

"We should probably get back out there," he says after kissing me breathless again. There's no way my lips aren't going to be swollen when we go back to the ice. "You go first."

"Me? Why me?"

"Um, because my dick is as hard as steel right now

and I should probably think of horrible things to get it to go down?"

I laugh, shoving him away when he tries to kiss me again.

"I think if you stopped kissing me, that would help."

"Or," he says, stalking closer, "I could just kiss you again."

And because I'm weak, I let him. This time when he breaks the kiss, I swear it's the last.

"We should probably get back out there," I repeat his words.

"Or…" His eyes spark with mischief.

"Adam," I warn.

I realize my mistake instantly as his eyes darken.

"Oh, honey…" he whispers before reaching for me again, and I can't help but giggle, excited for what's to come.

But it's not at all what I was expecting.

A throat clears. We freeze. Hayes stands in front of me, keeping me hidden as best he can, craning his neck to see who's there.

"Hey, Hutch," he says calmly, like he doesn't have his hand up my shirt. "What's up?"

"Flora's asking for you," the Serpents captain says.

"Okay. I'll be there in a second."

"And Quinn too."

I gulp.

Fuck. I got so carried away with Hayes just now, I forgot all about Flora for a moment. *This* is why I couldn't be a teacher. Not because I'm incapable of doing the schooling, but because I'm too unreliable, too flighty. Too irresponsible. Just like everyone's always said.

"Be there in a second," Hayes repeats.

He doesn't look back at me right away. He's too busy watching Hutch as he retreats back toward the ice, and there's no mistaking the panic in Hayes's eyes. He lets me go as soon as Hutch is gone, putting far more distance between us than we have in a long, long time. I miss him instantly.

He hitches his thumb over his shoulder. "We should probably…"

There's no playfulness behind his words anymore. He means it this time. Our stolen moment is over, and it's back to pretending we're strangers, pretending he doesn't know every inch of my body or how to turn me on with one simple look.

"Yeah." I nod, pushing off the wall and running my hands through my hair. "Let's get back out there."

I breeze past him, ignoring the look he's giving me, the one that says he wishes he never followed me back here. I drop down onto the bench, reaching for the skates I abandoned. I'm slowly lacing them up when

Hayes goes marching past me, ignoring me like I'm not even there.

I might as well not be. I don't belong here. I'm not family. I'm just the nanny.

And that's all I'll ever be.

"Pickles!"

I whip my head toward the ice and watch in horror as Flora flails around, chasing after a small black kitten that's slipping and sliding across the ice.

What the fuck?

"What the fuck?" Hayes voices my thought out loud, skating after them both.

Everyone scrambles to get out of the way, all watching the frenzied scene in front of us unfold. I run to the edge of the ice, snatching up the kitten just as it tries to run off.

"Pickles, what the hell are you doing here?" I ask, snuggling the frightened animal close.

"Flora, what the…" Hayes says, catching up to her as she stops in front of me. "Where did Pickles come from?"

"My pocket." She points to the front pocket of her hoodie.

"You had her in there the whole time?"

She nods. I thought her pocket looked heavy, but I just figured it was stuffed with snacks or toys or a book, not a damn kitten. I guess I should have known, though. She carries the little thing everywhere with her. Of course she'd want to bring her to the rink today.

"Where did you…" Hayes shakes his head. "Where did you even get the idea to bring her with you?"

Flora points across the ice, right at the guy standing with his arm around Rory. "Uncle Lawson told me I could!"

"Lawson!" Hayes growls, skating after him, and for the second time during family skate day, the guys have to wrestle someone off Lawson, Coach Smith getting right in the middle of it.

I stand on the sidelines watching it all go down.

Just like I always do.

Just like I always will.

CHAPTER 19

HAYES

"This has to be the worst idea I've ever had, and I'm sleeping with my nanny."

"Hey, I happen to think *both* ideas are good."

I hold up my scratched and bloody hand. "Tell that to Coach Smith, who is going to have some serious questions when I roll into practice tomorrow all banged up."

"Just tell him the truth—you suck at building."

"I don't suck," I say through clenched teeth as I try to pry free the nail I put in crooked as shit.

Sunday Funday at the Park with Just Quinn and Flora the Little Flower has become one of Flora's favorite days, and since I'm hardly ever able to make it there to hang out with them, I got a wild hair up my ass and thought it would be a good idea to bring the park here. So, I've been spending this cloudy, cold November day building a playset in the backyard.

Sure, I could have had it delivered already assembled, but when I saw the salesman flirting with Quinn, I got pissed and told him to skip the sales pitch, then declared I could build it myself.

I was wrong. I'm four hours into this, I'm not even halfway done, and Flora gets home from school in two hours.

"Just take a deep breath." Quinn inhales steadily. "Then let it go."

I do as she says, but as expected, it does nothing to calm me down. I pick the hammer back up and channel all my frustration into getting the damn crooked nail out. When it finally pops free, I toss the hammer across the lawn and lie back, drained from the world's saddest playset build.

Quinn crawls across the grass next to me, laying her head on my chest.

"You're right. A nap sounds nice right now."

"Why do you need a nap? You haven't done anything all day."

"Supervising is very tough work, you know."

"Is that so?"

"Yes. I'm *thoroughly* exhausted."

"Oh, I doubt that, honey."

She lets out a shriek as I roll over on top of her,

burying my face in her neck. I press my lips below her ear, then over her jaw, not stopping until my lips are on hers.

Butterscotch. Always fucking butterscotch.

I kiss her until she's writhing underneath me, silently pleading for more with her body. It's been like this a lot with us lately, stolen moments where we can't seem to keep our hands off each other.

Like the one where Hutch caught us. I still haven't talked to him about it, and I'm trying to put that off as long as possible because I know he'll have nothing positive to say about it. How could he? I hired Quinn to help me with Flora, not dry-hump me in the middle of the day. I know we should probably stop before we get carried away and nothing else gets done on this playset, but I can't seem to find it in me to break away from her.

So I don't. Instead, I slide my hand down her leg and bunch her skirt in my hand, pulling it up, up, up until her warm pussy is pressed to my cock that's been straining against my jeans all afternoon.

"Shit," she mutters, arching her hips into me. "That feels so good, Hayes."

She sounds so needy, like I didn't fuck her against the door the second she got home from dropping Flora off at school.

"We should probably go inside," she suggests when

I finger the edge of her underwear, seeking access to my favorite place.

"Why? You scared someone will see us?"

She nods, and I laugh.

"There's no one here but us. Mr. Potts, who lives to the left, goes out to lunch with his daughter every Thursday. And the Yorks to the right won't be back until at least five thirty." I kiss her softly. "So if you want me to fuck you right here in this backyard, just say the word."

Her hazel eyes, a little more on the green side today, spark with heat, and she nods frantically, pulling at the button on my jeans.

"Ah, ah, ah." I move my hips out of her reach, and she frowns. "Use your words, Quinny."

She rolls her eyes and sighs. "Shut up and fuck me, Adam."

She undoes my pants, shoving them down my ass just far enough, and I slide her panties to the side, slamming into her with zero finesse. I don't care that it's sloppy and has zero rhythm. I don't care that I'm kneeling on top of the playset instructions or that I lied and have no clue if Mr. Potts is at lunch right now.

All I care about are the sounds Quinn is making, the way her cunt is gripping me tightly, and the way she calls my name when she falls apart around me.

I'm starting to wonder if I should care about why I don't care at all.

"Motherfucker!" Keller slams his stick against the board, snapping it right in half.

Nobody reacts, completely used to his outbursts. I don't blame him. Once again, we're sucking when we should be winning. It's frustrating that we can beat some of the best teams in the league, then struggle against teams we should easily outplay.

"Come on, Fox. Come on, come on, come on," Lawson mutters beside me as the Chicago player barrels down.

We've both been benched for the last ten minutes, Coach Smith trying to send the message that we need to get our shit together.

"Son of a bitch!" he yells as the opposing player sends the puck soaring past our goalie.

Fox sits in the net on his knees, hanging his head. He's done for the night. Coach isn't going to let him stay in after that soft goal. Dash, our other goalie, puts his helmet on and readies himself to hit the ice. Fox skates slowly toward the bench, his shoulders sunken in, and I know the guy is going to be beating himself up over this.

It's just not our night. Sometimes you have games where you just suck, and this is one of them.

He skates down the tunnel, likely taking a break before the cameras are trained on him, ready to pick apart his game.

"Hayes! Lawson! Go!"

We jump over the boards in unison as our names are called, getting a second chance with the new goalie. The puck hits my stick, and I skate harder than I have all night, carrying it into the zone with minimal pushback from Chicago. They're taking it easy this shift, trying to suss out what they can and can't get away with now that there are new guys on the ice. They play it too safe, and I get my first shot of the night. I miss, but the puck soars over to Lawson, who shoots it back to me and I try again.

Still nothing.

We skate it around, taking a few checks from the Chicago players but winning the board battles. I zip it over to Lawson, who tries the same angle I did, and the lamp lights up, silencing the crowd.

"Fuck yes!" he cheers, and I skate up to him, bumping helmets. "Let's get to work!"

We run by the bench, fist-bumping everyone, even Foxy who is looking a little happier than when we left the ice, then we go again. We manage to make it within a goal, but in the end, it's not enough. We still walk back to the locker room with zero points on the night.

It's crushing.

The room is quiet as we strip out of our gear, missing that usual banter and fun as we go through our post-game routines.

"It was a tough loss out there tonight," Coach Smith says. "We fought back, but it wasn't enough. I'm still proud of you. You didn't give up when it got hard. That's the real struggle, you know? It's not losing. It's being able to walk away at the end of the night and still look at yourself and know you gave it your all. You boys did. Now rest up. We got work to do."

"Heard!" we all call out.

That's really the last thing most of us say as we file out of the room and onto the bus back to the hotel for the night. We have two days off, so we're not flying to Detroit until tomorrow.

When we walk into the hotel, I head for the bar instead of my room like I should so I can call Flora. It's just been one of those nights, and a drink sounds good to take the edge off. I'm unsurprised when Hutch slides onto the stool next to me a few moments later, and I sigh. I've been waiting for this conversation.

"I'll take one of whatever he's having," he tells the

bartender of The Sinclair Chicago, who nods and pours him a cold one.

They slide it over the bar top and hurry down the stretch as a few other teammates join us on the other end. Guess tonight is a good night to drink our feelings.

"So, the nanny, huh?" Hutch says after several quiet moments.

I nod. "The nanny."

He whistles lowly. "That's something. Not surprising, but still something."

I look over at him for the first time, narrowing my eyes. "Why is it not surprising? Because I'm an idiot who has no self-control and usually fucks everything up?"

"No. Because of the way you were looking at her that day Auden and I watched Flora."

"What do you mean?"

"What I mean, *dumbass,* is it was obvious you were into her."

I scoff. "I was not. I barely even knew her then."

Sure, I had kissed her, but I wasn't *into* Quinn. I was just a horny idiot. I'm *still* just a horny idiot.

"How long?"

I shrug. "A while."

"Before or after the season started?"

"Technically, the night it started. Unless you count our kiss."

He lifts his brows. "Damn, you wasted no time, did you?"

I want so fucking badly to punch him off his barstool right now, but I know if I do, it'll cause a scene, and there are too many people around for that.

"Like you have any room to talk." I wave my hand around the bar we're sitting in. "You fucked the woman who built this when it went against her contract."

His eyes darken. "Don't talk about Auden like that."

"Then don't talk about Quinn like that."

He smirks, and I want to punch that off too.

"Stop fucking looking at me like that," I growl.

"No."

"Yes."

"No," he counters, sounding too much like Lawson right now for his own good.

I roll my eyes with a huff. "Whatever."

He laughs. "Look, I'm not here to judge. I'm really not. We both already know I have no business doing so after what Auden and I did."

"Then why are you here?"

He shrugs. "I don't know. Just to let you know I know and I get it. Sometimes we meet people we shouldn't want, but we do anyway, and we do things we shouldn't do to have them in our lives. It's not the smartest decision, but it's still one we make, you know?"

I do know. Being with Quinn is a decision I make every day, and even when I know I'm making the wrong one, I can't help it. He's right. I am into her. Big-time.

I wish I could stop, wish I could go back to being annoyed by her inability to make a black coffee right. But I can't. Hell, I bet if she made one now and messed it up, I'd find it endearing. She's just gotten under my skin like that.

"I like her," Hutch says. "For what it's worth. You seem…different lately. I know you kind of got the shit end of the stick at the beginning of the summer with all the crap with your niece, and I know you were struggling with adjusting. But now, since Quinn came along, you've seemed a lot more like your old self. As much as I hated that guy in the beginning, I kind of missed him, and it's good to have the old you back. I think you have her to thank for that."

I have been feeling a lot like my old self lately. I chalked it up to getting proper sleep, not having to worry about Flora every waking moment, and being back on the ice, but maybe there's something to what Hutch is saying. Maybe it does have to do with Quinn.

"Anyway," he says, "your secret is safe with me. So if you were worried I'd say something to someone, I won't. I'll keep my lips sealed until you're ready to tell everyone else."

"Tell everyone else what?"

"That you're with Quinn."

"I'm *not* with Quinn."

He laughs as he stands up. "Right, Hayesy. Whatever you say."

He pats me on the back twice before heading up to his room. I don't realize until he's walked away that he never touched his drink, and I haven't touched mine either. Suddenly, a beer doesn't sound so good right now. At the moment, I kind of just want to call home.

I make my way up to my room, falling backward onto my bed and trying to shut out the shit game and even the conversation with Hutch. I inhale deeply, then exhale, and all it does is remind me of Quinn trying to coach me through building that playset I never finished. I smile, thinking of Flora and her.

I miss them.

I pull my phone from my pocket and hit Quinn's name. It rings only twice before she answers.

"Hello?" she says, sounding like she's out of breath. Like she ran to answer the call...*my* call.

"Hey. How's it going?"

She sighs sympathetically. "Better than your night, apparently."

I grunt. "I'd hope so."

"Flora's asleep already."

"I kind of figured. It's late."

"Oh."

I called for you.

But I don't say that. We've been doing this a lot lately. I call even when I know Flora is in bed for the night and Quinn tells me so, but we still talk anyway. I wish I could chalk it up to not liking being alone with my thoughts, but I don't think it's that. I think I just like talking to her.

I clear my throat. "So, how was your day?"

I swear I hear her smile. "It was good. Long. Flora and I baked cookies, *and* we didn't burn the house down, so you better say you're impressed, or we won't save you any."

"Who are you kidding? You weren't going to save me any anyway."

She laughs. "That's true."

"I'm impressed. And thankful. I'm not sure I could have handled a phone call from the fire department tonight."

"I probably would have just let you be surprised when you got home."

I chuckle because she so would. "I'm not sure if I should say thank you for that or not."

"You should."

"Then thank you."

We fall silent, and I scoot up on the bed, pressing my back against the headboard as I loosen my tie.

"Sorry you lost tonight," she says quietly.

"Me too."

"You tried though. That counts for something, doesn't it?"

"You sound like Coach Smith."

"He's a smart man. A very, very hot smart man."

"Quinn…" I growl in warning.

I know Smith is very dedicated to Emilia, and I know there is no way anything would ever happen between him and Quinn, but the idea still sends a wave of jealousy through me.

"What? You have eyes. You can't deny it, and you know it."

She giggles. She's totally fucking with me, and damn if it isn't working.

"You're doing a very good job of distracting me from playing like shit, you know."

"I'm trying. Tell me all the good things you like about the game."

"The money."

She laughs loudly, then I hear her slap her hand over her mouth. "Shh. Flora's sleeping."

"You always did have trouble being quiet."

"Hayes…" Now it's her turn to give me a warning.

"Anyway," she says pointedly. "I'm sure the money part is nice."

"Very much so, especially given how broke I was growing up. I can't tell you the number of times I stole peanut butter from our local grocery store just so I didn't starve because my parents always conveniently forgot to go shopping."

"That's…"

"Fucked up? Yeah, I know."

Though I can feel the sadness coming off her, I like that she doesn't try to tell me how sorry she is for me. I've always hated everyone's pity whenever they find out about my past.

"How—and please don't take this the wrong way— how did you afford to play?"

"I didn't." I laugh lightly. "We had this community center in town, and I used to go a lot because it was free and a safe place to hang out after school. Anything was better than going home, so I would sit and watch the practices and games. I fell in love with the sport without ever stepping on the ice. One night when I was about ten, during a particularly bad fight my parents were having where I got an ashtray lobbed at my head, I snuck out of the house and into the rink. I found an old pair of skates in the lost and found, and I took 'em for a spin." I smile, remembering it. "I could barely make it around the ice the first lap, but on the second?

I was golden. Flying all over the place. For the first time ever, I felt free, like nothing bad that was happening at home could touch me out there."

I blink rapidly, my eyes suddenly stinging. I try not to look back at the shit life I had too often, and right now, it's feeling a lot closer than it has in a long time. I have no idea why I'm telling Quinn all this, but I can't stop.

"Anyway, I got caught. I guess the coach was in his office working late, and I had no idea. He came out and busted me, then offered me the bargain of a lifetime—I could pay him back for using his rink by keeping his locker room clean, and in exchange, I could come out and skate whenever he wasn't using the ice."

"You spent way too much time out there, didn't you?" she guesses.

"Yep. I was out there every night and every morning, skating until my legs were screaming at me."

"Did you just skate, or…"

"Eventually, Coach noticed my dedication and gave me a stick and some gloves. It was used, ratty equipment that was way too big for me, but I didn't care. I worked hard for a year and saved every spare penny I had from mowing lawns so I could pay the registration fee and join the league. Of course, I hadn't thought of actually buying equipment that fit me. But I guess at that point, Coach had a special interest in me and gave me some stuff he said was 'defective' that just happened to be my exact size." I laugh to myself. "Of course, I realize now he bought it specially for me, but man, I was ready as hell to believe the lie back then. Anything that got me on that team."

"He sounds like a great guy," Quinn says.

"He was. The best. He coached me, spending extra hours at the rink to run drills with me to get me up to where I needed to be, and then he personally took me to and from games. He gave me a chance at a better life, and I wish he were here right now to see me living my dream. Probably wouldn't be proud of some of the shit I've pulled along the way, but…"

"Maybe not you throwing that statue into the pool."

I wince. "That was such a stupid move."

"It was, but we all make mistakes. We all do those things we aren't supposed to that sound good in the moment and come back to bite us in the ass later."

Like us. We aren't supposed to be doing what we're doing, but it sure did sound good when we agreed to this affair of ours. Now… Well, fuck, it *still* sounds good, even though we still aren't supposed to be doing it.

Guess I haven't quite learned my lesson, huh?

"But he'd be proud," she says. "There's no way he

wouldn't be. You're playing in the NHL, you have a niece who worships you, and you're no longer destroying hotel rooms just for the fun of it. I'd say that's something to be proud of."

She's right. That *is* something to be proud of. Sure, it's the bare minimum, but it's still something. Better than how I used to be, that's for damn sure.

"Thanks," I say.

"You're welcome."

We fall silent again, nothing but hushed breaths and running thoughts. And mine are definitely running right now.

Where is she? Is she curled up in her bed or on the couch, a muted TV show flashing across the screen? Is she wearing those ridiculously short sleep shorts she prances around in? Is her hair that feels like silk between my fingers up in a messy bun or hanging loose around her shoulders? Does she smell like butterscotch?

Oh, who am I kidding? Of course she smells like butterscotch.

"Well…" she says after several minutes. "I should probably head to bed, and you should too. I know it's late there."

It *is* late, and I *should* get to bed. But I want to keep talking to her too.

Then she yawns, and I know there's no way I'm going to keep her up.

"Probably, sleepyhead."

"Hey, I've been wrangling a seven-year-old and a cat named Pickles who she tried to sneak into school all day. What have you done?" She pauses. "Wait. Don't answer that."

I laugh. "That's what I thought. Just one more question…"

"Yes?"

"What are they?"

She definitely smiles this time. She always does when I ask about her earrings. "Sushi rolls."

"But you don't even like sushi."

"So? They're still cute."

I shake my head. *Quinn logic.*

"Good night, Adam," she whispers.

"Night, honey."

When I finally crawl into bed, I don't even spend the time falling asleep thinking about my horrible game. I think about Quinn and her sushi earrings and all the other things about her that make me smile. What we're doing might technically be wrong, but I can't help but think it feels so, so right.

And I have no idea what to do about it.

CHAPTER 20

QUINN

"You cannot be serious right now."

Hayes shrugs like it's no big deal. "It's fixed."

"I can see that. I just…" I put my hands on my hips. "How the hell did you do this?"

"I went to the shop and paid for it and the guy handed me the keys and then I drove it here last night."

I thought his SUV sounded a little loud coming up the driveway, but I was so excited to see him that I didn't even give it a second thought. Now I'm thinking I should have.

I glare at him. "You know exactly what I mean. They've been running me around for the last two months. How did you get them to actually work on it?"

He points to himself. "Big scary hockey player." He

turns his finger to me. "Pint-sized grown woman wearing fish-stick earrings."

I finger the jewelry hanging from my ear—the top half is a fish, the bottom is a tree branch. "How dare you insult these beauties!"

"They're hideous."

"I like them," Flora says as she runs her hands over Pickles's back. The two are so attached to one another that Flora can bring her outside and the cat doesn't even try to run. She's too busy being in love with the kid.

I give Hayes a look that says, *See? She gets it.* He rolls his eyes.

"This is too much," I tell him. "At least let me pay you back."

"No."

"Hayes."

"No," he repeats.

I stomp my foot. "Fine. Then take it out of my salary."

"I'll get right on that."

But he says it in a way that most certainly tells me he will *not* be doing so.

"Fine. Then I'm driving to Thanksgiving dinner and I'm using *my* card to fill up the gas tank."

"Fine."

He marches over to the SUV that, only if the

information were tortured out of me, I'd admit I'm going to miss driving around and pulls Flora's booster seat from the back, then buckles it into the back of my cherry-red VW Bug.

He nods toward my car. "Get in, kid. Don't want to be late for dinner."

She picks up the cat. "Pickles *loves* Thanksgiving. She's so excited to eat turkey."

"You're not bringing the cat."

"But Mrs. Bess said I could."

"She did not."

"Actually," I interject, "she did. In fact, she said, 'Now you make sure to bring Pickles to dinner. I want to snuggle that sweet little baby.'"

It's a lie. *I* was the one who told Flora my mother said she could bring the cat, mostly because I know my mother won't care at all if she brings Pickles along.

Hayes huffs. "Then bring the damn cat. But we have to go, especially if we're stopping for gas."

"And dessert," I call over the hood of the car as I make my way to the driver's side.

"What dessert?"

"Cookies," I explain as I take my spot behind the wheel.

He looks completely confused but opens the door for Flora—and Pickles—then climbs in behind us. He doesn't say anything else until we stop in front of George's.

"You're kidding me."

I shrug as I parallel park the Bug effortlessly. "Trust me, this is exactly what she expects."

"For you to bring *someone else's* cookies into her home for Thanksgiving dinner when she's been sweating over the stove all morning?"

"Yep."

"You're horrible." He pouts in the front seat as I exit the car and run inside George's.

"You fixed it!" the old man calls from behind the counter as I run toward the back.

"Hayes did!"

I snatch up a box of butterscotch cookies, then think better of it and grab two because I just know it's going to be a long day. When my mother found out Hayes hasn't had a proper Thanksgiving in far too long, she was not having it. She insisted he and Flora come to ours, and I won't lie, it made me love her even more. They both deserve this, to have some good homecooked food and to feel my mother's love.

"How'd he do it?" George asks as I approach the counter, but not before tossing a bag of butterscotch candies onto the cookies.

"Apparently," I say as I dig through my purse for the wallet I know I shoved in there, "he used his big, broad muscles that look far too good in a shirt and threatened them or something."

George doesn't say anything, which is incredibly unusual. I peek up to find him staring down at me, his bushy white brows nearly kissing his hairline.

"What?" I hand my card over. "Can I get some cash back too? Twenty bucks in small bills. I owe Flora five dollars because I bet her uncle would cave and let her bring Pickles to dinner."

He still doesn't say anything. He doesn't even move to grab my card. He just stares.

"Uh, Earth to George." I wave my hand in front of his face. "You're not having a stroke, are you?"

The side of his mouth kicks up into a grin. "You're playing house with him."

I jerk my head back. "Excuse me?"

"The hockey player. You're playing house with him, aren't you?"

I scowl. "No. Now ring me up, old man."

Slowly, he grabs the cookies, running them under the scanner. "You're lying, kid. To me, and to yourself."

"I am not."

But the words don't come out as strong as I hoped they would. Is he right? Am I playing house with Flora and Hayes? I know the lines are a little blurry given what's going on with Hayes and me, but do I look at us like we're one big happy family?

Yes.

They're coming to Thanksgiving with me, for fuck's sake. I mean, sure, that was mostly my mother's doing, but I didn't even try to fight her when she suggested it. In fact, I was thrilled by the idea of bringing someone to dinner for the first time, having someone there just for me because they're mine.

Shit.

George is right. I'm playing house with Hayes and Flora.

And I think I wish it wasn't playing anymore.

"Whatever," I mumble, grabbing my stuff and heading out the door before he analyzes me any more. "Happy Thanksgiving!" I call over my shoulder.

"Quinn! We aren't done talking about this!"

"Yes we are!" I say back, running out of the store and straight to the car.

"You good?" Hayes asks as I hand him the cookies, completely out of breath.

"Yep."

But I'm not good. I'm not good at all.

"Are you nervous?"

I nod, blowing out a heavy breath as I stare at the

lilac-painted door, the same color that welcomes you to B's Bakes. My mother's favorite, as Hayes will soon find out.

"To visit my family? Always."

I'm always on edge when we have family dinners, but today my nerves are extra frayed. It's all George's fault, that grouchy old man I love so dearly. He had to go and get all in my head about "playing house" with Hayes and Flora, and all I did on the ride over here was overanalyze absolutely every last second of the past two months.

Am I spending more time with them than I realized? Yes. Would I rather spend my off days hanging out and doing something with them than going somewhere on my own? Yeah. Is there a chance I'm inserting myself into their lives so deeply that when this is all over, I'm going to be irrevocably changed and completely crushed? Absolutely.

Yet I can't find it in me to stop. I love Flora. Being with her is the highlight of my day. I drop her off at school with a frown and pick her up with a smile, so excited to get to spend more time with her.

And Hayes? Well, it's safe to say I am immensely enjoying my time with him. Perhaps a little too much. We've gone from stolen nights to spending our time without Flora together doing the most mundane things like building a swing set and painting Flora's room a pretty blush and even doing laundry together. It's so… normal. And not at all like two people who swore it was just sex and nothing else.

"I thought you loved your mother," Hayes says, pulling me out of my head.

"Oh, I do. Very much so. My father too. It's my siblings that are the nightmare."

"That bad?"

He doesn't even know. Well, maybe he does a little since he has an awful brother too. It's not that my siblings are truly awful people. They have their faults, sure, but at their roots they're good. I think they just forget about being good where I'm concerned.

"Can I press the button now?" Flora asks, Pickles tucked safely in her arms.

"Just a minute."

I draw in another breath, then release it slowly, feeling Hayes's eyes on me the whole time. I'm sure it probably seems like I'm blowing this out of proportion, but he doesn't know what it's like to be the screwup in a family full of otherwise perfect children. I'd like to believe they're going to be on their best behavior with Hayes here, but I know they'll still take jabs at me. They might be jabs only I'll understand, but they'll hurt all the same.

"Whenever you're ready," Hayes says soothingly.

I nod. "I'm ready."

"You sure?"

"Yep. Let's do this. Flora, go ahead."

I'm sure my mother will have something to say about how family doesn't have to ring the bell, but Flora loved the idea so much, so she's going to have to live with it. As we wait, I work through the breathing exercises I learned during that one yoga class I took.

In through your nose, out through your mouth.

In through your nose, out through your mouth.

In through your—

Then I'm not breathing at all. Instead, I'm looking down, down, down to where Hayes has taken my hand in his, his long fingers curling between mine. He squeezes once, twice, then three times, and my worries slowly slip away. My shoulders relax and my breathing goes back to normal, not forced. It's like a weight has been lifted, and I have him to thank.

"I'm here," he whispers so low only I can hear.

I smile up at him, having no doubt he means it. He didn't let the body shop bully me around. He's certainly not going to let my family do it.

The front door clicks open, and I drop his hand, shuffling an inch away and trying to make it look as natural as possible, but it doesn't matter. My mother isn't looking at me. She's beaming down at Flora and Pickles.

"Oh my goodness! You brought a cat!"

"Wait," Hayes says. "I thought—"

"Just like you requested, Mom," I say, stepping forward and widening my eyes, hoping she'll understand.

She nods. "That's right. I *did* ask to meet this adorable, lovely little thing. And the cat too, of course." She winks at Flora.

The kid giggles. "You already know me, Mrs. Bess." She holds the cat up. "This is Pickles. She's my best friend." Flora looks back at me. "Sorry, Just Quinn."

I grin. "That's okay. I'll allow it. Pickles is awfully cute."

"She is." She thrusts the cat toward my mother. "You want to hold her?"

"You know what? I do, but not right now. I've got some potatoes on the stove that need stirring and a turkey that needs basting. Can I hold her later?"

Flora nods. "I'll allow it."

My mother chuckles as she rises back up to her full height, smiling over at me and Hayes. "I'm so glad you came, though you could have just walked in."

Knew that was coming.

She waves us inside. "Come on in. Everyone else is already here."

Great. Even though I made sure we left ten minutes earlier than we needed to, I still managed to somehow be late. Can't wait to hear my siblings get on me for that.

We follow my mother inside, taking our shoes off by the door, and I watch as Hayes takes the house in. It's nearly the same size as his, but he's looking at it like it's a mansion or something, and I wonder if he thinks this is where I grew up.

"My parents moved here about two years ago," I tell him. "I grew up in a small town on the Peninsula."

"Gosh, I miss that house sometimes," Mom says. "Don't get me wrong, I love this one, but that one just had a coziness to it, you know? It was well loved."

"Small. She means small. I lived in the attic until I was fifteen."

"Because you *chose* to, Quinn Penelope."

Hayes smirks at me. "Penelope?"

"What? It's better than Adam Carlisle Hayes. I mean, you're named after a vampire doctor."

He rolls his eyes, and I stick my tongue out at him.

"This," my mother says, stopping at the hall closet door, "is my favorite piece of the house. I wanted to bring a bit of the old into the new and made poor Chuck pull it off the hinges and bring it with us."

She opens the door—also lilac—and proudly shows off the scratches on the inside, each one marking a different kid's height over the years. I don't miss his rough swallow as he takes it in. He hasn't gone deep into the particulars of what his home life was like, but I've surmised enough to know it wasn't anything like mine, and he certainly didn't have his parents marking his growth when he was younger.

"Can you guess which one was Quinn?"

"Well, considering it hasn't moved in twelve years, I'm guessing that one." He points at the line that is indeed mine.

"I swear I ate all my vegetables."

"That's a lie. I saw you put your Brussels sprouts in your napkin at our last family dinner."

I shrug. "Not all of them. I ate...two."

My mother shakes her head, waving us forward. "Come meet my other kids. They can't believe *the* Adam Hayes is having dinner with us."

I bet they can't. I guarantee each of them has charged their cell phones to the max and are ready to take pictures to post all over social media. I bet we don't even get the turkey carved before someone is asking for free tickets to a game. It's the thing they do with Brody. I'm sure they're proud of him in their own way, but they're mostly worried about what Brody can do for them, not what they can do to show up for him.

I wish he were here. He'd get the biggest kick out of me bringing Hayes to dinner.

"Chuck!" Mom calls as we enter the kitchen that has more lilac items spread around it. From the mixer to the custom-painted fridge, the color is everywhere. "Get your dang fingers out of that pumpkin pudding!"

"Sorry, sorry." My dad scoots away, holding his hands up as my mother swats at him. He catches sight of me, Hayes, and Flora and grins. "Quinnicorn!" He wraps me in his arms. "Good to see you, kid."

"Hi, Dad." I hug him tightly, then step back and point to Hayes. "This is Adam Hayes, my *boss*."

Hayes coughs loudly, side-eyeing me because he's certainly not *just my boss*. He extends his hand to my father.

"Nice to meet you, sir."

"Ah, no sirs. Just Chuck. I understand you prefer Hayes?"

"Please. I've never been a fan of Adam."

That's a lie. He likes Adam just fine when I'm screaming it.

I push that thought away. No sense in getting worked up with family around.

I point to Flora, who is trying to hide behind Hayes's leg. "And this is Flora."

"Flora. Oh, I've heard so much about you, little flower."

Her eyes widen. "That's what Just Quinn calls me."

"She does? Well, ain't that something. Say, is that a cat you're holding?"

"This is Pickles. Do you want to hold her, Just Chuck?"

My dad laughs at the name. "You bet I do! Come on. Let's go meet my grandkids. I think you're going to like them."

Dad takes Flora's hand—which she's surprisingly okay with—and leads her into the family room, which I have no doubt my nieces and nephews are having the time of their lives tearing up.

"Mom, do you need any help?" I ask her. She's already back at the stove, stirring this and mixing that.

"*You're* offering to help? Considering I'd like to eat sometime today, I don't think that's such a good idea, *Quinny*."

I groan inwardly as Matthew walks into the kitchen, a beer in his hand. I have no problem with Hayes calling me *Quinny*—in fact I love it—but when one of my siblings does it? I loathe it. It's always so… condescending.

"Matthew. Hi."

"Hey, little sis. Want to introduce me to your friend?"

I feel Hayes step up behind me, his warmth spreading over me. He extends his hand over my shoulder, brushing up against me in a way that appears innocent yet is anything but.

"Hayes."

I see Hayes's forearm muscles tense with how hard he shakes Mathew's hand, and I can't help but smile when my brother winces a little.

"Seattle Serpents, right? Heard you're kicking ass this year. You're what? Second overall?"

"I have no clue. I don't pay any attention."

Matthew laughs heartily. "Right, right. Sure you don't." He winks like it's some big joke, but I know otherwise. Hayes really doesn't pay attention to the standings like that, especially this early in the season. "Say, you ever need someone to come keep my sister and your niece company at the games, I'm always available."

Wow. That was fast.

Hayes gives him a tight-lipped smile. "I'll keep that in mind."

He won't.

"Hayes, dear, would you like something to drink?"

"I can grab him something, Mom." He gives Hayes the same slimy grin I bet he gives all his clients who pay him way too much money. "Guess Quinny left all her manners at the door." He rolls his eyes as he turns to the fridge. "What's your poison?"

"I'd like to poison him," Hayes murmurs into my ear.

I stifle a laugh—barely.

"Water is fine, thank you."

Matthew grabs two from the fridge—one flavored and one not—and hands them over to us before leading us into the dining room where the rest of my siblings are gathered. On the way, Hayes takes the plain water from my hand, trading it out for the flavored one my brother handed him. I smile up at him, making a mental note to kiss him extra long later for the gesture.

Hayes meets the rest of my family, all of them somehow managing to sneak in a way to ask for free stuff within the first sentences spoken to him. All the while, Hayes sits by my side, his knee pressed tightly against mine under the table. Tension rolls off him in waves, and I know him well enough to know there are so many things he wants to say to each of them, but he's biting his tongue.

When my mother announces that dinner is ready, I offer to grab Flora and get her washed up. Truthfully, I just need a break. If I have to hear one more time about how perfect Liza's, Ruthie's, Daniel's, or Matthew's lives are, I might scream.

"Are you having fun?" I ask Flora as I stand in the hallway while she's rubbing soap all over her hands. "Is everyone being nice?"

"Yes. The one with glasses let me take his turn on the Nintendo. He's nice."

"Good. I'm glad."

As much as their parents drive me insane, my nieces and nephews are all actually good kids. I guess those nice genes skipped a generation.

Flora rinses the soap off her hands, then dries them, and we reluctantly make our way back to the dining room. I take my place next to Hayes, who eyes me carefully. I send him a smile that says *I'm okay*, but he looks like he doesn't believe me, and I don't blame him. If I thought sitting through introductions was hard, small talk during dinner *always* turns into chaos, and I have no doubt this will be the same.

My dad carves the turkey with little fanfare, and we all pass the dishes around. Hayes even skips me when it comes to the Brussels sprouts, and I decide he's getting *two* extra-long kisses now.

"So, Hayes, how are things? I don't see you at the bakery much anymore."

"Good, Bess. Been trying to feed this kid less sugar."

He ruffles Flora's hair, but she doesn't care. She's busy stuffing her face with my mother's famous mashed potatoes that are perfectly buttered and seasoned.

"You've been staying away too, Quinn."

Because I've been spending all my free time with Hayes.

I shrug. "Sorry. Boss's orders."

My mother huffs like she's offended, but I know

she's not. I just hope she doesn't suspect the real reason I haven't been around much lately.

"I take it you're enjoying nannying, then?" she asks.

I nod around a forkful of turkey, chew, and swallow. "Very much so. Flora's the best."

"I love Just Quinn," the kid says, and I swear my heart stops.

It's the first time she's said that to me, and it makes my eyes burn and my chest feel like it weighs a hundred pounds. *She loves me?*

"I love you too, little flower."

She nods, never once taking her attention off her mashed potatoes. I look over at Hayes, and he's staring down at her too, his eyes wide with surprise. I can't help but wonder how he feels hearing her say that.

Is he upset? Does he care that she's said it to me but not him? Is he worried we're getting too close? If he is, he doesn't say anything, he just takes a bite of his roll and continues with his meal like nothing happened.

Huh.

"Well, I bet you're glad I had the idea now, aren't you?" My mom reaches over and squeezes my hand, then winks at me, knowing what a big moment that just was.

"I am. So much so that I've, uh, been thinking about maybe going back to school."

It's the first time I've said it out loud. Ever since Auden mentioned it at the family skate, I've been mulling it over, even going so far as to fill out half an application for classes before chickening out and shutting down my laptop entirely.

Matthew's fork clatters to his plate as he sits back and takes a swig of his beer. "Can't wait to hear what this is for now. Let me guess—clown school? Isn't that the only thing you haven't tried yet?"

I want to flip him off so badly, but it's a holiday, and I know my mother would kill me.

Instead, I settle for a glower. "Early childhood development, actually."

"You're kidding. You, a teacher?" This from Liza. She looks at her husband. "Can you believe that?"

He shakes his head.

"You've had one babysitting job and now you think you can be a teacher?" Matthew scoffs. "That's not how it works, Quinny. Teaching is a lot harder than that."

"I know that, *Matty*. I'm very aware it's different. It's just... Well, I've had so much fun with Flora and seeing her learn new things, so I thought, why not?"

"Why not fly to the moon? Why not go live on Mars? Why not eat ice cream for dinner every night?" Matthew rolls his eyes. "Give me a break. Right, Daniel?"

He shrugs. "I mean, it's kind of your thing, Quinn. You find something you like, then make it your whole personality. Like those stupid earrings of yours."

I clutch the turkey-shaped earring hanging from my right ear. It's not stupid. It's festive. I look at Hayes, but he's still staring down at his plate, and I don't know what hurts more—the fact that he's allowing them to pile on me or that he's staying silent, clearly agreeing with them.

"That's a big decision," Ruthie says. "You need to be really sure before you dive into that."

"I know that. I—"

"Not to mention how much that's going to cost. Surely you can't afford to go back to school *again*. You're still paying on your loans from before, aren't you?"

That is true. However, I have what Hayes has paid me so far and then some in my savings account. I could pay off a decent chunk of them now, and when I get the other fifty grand, I can pay the rest.

"Yes, but—"

"There's always a but with you, Quinny." Matthew scoffs, gulping down his beer.

I get it. I do. I haven't been reliable in the past. I've shirked my responsibilities and have changed what I want to do so many times over. I've thought about this a lot more than any of them realize, though. Being with Flora, teaching her…it's been the most rewarding experience of my life, and I want to help other kids too. I want to show them that someone cares about them. I want them to know they matter.

I want to tell them all of that, but I can't seem to find the words. So I don't. I finish my Thanksgiving dinner in silence, barely touching my favorite meal of the year. All the while, Hayes sits beside me, still not saying anything, and I know without a doubt he's thinking what they've thought all along—I'm not good enough.

For them or for him.

I'm not sure which part of that hurts the most.

CHAPTER 21

HAYES

"Man, can you believe our little sister?"

Matthew, Quinn's fuckhead older brother, takes a swill of what appears to be his sixth beer, rocking back on his plastic lawn chair as we all sit out back, dinner settling in our bellies.

Well, mine's not settling. It's sitting at the base of my throat, waiting for me to barf it all back up because all I did was sit there while they shit on her so I didn't ruin Bess's holiday meal. It took everything I had not to say something, not to reach over the table and punch that stupid fucking smirk off Matthew's face. Hell, it's taking everything I have now.

These people have no idea who Quinn really is. They don't know she stays up every night to help Flora with her homework with nothing but patience and kindness, don't know she reads to her nightly, helping her sound out the words she doesn't know and giving her definitions when Flora has questions. They don't know Quinn single-handedly taught her the multiplication tables *and* is learning how to cook by watching YouTube all so I can eat better during the season and Flora doesn't have to survive off grilled cheese and pickles—though I doubt the kid would complain about it.

They don't know shit about her, and they certainly don't know that Quinn would make a fantastic teacher. I'd pay all the money in the world to put her through school and make it happen for her.

"She really thinks she can be a teacher, huh? She can barely take care of herself." Her douchebag brother looks at me, rocking back in his chair again. I wish I could sweep the legs right out from under him. "Honestly, between you and me, I wouldn't trust her around your niece. She has no sense of what's right and wrong. She'd probably allow her to run off in a crowded mall or something. Too busy looking at more hideous earrings she can scare men away with."

I grip the edges of my chair so hard I can feel the plastic bending beneath my fingers.

Don't hit him. Don't hit him. Don't hit him.

I really, really want to hit him.

The back door swings open and out walks Quinn, Flora by her side, that damn cat in one arm and a plate stacked full of desserts in the other. I relax at the sight of them, but only a little.

"Speak of the devil… What are you doing, Quinny? Practicing corrupting the youth for when you become a 'teacher'?" He rolls his eyes. "I—"

I rise out of my chair so fast it topples over, all eyes shooting to me. I think one of her sisters even gasps, though I couldn't tell you which one. They've both had their noses turned up all night, so I can't really tell them apart.

"Don't," I growl.

"Excuse me?"

"Don't. Don't you dare say another fucking word to her."

"I can say whatever I want about her." Matthew rises from his chair, stumbling ever so slightly. "She's *my* sister. She's just your nanny."

The fuck she is.

I march toward him, done listening to his bullshit and definitely done worrying about screwing up Bess's holiday. This guy needs a good ass kicking, and I just happen to be willing to deliver it.

"Hayes!"

I ignore the call.

"Hayes!"

I don't fucking stop. I can't. I want to hit this fucker way too much to stop.

"Adam!"

My feet halt of their own accord, and I turn to Quinn, who is halfway down the stairs, her eyes filled with fear. I remember how Hutch and Auden were able to have a whole conversation with just a single glance, and that's what Quinn and I are doing right now.

Don't do this, hers begs.

Fuck that guy, mine says back.

I look back at Matthew, who is standing there smirking at me, so close I *could* reach out and punch him and I wouldn't lose a wink of sleep over it. But then I look to Flora, who is watching with wide eyes, then to Quinn, who is still staring after me.

Please, her hazel eyes implore.

As much as I don't want to, I cave. I won't hit her brother. Not here. Not now. But that doesn't mean I'm leaving without saying something. I turn to him, closing the distance between us until my nose is damn near pressed up against his. At least the prick is smart enough to look scared.

"If you're going to insist on talking to her like that, this is the only warning I'm giving you—do it again, and you'll be bleeding all over your pretty Prada loafers, *Matty*."

Matthew's eyes widen like *he's* the one being put out here. Me? All I can do is remember the look in

Quinn's eyes to keep me from making it happen anyway.

I look at the rest of her siblings. "That goes for every last one of you pricks too. One more bad word about her and we're going to have problems."

"What's going on here?"

I turn to find Bess and Chuck coming down the stairs, their eyes bouncing from me to Matthew to Quinn.

"Everything okay, Hayes?" Bess asks.

"It's fine, Mom. I—"

"No, Bess." I cut her off because I *know* she was about to apologize, and that's bullshit. She has nothing to apologize for. "Everything isn't okay. It's not okay for this to continue. For your other children to rag on Quinn because she's trying to find something she loves to do instead of taking the first soul-sucking job that comes her way. You know I like you, so please forgive me for causing a scene with your children, but we're leaving."

"We are?" Flora asks as I grab her hand, tugging her up the stairs. "But dessert!"

"We'll eat it in the car," I say, holding my other hand out to Quinn.

She looks down at it, then back up at me.

"Quinnicorn?" Chuck eyes his daughter. "Dear?"

Then she grins and slides her hand into mine.

"Mom, Dad, thank you for dinner. It was delicious as always, and I'm sorry we can't stay any longer." She turns to her brothers and sisters. "As for all of you…" She flips her middle finger up at them, and I laugh, holding her hand the whole way to the car.

I sit on the edge of my bed, watching the minutes tick by. Every ounce of me is *screaming* to run to Quinn, to check and make sure she's okay, but she just put Flora down not even ten minutes ago, and the last thing I want is for her to get up and wander out looking for one of us and find us together.

Especially not after Flora's confession. She loves Quinn.

I'm not stupid. I know they've grown very close, and I knew the likelihood of Flora getting attached to her nanny was extremely high. But to actually hear her *say* it? That was something else entirely.

It's not even because I'm jealous of their love. I know deep down Flora loves me in her own way. It just made me feel absolutely racked with guilt over what Quinn and I have been hiding. I've been so wrapped up in Quinn and how good she feels that I've stopped thinking of how this could impact Flora heavily if things were to go south. She should have been my first thought this entire time, not my second.

Yet…I watch the clock, counting down the minutes until I can go to Quinn. It's funny. My parents were addicted to alcohol, and my brother was addicted to drugs. Me? I'm addicted to Quinn Benson, and it's one habit I don't want to kick.

Tap, tap, tap.

I jerk my head up.

Was that…?

Then I hear it again.

Tap, tap, tap.

I scramble across the room, wrenching open the door.

"Hi," Quinn says quietly, standing before me in a Serpents t-shirt that's so big I can't even see the sleep shorts I know she's wearing underneath.

She's wearing my shirt. She's wearing my shirt and she's standing at my door and fuck if I don't want to kiss her.

She slips into my room, pressing her back against the door as she closes it. I want to close the distance between us and kiss her so fucking bad my fingertips literally *ache* to touch her.

But I don't. We need to talk first. The ride home was silent save for Flora happily eating her dessert in the back seat of Quinn's Bug, and we were just as quiet when we got home. She did her nightly routine with Flora while I hid away in my room, trying to talk myself out of driving back over to her parents' place and really giving them a piece of my mind before pummeling Matthew.

Fuck, I still want to do it.

"Are you okay?" I ask her.

She nods, but it doesn't match the tears shining in her eyes.

"Honey…"

And now they're no longer just shining. They're running down her cheeks, one little tear, then another big one, and I fucking hate it. Her chin wobbles and she sniffles, brushing the streaks away.

"I'm sorry. It's nothing. It's just…"

"Just that they're all assholes?"

She laughs lightly. "Yeah, that. It's nothing new though. They do it all the time. I should be used to it by now."

"No, Quinn, you shouldn't. You should *never* be used to something like that, and they should never be talking to you like that. And your parents should damn sure never let it happen."

That part pissed me off nearly as much as the shit her siblings were spewing. How could Bess and Chuck just sit by while their kids tore into her? I never would have expected that from Bess.

Quinn shakes her head. "No, no, don't blame them. My parents are great. They love me. Sure, they're totally exhausted by me always jumping from one thing to the next, but they love me no matter what."

I have no doubt she's telling the truth, but what I witnessed today still wasn't right.

"They should still say something."

She shrugs. "Maybe. But Matthew and them wouldn't have gotten nearly as ugly as they did if my parents were in the room. They're dumb but not that dumb."

"I'm not sure dumb is the word I'd use for that prick. Maybe a douchey piece of shit or asswipe or something to that effect. Actually, I *should* bring him to a game. Let the guys have a go at chirping him for a bit. He'll change his tune real quick."

"That does sound really nice." She smiles at the thought. "But that's not what I came in here for. I don't want to talk about them."

"Then why'd you come in here? I mean, I have an idea why, but..."

"Well, *that*, and for another reason. I, uh..." She tucks a stray hair behind her ear. "I wanted to say thank you."

Okay, I was *not* expecting that.

"Thank you? For what?"

"For standing up for me."

Her words are like a punch to the gut. While I *did* say something to her fuckface brother, I still sat there and let her get ragged on for far too long.

"I should have said something sooner. I should have stopped them before I did. I—"

She shakes her head. "You didn't because you're a gentleman, Hayes. Because you're starting to think before you act and you didn't want to ruin my family's Thanksgiving. I didn't realize it at first, but the moment you stood up from your chair, I could see it, could see how much you'd been holding back all day. So, no, while you didn't say anything right away, you still said *something*, and that's a hell of a lot better than not saying anything at all."

She's wrong. It's not better. I still should have said something. I—

"Stop," she says, sliding her arms around my neck. "Stop beating yourself up."

"I'm not beating myself up. I'm—"

"Adam?"

"Yes?"

"Shut up and kiss me already."

I crowd her against the door, not wasting a single second, and press our bodies together tightly, taking her mouth in mine, kissing her hard and fast like I can't get enough because *I can't get enough.* But that's how it's always been, hasn't it?

When I finally release her, she sighs, like she's been waiting for the kiss all day, and I feel like I have too.

"That's better," she mutters, and I couldn't agree more. "Now, I'd like to be fucked hard and fast, please."

I smile down at her. "Is that so?"

"Yep. You said I should use my words, right?"

"I did say that, huh?"

I kiss her again but slow this time, softer. She's having no part of it, pulling at my shirt, trying to take it off.

"Easy, easy," I say, holding myself away. "We'll get to your thing, but I want to do my thing first, okay?"

"Hayes…" she whines.

"Just trust me, okay?"

She nods, and I kiss her again, sliding my lips against hers with a gentleness I'm not sure I've ever used before. I don't know why I want to take this so slow. I don't know why I'm not just ripping her clothes off and fucking her as hard and fast as she requested. But this feels important right now. Taking my time and worshipping her feels right.

I've always struggled with that—knowing what's wrong and what's right. But not this time. This time I'm following my gut, and it's saying to drive this woman mad with pleasure until she forgets all the awful things about today. I trail my lips over her chin and down her neck, sucking her collarbone before moving lower until I can't kiss her any more. Then I drop to my knees.

She holds the t-shirt up, watching me with hungry eyes as I hook my fingers into the waistband of her tiny sleep shorts and pull them down. She steps out and I toss them aside, never once shifting my attention from the sight before me.

"No panties?"

She shakes her head. "Seemed unnecessary."

She's right.

I lean forward, pressing a kiss to her right thigh, then her left. I do it again, inching closer and closer to where I know she really wants before pulling back and starting again until she's a panting mess above me.

I love it. I love seeing her like this, splayed out before me, needy.

"Adam…" She says my name like a plea. "Put your mouth on me."

"My mouth's been on you, honey."

She growls. "You know what I mean."

I laugh darkly. "Yeah, I guess I do."

I slide my tongue over her, and she arches off the door with a sigh. It's the most beautiful sigh ever, so good I'm dying to hear it again, to taste her again. I run my tongue through her folds over and over, licking every inch of her I can. I swirl my tongue around her clit, sucking it hard before backing off. I do it repeatedly until her legs are shaking around me and I'm certain she's about to fall over if she doesn't come soon. I curl a single finger into her, and she groans, her head slamming back on the door with a loud thud.

"Yes, yes, yes. So close. I need…"

I know exactly what she needs. I slip my finger from her pussy and glide the soaked digit back to her ass, pressing against the tight ring we've only explored a few other times. I push against the muscle, and she tenses for only a second before relaxing, allowing me to glide in with ease as I suck her clit hard, this time not relenting.

It's only a few moments before one hand is crashing through my hair and dragging me closer while the other is slapped over her mouth as she screams into her palm. I smile when I hear her muffled cry of my name. I pump my finger in her ass, dragging out her orgasm as long as I can before sliding it out and rising to my full height.

I take her tired body in my arms and carry her to the bed, placing her in the middle before stepping back to lose my sleep pants and shirt. She watches me with sleepy eyes, and I can't help but stroke my cock as I take her in, body spent and breaths ragged. She's gorgeous like this. Hell, she's gorgeous all the time, even when she's walking around in a messy ponytail and leggings that have seen better days with mismatched socks. I swear I could stare at her all day.

"Please don't," she says, and I realize I must have said that last part out loud. "I need you."

Fuck if that doesn't get me moving. I crawl up the bed, fitting myself between her legs and sliding over her slick heat.

"I'm going to fuck you hard and fast now, Quinny," I promise, brushing my lips over hers.

She nods, barely listening as I press just the head of my cock into her.

"But I want you to know something first, okay?"

"Tell me."

I grab her chin, staring down into her eyes, and she stills, her attention solely focused on me now, not what's happening between her legs.

"You're smart, Quinn Benson. You're good enough. And you're absolutely fucking capable of doing whatever you put your mind to. Fuck anyone else who says otherwise, understood?"

She doesn't say anything. She just watches me, the hazel eyes I love so much glossy, and I'm not sure if it's with lust or emotion or what.

Then she gulps audibly. "Understood, Adam."

And I fulfill my promise.

"Coming!"

I run a towel over my hair as I speed-walk toward the front door with a grin. It must be Quinn. She left her phone in my bed, and I'm betting she realized it and forgot the door code again, even though I've texted it to her ten million times over the last few months.

"Forget something, honey?" I ask as I pull open the door.

Only it's not Quinn.

"Bess."

Her purple-painted lips pull into a smile. "Well, hey there, *honey*."

Heat warms my cheeks. "Uh, sorry. I thought you were someone else."

She lifts a brow at that, likely deducing exactly who I thought she was. I'm sure after the way I left things at her house, Bess has been able to deduce a lot of things. You don't usually almost get into a fight over someone who is "just your nanny."

"How are you? Come on in."

I step aside and she squeezes by me, her hands full of several different-sized bowls, each a different shade of purple. I toss the towel onto the couch, making a mental note to pick it back up later before I leave for the game. I lead her into the kitchen, grabbing a few things off the stack of dishes and holding them as she makes her way over to the fridge and begins loading them in there.

"Thank you," she says.

O...kay?

When she's finished, she faces me, folding her hands together in front of her.

"I brought you dessert since you never got the chance to have any."

"Oh. Well, thank you. Flora will be excited to hear that. She was raving about the slice of pumpkin pie she snuck away with and let nobody else touch."

Bess smiles. "That little girl is the best."

"She is," I agree. "So, how are you, Bess?"

"I'm...well, not so great."

I frown. "Is everything okay? Chuck okay?"

She waves her hand. "Oh, yeah. We're fine. It's just... Well, I noticed you haven't been to the bakery in a while, so I figured I'd stop by. Make sure everything is okay."

We both know she's not here asking after Flora and me. She's asking if *we're* okay after what happened at her house last week when I nearly decked her son over her daughter. Her daughter who makes me smile. Who makes me laugh. Who makes me feel like I've never fucking felt before.

"We're good, Bess. But what happened last week was out of line."

She sighs. "I know. Matthew is…" She rolls her eyes. "Well, he's a little much sometimes."

"I don't mean just with him."

Her brows shoot up. "Oh?"

I lean back against the counter, crossing my arms over my chest, not caring if I wrinkle my dress shirt. "I mean with you and Chuck just letting your other kids dump on Quinn like that. It was wrong. She doesn't deserve that."

"Well, I know that. Chuck and I love Quinn. We love all our kids. We—"

"You let her down is what you did. You should have stopped them. You should have stepped in and shut it down and told them they were wrong for talking to her the way they did."

"They've always been like that, ribbing each other and whatnot. They're siblings. That's how it goes."

"Did you know Quinn believes them?"

She rears her head back like I've just slapped her. "What?"

"Quinn believes them," I repeat. "She thinks she's not good enough because they say she isn't. She thinks she's irresponsible because they say she is. She thinks she can't be a teacher because they say she can't."

"That's… That's ridiculous. She's completely capable. Chuck and I talk all the time about how much we love her sense of adventure and how she's not afraid to try new things or go after what she wants. We envy her for that."

"Have you told her that lately? Has Chuck?"

"Well, of course we have. We've…"

But she doesn't finish her sentence, and I have a feeling she's realizing right now that while yes, she loves her daughter, she hasn't quite supported her in all the ways she should.

"I guess it has been a while since I've talked with her about it, you know? Made myself clear. I love Quinn and I think she'd make an amazing teacher. Sure, she's needed more time than my other kids to figure out what she wants to do, but I've never doubted for a second that she would. We've always believed in her. We always will."

"Do you mean that?"

I spin around to find Quinn standing at the edge of the living room.

"What are you…"

"I forgot my phone." She shrugs, then looks at her mother. "Do you mean that?"

"Yes, dear," Bess says, rushing over to her. She

takes her hands. "Yes, of course I mean it. You are capable of so many great things, Quinn Penelope, and I want you to know that even if you change your mind about becoming a teacher or if it takes you another ten years to find what you want to do, your father and I will still be here to support you. Every dang step of the way."

Even from here, I can see Quinn's bottom lip quiver. She wraps her mother in a hug, squeezing her eyes shut tight, but I see it anyway, the lone tear that streaks down her face, the weight she's been carrying around being lifted from her shoulders.

I see it.

I see her.

And I know in this moment I am completely fucked because I've gone and done the most irresponsible thing I've done yet.

I've fallen in love with Quinn Benson, and there's no turning back.

CHAPTER 22

QUINN

"How come you don't live with your mommy?"

My feet catch on the sidewalk, Flora's unsuspecting question throwing me for a loop.

"What do you mean?"

"Well, I know I don't live with my mom because she's dead and my dad is in jail for being bad, but I don't understand why you don't live with your mommy if she's so amazing."

It's not the first time Flora's mentioned her parents, but it is the first time she's referenced where they are. I imagine she asked Hayes about them at some point since she seems to be very aware, but she's not talked about them with me. Not like this.

Until now, on a nice quiet walk back from the library, her little backpack full of books while she clutches a sucker the size of her head in one hand

and mine in the other. Giving her so much sugar probably wasn't a good idea, but when her eyes grew to twice their size at the sight of it, I knew she had to have it.

It's exactly what my amazing mommy would have done. We've been talking every day since I walked in on her and Hayes in his kitchen. I had no idea how much I needed to hear what she said, but it gave me a renewed sense of worth.

Well, that and Hayes's words. He's been tossing a lot of compliments my way in the last week or so. If he wasn't already getting laid so often, I'd say it's because he's trying to score, but I know it's not. It's all genuine, and it makes my heart go *thump thump thump* just thinking about it.

"I'd live with Mrs. Bess if I could, so why don't you live with her?"

I smile. My mother would *love* it if Flora lived with her.

"Well, it's because I'm a grown-up, and grown-ups don't usually live with their parents."

A poor excuse for one who does bad things like sleep with her boss but is still a grown-up.

"Oh." She nods like it makes so much sense. Then she wrinkles her nose, looking up at me. "Then why do you live with me and Uncle Adam?"

Adam. Just hearing his name does something funny

to my insides, *especially* since he makes me say it whenever I come.

I shove the totally inappropriate thought away and answer the curious child. "Because I work for your uncle and we figured with *his* work schedule, it would make more sense for me to live with you guys." I squeeze her hand. "Why? Do you not want me to live with you anymore? I thought we were having fun."

"Of course I do! We *are* having fun. I love you."

I smile. "I love you too, little flower."

"So does Uncle Adam."

I trip again. *Damn these sidewalks.*

"What?" I ask as I recover. "What do you mean?"

"Well, he looks at you."

"Okay?"

It comes out as a question because I don't really understand what she means.

She huffs like she's annoyed by my confusion. "When you aren't looking, Just Quinn. That's when Uncle Adam looks at you the most. He loves you."

I don't have anything to say because I don't know *what* to say. Hayes looks at me? And he does it enough that Flora's noticed? What does that even mean? *Does* it even mean anything? The lines between us have been blurred for quite some time now and even more so since Thanksgiving, but could Hayes *love* me?

Could I...love *him*?

No. It's completely crazy.

I shake away the thought before it can develop any further, but no matter how many times I shake, it doesn't go away. I like Hayes, yes. I like spending time with him, and I like how much he makes me laugh. I like watching him with Flora and the way he takes care of her in ways she doesn't even realize, like *always* keeping pickles on hand for her. I like how he buys me butterscotch candy without me ever asking and how he always orders extra spring rolls because he knows I love them. I like Hayes. I like Hayes a lot.

But love him? No. It's not possible. It goes against all the rules.

So why can't I stop thinking about it? Even as we make our way back home and Flora asks for grilled cheese for dinner, it's there in my head. As I brush her hair after her shower and twist it into a braid, it still won't go away. And even when I read her a bedtime story and should be focusing on doing all the amazing voices I've come up with, it's all I can think about.

The thought doesn't leave me even when I tell her good night, or when Hayes calls from Boston like he always does when he's on the road. For the first time, I don't answer. Instead, I shoot him a text and tell him I have a headache, Flora is already in bed, and I'll talk to him tomorrow.

When I lie down and close my eyes, I'm still

thinking about it, especially because loving Adam Hayes doesn't sound like such a crazy idea after all.

"I think we should do this more often."

"Have sex? Because I think we do that fairly often already."

It's true. The second he got home from his latest road trip, during which the Serpents won three of their four games, our lips locked together, and we stumbled through the house to his bedroom. It's where we've been for the past several hours.

"No. Well, I mean, yes—always that. But I mean sleep in my room. My bed is so much more comfortable than yours."

I gasp. "Hey! I worked hard to pay for that mattress."

"While I'm sure you did, that doesn't make it any more comfortable. I've even had to have our team chiropractor do some extra work on my neck."

"You could always just sleep in your own bed, you know."

He doesn't have a rebuttal for that.

He loves you.

I slip the thought right back into the box I placed it

in when Flora mentioned the crazy idea a few days ago. I've been trying hard not to think about it since, but I'd be lying if I said late at night, when everyone is asleep, I don't pull it back out and mull it over and consider the fact that I just might love him, too.

"So, I noticed you were looking up colleges the other day."

I lift my head off his chest, looking down at him. "Adam Hayes, are you spying on me?"

"No." He twists his lips. "Well, sort of, but it's unintentional. You left your computer on the counter when you went to braid Flora's hair, and I was cleaning up and accidentally bumped it, and the screen booted back up."

I raise my brows at him.

"What?" he asks. "That's totally what happened."

"I'm just struggling to believe *you* were cleaning."

"Hey, my cleaning lady has been very impressed with the state of this house lately. She joked about wondering if her services are needed anymore. I kept her on. You're welcome for that."

I pinch his nipple, and he yelps.

"Shh!" I tell him. "Flora's sleeping."

"Then quit pinching me!"

"Quit needing pinching!"

"I didn't." He rubs at his nipple, smirking because he damn well knows he deserved that just now.

"Anyway, you're still thinking about going to school, huh?"

I settle against him, loving how he grazes his fingertips over my naked back, like he's not capable of *not* touching me.

"It's just a thought."

"Why?"

"What do you mean?"

"I mean, why is it just a thought? Why haven't you enrolled?"

"Well, for starters, college costs money."

"So?"

"So," I say pointedly. "We're not all rich hockey players, you know."

"No, but I'm sure there are grants or loans or something you can use to get you started, then you can figure out the rest later."

That's always been my life—figuring out the rest later. For once, I don't want to do that. I want to jump in with both feet and be completely secure in what I'm doing. I want to be sure. Absolutely so.

It would be a lie if I said my siblings' words weren't still haunting me. I can't help but think about them because what if they're right? What if I fail at this too? What if I am rushing into it? What if I—

"Stop."

"Stop what?"

"Overthinking it," Hayes says, his touch still light against me. "I know that's what you're doing. I can hear you all the way up here."

"You cannot."

"Can too."

I don't miss how he covers his nipple…just in case.

"For what it's worth," he says, "I think you should do it."

He does? "You do?"

"Yeah, I think you'd be great at it. And you'd look totally hot in those buttoned-up teacher's outfits."

I roll my eyes.

"Plus, you already have the silly earrings the kids will undoubtedly love. It's perfect for you."

"I do have some pretty amazing earrings."

"I said *silly*."

I lift my hand to pinch him again, but he's too quick, covering up before I can. *Damn those hockey reflexes.*

His chest rumbles with a low laugh, and I can't help but smile. Sometimes, I think I like moments like these where we're lying in bed and just talking as much as I like the sex.

He loves you.

"But in all seriousness," Hayes says, distracting me before my brain can descend into overload again, "I think you'd be great, and I'm not just saying that because I'm a little biased since Flora loves you so much. I'm saying it because I mean it. I see the way you look at her when she gets an answer right on her homework or recites something you've taught her. Those hazel eyes of yours light up, and you give her a secret grin like *you* just did something right—and you did. You taught her. So, yeah, I think you'd be good at it, and I think you should do it. If you want to, of course."

I don't have the words. I'm too busy trying to choke down the sob that's attempting to work its way free. I have no idea why it means so much to me that Hayes supports me in this decision and thinks I can do it, but it does, and it gives me just a little more confidence that I *can* do this.

Maybe I should.

"Okay."

"Okay?"

"Yeah, okay. I'll re-enroll. I'll go back to school. I'm going to become a teacher."

Just saying it out loud makes my heart thunder with excitement.

"Good. I'm glad. We can figure out all the other details later."

I'm sure he means Flora and her schedule and his. We'll work on that after I know when classes will actually start.

Hayes presses his lips to my forehead. "Now that we have that settled, you need to get some sleep. I'm planning to wake you up very early with my tongue between your legs."

Who could possibly argue with that plan? I close my eyes, letting sleep wash over me.

He loves you.

This time when the thought comes, I don't push it away. I don't hide from it. I let it happen. I let it sink in.

All I can think is, *I love him too.*

"You're doing it wrong."

"I am not."

"You are too."

"I am *not.*"

"Are too."

I laugh as I watch Flora and Hayes argue back and forth while they work on building her swing set that's been sitting in pieces in the backyard for far too long now. With the weather not cooperating and Hayes's hockey schedule, it's been next to impossible to get anything done on it. So why not build a playscape outside in the middle of a random sunny Saturday in December?

"You're supposed to put E and F together, not E and H. Don't you know your ABCs?"

"I guess not. Want to teach them to me since you're so smart?"

Flora rolls her eyes at her uncle and hands him the correct piece while I sit on the patio, sip my butterscotch hot chocolate, and enjoy the show they're putting on. They're never going to get this done, but I'm not sure I mind. I like watching them like this. I probably shouldn't be so excited to see them arguing, but it's such a far cry from where they were when I first met them that I can't help but love it.

I love him. I love her. I love them.

The thought doesn't scare me as much as it once did. It probably should, especially since I have no idea how Hayes feels, but it doesn't. For once in my life, I feel like everything is going okay. I re-enrolled in school the night after Hayes told me to. He even helped me with the forms. Sure, for every answer I filled out, he would lick my pussy, so there was definitely some incentive there, but still.

I'm officially going back to school. Again. Something about it feels different this time, like I can do it. It feels *right,* and I'm so excited to get started. I still have several weeks until classes start, but January can't come soon enough.

The doorbell chimes, and I rise from my chair. I let

them continue arguing while I trek through the house to the front door. I pull it open and take a surprised step back.

"May I help you?"

"Hi." The gorgeous woman with long blonde hair steps forward, extending her hand. "I'm Rachel Carr. I'm here to interview for the nanny position."

Interview for the what?

"The…nanny position?"

She frowns. "I'm sorry. Do I have the wrong house? I could have sworn this is the address Mr. Hayes sent."

Mr. Hayes.

Nanny position.

What the hell is going on? Am I…getting fired? Or is this some horrible, awful prank Hayes is trying to pull?

"Oh, you're early."

I turn to find Hayes waltzing up, a smile on his face directed at the woman standing on the other side of the door.

Not at me. At her.

And man, does it make my blood boil.

"Come on in." He waves her inside. "It's nice to meet you, Miss Carr."

"Likewise," she says, stepping in, shooting me an innocent smile as she passes like she's not here to steal my job. "Thanks so much for inviting me over today. I can't wait to meet little Florence."

"*Flora*," I correct. "Her name is Flora."

"Oh, I'm so sorry. I thought Flora was short for Florence."

That doesn't even make sense!

"Nope. Just Flora."

"That's such a lovely name." She looks at me like *I'm* the one who named her, like I'm Flora's mother. Does this woman not realize she's here to take my job from me?

"Rachel, this is Quinn. She's—"

"Going to go lie down. I have a horrible headache."

Hayes frowns, likely because I was just sitting outside with him and Flora and I was fine then.

That was before you brought someone here to steal my job.

I don't wait for either of them to respond before turning on my heel and racing away, hoping Hayes didn't just see the tears that are threatening to spill free. I have no idea what's going on right now, but I know one thing for certain—I'm done here.

I close my door, pressing my back up against it just as the tears spill over. I hate that I'm crying, hate that I'm feeling the way I am. But even more, I hate Hayes for blindsiding me with this.

I shove off the door, marching over to my dresser

and grabbing a handful of clothes before throwing them on the bed. I'm not staying here. I can't. Not right now. Not after Hayes just brought some other woman into this home to take my job away from me, to take Flora away from me.

Wait. No. She's not mine. I know that. She's Hayes's, but I...I love her like she's mine. These last few months with her have been nothing short of spectacular. That little piece of my life that always felt like it was missing something... It was her. It was them.

And now it's all being ripped away.

I grab a bag from the closet and start shoving clothes inside. I don't even pay attention to what I'm grabbing—I just want *something* so I can be gone.

Gone.

Ugh, I don't even know where I'm going. I haven't thought that far ahead. But that's sort of my MO, isn't it? Just do as I please and worry about the consequences later. Like sleeping with Hayes. Now look at me—completely in love with him and crying because he's cast me aside, decided he's moving on and forgot to tell me.

When my bag is filled to the brim, I zip it up, then sling my purse over my head and march out of my room. I stop in the hall just before I reach the living room, straining to hear. I didn't really think about waltzing out of here holding my clothes and the scene that'll cause with the new nanny.

But there are no voices, just the low hum of the refrigerator. I peek around the corner, then look through the kitchen and out the large glass door leading to the backyard. Hayes is standing on the back porch, his back to the house. Rachel's out in the yard with Flora, bent down and chatting with her, laughing about something.

My chest aches watching it. That should be me out there. That should be *my* laugh from Flora. But I'm not out there, and that's not my laugh anymore. I thought I'd finally found somewhere I was accepted, somewhere I could be myself and that made me feel like *me*, somewhere that didn't make me feel like a complete mess.

But I was wrong. This isn't it. I'm being replaced. I don't belong here anymore.

I'm not sure I ever did.

As if he can sense my eyes on him, Hayes turns, staring into the house. He can't see me, tucked back into the hall like I am, and I'm glad for it. I don't want him to witness this. I just want to press my shoulders back and hold my head high and walk out of here with a bit of my pride intact.

So, that's exactly what I do. When the door clicks shut behind me, I exhale shakily and look around.

What the hell am I going to do now?

CHAPTER 23

HAYES

"Flora! Dinner's almost done!"

"Coming!"

I leave the sliding back door open, then return to my spot at the stove as I stir the mac and cheese. It's nothing fancy, but it's the best I've got, and I know Flora loves it, so that's all that matters. I did have grander plans for tonight, but with Quinn's headache, I'm going to have to hold off on those.

I look down the hall with a frown. Quinn's been in her room all afternoon, and I'm starting to wonder if she's ever going to come out. I've had to stop myself so many times from going in and checking on her. She seemed like she was in a lot of pain earlier, and I just want to let her rest, even if it does mean I'll need to re-evaluate tonight. Our plan was to put up the Christmas tree—with Flora's help, of course—and I was going to ask Quinn to move in with us in an official capacity.

I don't want Quinn to just be Flora's nanny anymore. I want her to be mine. I want her to be ours.

I simply want her.

"Oh my gosh, I'm starving," Flora says as she steps back inside, depositing her dirty shoes right by the door.

We've been working on building the swing set most of the day and have still made little progress. Mostly because we kept getting distracted doing anything *but* building, like playing tag and tossing around a little felt mouse for Pickles to chase. That's what Flora's been out there doing for the last half hour on her own as I get dinner ready.

"Go wash your hands, then check on Quinn, will you?" I ask as I grab some bowls out of the cabinet. "See if she wants dinner or just wants to keep sleeping."

"Aye aye!" She salutes me before racing off. I have no idea where she got that from, but it still makes me grin.

It's still so wild to me to see the difference in her from when she first got here to now. That was my biggest sign earlier that it wasn't going to work out with Rachel. Flora instantly retreated into her shell, only giving the woman short and quiet answers if she even answered her at all. I stood back and watched, noticing how flustered it made the potential new nanny. Quinn never gets flustered. She just rolls with whatever mood Flora is in.

I know there's no way I'm going to be able to find another Quinn, but I at least hope there's someone else out there with just a fraction of her charm who Flora can connect with. We're going to need them with Quinn going back to school. That's why I'm doing this, why I'm searching now. I want her to be able to focus solely on her classes that start in January and leave the rest to me and the new nanny. She deserves the best shot at this, and I'm going to do everything in my power to give it to her.

"Uncle Adam!"

I drop the wooden spoon I'm using to scoop dinner into bowls, macaroni flying everywhere at Flora's sudden outburst.

"Uncle Adam!" she screams across the house again.

I spring into action, throwing the pan onto the stove, then sprinting down the hall. She's standing in front of Quinn's room, her mouth hanging open, her eyes wide like she's frozen in horror.

"What?" I ask, dropping to my knees beside her, checking her over even though I doubt anything could have happened to her between the bathroom and here, but what else could it be? "What's wrong?"

She points to the bedroom, and I turn to look. It's empty.

Why is that so scary? Why does that require a scream? Why—

That's when it hits me.

It's empty.

It shouldn't be empty. Quinn should be resting in her bed. She should be sleeping off the headache she has. She should be *here*, but she's not.

Where the hell is she?

I step into her room. Her dresser drawers are half open, clothes hanging out of them like she was rifling through them and packing a bag. My eyes shoot to the closet and—yep, her bright pink bag is missing. I wouldn't have caught it if I hadn't spent so many nights tangled up in the sheets in here.

Quinn left.

Why did Quinn leave?

"Where's Just Quinn?" Flora asks.

"I...I don't know," I say, looking around the room for any other clues, something—*anything*—to tell me where she could have possibly gone. Other than her purse missing, there's nothing. She's just gone.

I walk out of the room, heading to my own, Flora's

footsteps behind me the whole time. I pull down the blinds, looking out to the driveway and confirming my suspicion. The cherry-red VW Bug is missing too. I run my hand through my hair, pulling on the roots as I begin to pace my room, thinking of all the places she could have gone and all the reasons she could have left.

Why did she leave? Where did she go?

"Where's Just Quinn?" Flora asks again.

"I don't know."

"But why would she leave without telling us? Where did she go? Did she take a suitcase? Is she coming back? Does she not love us anymore?"

"Fuck!" I throw my hands in the air. "I don't know, Flora! Okay? I don't know where she is!"

My niece's eyes widen, and she takes a step back. I don't blame her. I've never raised my voice at her like this before, and she doesn't deserve for me to do it now. I'm just stressed and worried and completely fucking confused.

"I'm sorry," I tell her, dropping my hands to my hips. "I'm sorry. I didn't mean to yell. It's..."

She nods like she understands. "You're worried about Just Quinn."

"Yeah. That." I scratch at my beard. "I don't know why she left."

"It was Miss Rachel."

"Rachel?" I tip my head. "Why did she leave because of Rachel?"

"Because you're trying to replace her."

"What?" I scoff. "No I'm not. I'm trying to help her. We talked about her going back to school, remember? Quinn is going to need help when that happens."

"Does *she* know that's why Rachel was here?"

"Of course she does."

I mean, she has to, right? I told her I'd take care of everything. Her classes are starting next month, the holidays are coming up, and my hockey schedule is about to get even more chaotic. I want to get this worked out before I'm back in the same position I was in before the season started.

"She has to know," I mutter aloud. "I would never just replace her. I *could* never just replace her. She knows that, right?"

Flora shrugs. "Did you tell her? Did you use your words?"

Use your words.

Isn't that what I'm always preaching? To both Flora and to Quinn? But I didn't use my words. I just assumed we were on the same page, assumed Quinn would know why I had Rachel stop by and why I was looking for someone to help her.

Fuck. Fuck, fuck, fuck!

I messed up. I messed up big-time, and I need to fix it—*now*. I run my hand through my beard again, trying to think of places Quinn could have run away to, but there are too many.

"Come on," I say, marching past Flora.

"Where are we going?" she asks, hot on my heels.

"To find Quinn."

"And tell her you love her?"

I stop, turning. "What?"

"You love her." She wrinkles her nose. "Don't you?"

I nod. "I do. I love her a lot. How… How did you know that?"

"I'm seven, not stupid. I have eyes." She points to them like I don't know where they are. "You guys look at each other all funny like people in movies look at each other when they're in love. Plus, I've seen you kiss."

"You have? When?"

She tucks her lips together, rocking back on her heels like she's afraid to say.

"You won't get in trouble if you tell me."

"You promise?"

"Promise."

"I…I snuck out of my room one morning to get

some pickles because I was really hungry, and I knew you weren't awake yet because you flew in super-duper late. I saw you sneaking out of Just Quinn's room, and you kissed her."

Shit. That could have been any number of mornings since I've barely spent a whole night in my room since we finally gave in to this thing between us.

This thing. Like I haven't completely fallen for the woman. Like she's not on my mind every waking hour of the day. Shit, she's even in most of my dreams too. I am totally fucked when it comes to her, and I couldn't imagine a better thing to be.

"Well, maybe no more sneaking around the house," I tell Flora. "But…you're okay with Quinn and me being together?"

"I love Just Quinn. Why wouldn't I be okay with it?"

I shake my head, not wanting to get into the power dynamics of it all with a seven-year-old. "Never mind. I…I guess I was just worried how you would feel about it."

"Happy. I'm very happy. Are you happy, Uncle Adam?"

"Very happy," I echo. "The happiest I've been in a long time."

Maybe even ever, including winning the Cup with the Carolina Comets, a defining moment of my life.

With Quinn…*all* the moments feel like defining moments. They all feel so important, and I want more of them. I want her mornings and her nights. I want her angry and I want her happy. I want to be there when she's had a rough day so I can do everything in my power to make it better, and I want to be the one who gives her so many good days.

I just want *her*. Back in our house, and back in our lives for a long, long, long damn time. I don't know where she ran away to, but I will find her. I don't care if it takes me running around this city all night.

"Let's go bring our girl home," I say.

Flora claps her hands together. "Yay! Finally!"

Finally, indeed.

I get that Seattle and the surrounding suburbs are big, but I never thought it would be so hard to find someone.

I drove straight to Bess's to see if Quinn had gone there. Chuck answered and told me he hadn't seen her in days, but to maybe try the bakery, so I went there next.

She wasn't there either. Bess, of course, was, and I got a twenty-minute lecture from her about the importance of communication and a very, very detailed outline of what will happen to my body should I ever hurt her daughter intentionally or unintentionally again. Then I got a hug and Flora got a free donut. It was a weird visit.

Next, we tried the park per Flora's suggestion. I wasn't surprised when she wasn't there either. I think Flora just wanted to go so she could swing.

I even stopped by her storage unit since I know she's been spending some time cleaning it out, but then I realized I had no clue what the code was to get through the gate. I tried bribing the front office clerk with hockey tickets, but he wasn't biting. I was actually grateful for that.

"Nothing?" Flora asks as I climb back into the SUV after Tex tells me she hasn't been by the diner either.

I sigh. "Nope. She's not here either."

"Ugh." She flings herself back against the seat with a groan. "We're never going to find her. You made her leave."

"I didn't make her leave."

"Yes you did. You didn't tell her you love her and now she's gone."

She sniffles on the last word, her eyes rimmed red with unshed tears. I've never once seen this kid cry before, not in everything she's been through, and she's too damn close to it now.

"I was so close to having a mommy," she whispers, and fuck if those quiet words don't break my heart.

"Flora...Quinn isn't your mom, you know that, right?"

"I know."

"And I'm not your dad."

"I know. You're Uncle Adam. But sometimes..." She trails off, her little lip trapped between her teeth. "Sometimes I pretend you are my dad and I pretend Just Quinn is my mom and I feel so happy I could burst."

Now it's my eyes that are lined with tears. How could they not be after that? It's what every kid wants —a family. To be loved. To be happy. Flora's gotten a glimpse of that over the last few months, and now there's a chance it's being ripped away from her all because I'm a big idiot who messes everything up.

If I'm being honest with myself, I sometimes pretend I'm her dad too. It *feels* like I'm her dad, like she's mine. I was so scared when she first got here, so fucking worried I'd resent her for screwing my life up, but now? Now I can't imagine it without her.

And I can't imagine it without Quinn either, wherever the hell she is.

"Flora..." I clear my scratchy throat. "I'm...I'm sorry. What can I do to make this better?"

She sniffles again. "Butterscotch candies would help."

I chuckle lightly. "I can do that."

"We can stop by George's on the way home and get them."

"Yeah, we can stop by—*George's?*"

"That's what I said."

"No. George's! We haven't checked George's."

She gives me a look that says *Why would Quinn go there?* I can give her two words that explain it just perfectly.

"Butterscotch cookies."

I throw the car into reverse and go find my girl.

"You got a lot of nerve walking in here."

George rises from his stool behind the counter, the big white-haired burly man pushing to his full height. And it's...well, underwhelming. I've never *not* seen George on his stool, and seeing him now? It's not what I was picturing. He's so...*short.*

"You, however, are welcome."

He winks at Flora, who grins up at him.

"Hi, George," she says. "You got any candy?"

"Kid, this is a store. Of course I have candy. For you." His stare goes from warm to icy in one second flat when he looks over at me. "Not your uncle."

"Is she here?" I ask, ignoring the glare he's tossing my way.

"Is who here?"

I want to be annoyed by this game he's trying to play, but all I can do is love the way he's protecting her.

"I'm taking that as a yes."

"I didn't say yes."

"You didn't need to." I point to the back of the store where I know he keeps the cookies. "She's back there, isn't she?"

He shrugs. "Depends on if you're about to go break her heart some more or not."

I sigh. "I'm not, George. I didn't mean to hurt it in the first place. I'm just stupid."

"You got that right." He lifts his chin toward the back. "She's back there all right. Probably eating all my damn cookies too."

"I am not!"

Quinn.

"Flora, stay up here, okay? I want to talk to Quinn alone."

She nods. "Don't forget to use your words."

Trust me, kid. I won't forget this time.

I turn toward the back, making my way past the baking supplies and toilet paper—why they're together in one aisle, I don't know—and breathe a sigh of relief when I round the corner and see her. She's sitting beside the cookie display, her back pressed against the wall as she takes a bite of butterscotch cookie. I smile at her, but she doesn't return it.

Fuck. This might be harder than I thought.

I settle down in the spot next to her, stretching my legs out with a sigh. I did not at all anticipate my night going this way. I was planning to cuss a few times while putting up the tree, maybe complain as Quinn inevitably made us listen to Christmas music, and then I was going to ask her to move in, and she'd say yes. We'd put Flora to bed, then make love right under the tree.

That's how it should have been. Not me sitting on the floor of some dingy, outdated grocery store because I didn't do the one thing I've lectured her about over and over.

Use your words.

"I remember the first time I saw you in this store when you were trying to kidnap Flora."

Quinn huffs. "I was not trying to kidnap her. I was trying to help her because *you* were kidnapping her."

"I wasn't."

She rolls her eyes, taking another bite of the cookie. "Well, obviously."

"But that wasn't the first time we met. You remember that, right?"

"You were an asshole about coffee."

I laugh. "Yeah, I was an asshole about coffee." I shake my head. "But that's not the *real* reason I was an asshole."

She stops chewing, then swallows. "It's not?"

"Nope. I was an asshole because I thought you were the most beautiful girl I had ever seen even though you were wearing earrings shaped like baby goats in pajamas and they were the ugliest thing ever."

"They are *not* ugly! That's one of my favorite pairs!"

"Why does that not surprise me?"

"Because I have good taste, and you know it." Her lips twitch. "So, you thought I was beautiful, huh?"

I nod. "I did. And it pissed me off so bad because I knew if I wasn't dealing with all the shit with Flora, I would ask you out and you would say yes, and the rest would be history."

"Wow. Confident we were a sure thing, huh?"

"Yep. Still am too."

I reach for a cookie, and to my surprise, she lets me have one. I take a bite, chew, and swallow. This is the routine for the next minute.

Then finally, when I've dusted all the crumbs away, I sigh.

"Why'd you pack a bag and run away, Quinn?"

"Why'd you invite her into our house, Hayes?" She squeezes her eyes shut. "I'm sorry. That was uncalled for. It's not my—"

"You're right. It *is* your house too, and I should have said something to you. I thought...I thought we were on the same page."

"That we were breaking up? Um, no. I mean, can we even break up? We're not really together."

"Are we really still feeding each other that bullshit? We're together. We've *been* together. You know, I know, and apparently Flora knows it too."

Quinn gasps, sitting up and looking over at me for the first time, and *fuck.* Could I have really missed her hazel eyes so much in such a short amount of time?

Yes. This is Quinn we're talking about. Of course I did.

"Flora knows?"

"Flora knows. I guess we aren't as slick as we thought. She slipped out of her room one morning for a pre-breakfast pickle fest and saw me leaving your room. I guess she's known for a while now and it never made a lick of difference to her."

"I... Wow." She rests her back against the wall once more. "She said something to me last week, but

I brushed it off as nothing. Now it makes me wonder."

"What'd she say?"

"That you *look* at me, whatever that means. To her, it means you're in love with me. I didn't really indulge her because I had no idea what *to* say. But now…"

"She said the same thing to me, about how we look at each other. She said that's what tipped her off first before she even saw us kiss. That just sealed the deal."

Quinn laughs lightly. "All this time we've been worried about what she would think and how this would affect her, but she's been fine."

We've been more stressed about it than she has, or at least I know I have. The last thing I wanted was for Flora to think I wasn't putting her first. I have been since she came to live with me. The stuff with Quinn…it never should have happened. It was wrong the way we went about it.

But now, sitting next to her, I'm glad it did happen.

"She was right, you know."

"About what?" Quinn takes a bite of another cookie. I've lost count of how many that is now.

"About me loving you."

She freezes, cookie halfway to her mouth, then she gulps down her bite roughly.

"What?"

"Are you really that surprised?"

She turns to me. "Yes! How could I not be? You… We… This wasn't supposed to happen."

"No, but it did. I love you. I know it's not what we agreed on, but I lo—"

Quinn is kissing me. She's kissing me and she tastes like butterscotch and sugar and everything good about life. She tastes like mine.

She crawls into my lap, crushing the cookies between us, and I don't think either of us cares. We're too busy with our mouths fused together, trying to get as close as possible, even though it'll never feel like enough.

When we finally break away, we're both breathing heavily, our chests brushing as Quinn peers down at me with a grin.

"What?" I ask in a whisper.

"Nothing. I…" She sighs. "I love you too."

"You do?"

She nods. "Yeah, I really do. I don't know when it happened exactly or how or why, but I do. I love you even though I'm not supposed to. Even though it's not what we agreed on. Even though I'll probably screw this up somehow too."

I pinch her side lightly. "Stop that. You're not going to screw this up. If anything, I probably will."

She pinches me back. "*You* stop that. You won't screw it up."

"Uh, hello? Do you remember why you're sitting on the floor of George's eating two dozen cookies?"

"It was *not* two dozen. It was only like six cookies… or nine. I don't know. I lost count." She shrugs, then twists her lips. "Why *did* you bring another nanny over?"

"For you."

"Come again?"

"For you," I repeat. "You start school next month, remember? I told you I was going to take care of things when it came to Flora. That includes getting a new nanny so you can focus on school and follow your dream."

She stares down at me, her mouth slightly ajar. She blinks. Then again. And again.

"You fired me so I can go to school?"

"I didn't *fire* you. I was just hoping you'd take on a different position. A promotion, if you will."

"A promotion? From live-in nanny to what?"

"Live-in *girlfriend*. Like officially. I figured you could move into my room."

"You…" She shakes her head. "You want me to move into your room? To be your official girlfriend? After everyone already knows I was your nanny first?"

"Yeah."

"That's… That's ridiculous! They're going to know, Hayes."

"So? Do you think I give a shit what they think? I don't, Quinn. I don't care because I love you. I fucking love you, okay? I've never done that before. I've never loved someone. I've never cared enough to love someone because why should I? People are shitty. But you… You're not. You're everything I didn't know I needed. You're smart, and you're funny, and you're so good to Flora. You wear stupid earrings that drive me nuts, and you eat way too much fucking butterscotch, but you have a big heart and an even bigger ass, and I just love you, okay? I'm just madly fucking in love with you. Can't you believe that?"

A slow smile curves her lips.

"What?" I ask softly, not sure I want to know the answer when she's looking at me like she is.

"You just somehow managed to insult me *and* compliment my *big ass* while also telling me you're madly in love with me."

"I'm…sorry?"

"Don't be. It was perfectly you. It's what I love about you." She sucks in a deep breath. "I think I might have fallen for you when you came over to my apartment and forced me to eat pizza."

"When I found your *box* of sex toys, you mean?"

"If I remember correctly, you're quite fond of those sex toys."

I smirk, remembering the last time we played with

them when I fucked her from behind while torturing her clit with a wand. She was so spent afterward I had to carry her to the shower and wash her myself.

"Anyway," she says, "you barged into my apartment and helped me pack. You yelled at me for inviting strangers into my house, then you fed me pizza and I was so confused. I couldn't understand how you could be such a jerk one minute, then sweet as hell the next. But then I realized that's just who you are. You act like you don't care, but you do. You probably care way more than anyone else. You care about Flora, you care about me, you care for your teammates. You're a good guy with a big heart that you hide behind this façade. You let everyone think you're just an immature, irresponsible moron, but you're not. You had a shit life. You were dealt horrible parents and possibly an even worse brother, and yet, you still made something of yourself. Yeah, you've made some mistakes along the way, but who hasn't? All through that, you've owned up to it. You've never shied away or pretended to be anything other than who you are, and it's admirable, really. You're just *you*, and that's what I love so much. Well, that and the way you whisper honey in my ear when you're deep inside me."

I laugh, loving that she had to ruin her speech like I ruined mine. That's who we are. We're both messes, and that's why we work so well together.

I slide my hand around the nape of her neck, pulling her to me and brushing my lips against hers in a soft kiss.

"I love you, Quinn Penelope Benson."

"And I love you, Adam Definitely Named After a Vampire Doctor Hayes."

I roll my eyes. "You're so annoying."

"I know. But you love that about me."

"I do. I really, really do."

She kisses me again. Hard and fast, then soft and slow. It's chaotic, but that's just how Quinn is. It turns out the thing I hated about her at first is the part I love the most.

"So…" I say when we pull apart. "I guess that means you're coming home, right?"

"What about Rachel?"

"Nah. She's not going to work out."

She looks surprised. "Why not?"

"Well, for starters, she kept calling Flora *Florence*."

"You can learn a person's name."

"Sure, but Flora didn't seem that into her."

"No? I'm surprised. I'm surprised *you* weren't into her."

She mutters that last part, and I pull my brows together. "What do you mean?"

"She was hot, Hayes."

"I wouldn't know."

"Oh, please." She rolls her eyes, her gaze dropping to my chest—anywhere but at me. "You can't tell me you didn't notice."

I grab her chin, pulling her face toward mine.

"I wouldn't know," I repeat. "All I see is you, honey."

I know in the deepest part of my heart, she's all I will ever see, and I'm going to spend the rest of my life proving it to her.

CHAPTER 24

QUINN

Much to my mother's chagrin, Hayes and I decide to spend Christmas with just us this year. I had to assure her no less than fifty times it had nothing to do with how awful Thanksgiving went and we truly just wanted to be alone and get Flora acquainted with a holiday she's never really experienced before. Now, sitting in the middle of the living room surrounded by so much wrapping paper I swear we could cover the Space Needle, I know it was the right choice.

I look at Flora, who is currently organizing the new paperbacks she got—all thirty of them—in stacks by genre, author, then title. I think we might have a future librarian in our midst. She wasn't feral this morning like you typically see kids act on Christmas. No, she opened each present nice and neat, so careful not to damage the paper. It was sweet, but it also took three hours to get through everything.

Hayes smiled the whole time. He's smiling even now, watching her. Feeling my gaze, he shifts the silver stare I love so much over to me.

What? his eyes say.

I love you, mine say back.

A whole conversation with just one look.

I went back home with him and Flora after he found me eating my weight in cookies at George's. After cleaning up the mess of macaroni and cheese in the kitchen—don't even want to know what happened there—we ordered Chinese and sat around the living room, answering any and all questions Flora had about us being together.

She had two.

1. Does this mean Hayes and I are getting married?
2. Are we going to kiss in front of her now?

She was really grossed out by the thought of our answer to that second question being yes. I wasn't. The fact that I can kiss Hayes freely now is so…well, freeing. I won't lie and say a part of me didn't love the secret aspect of our relationship. It was fun sneaking around, but loving him in the light? It's so much better than loving him in the dark.

"So, Flora, did you have a good Christmas?"

She nods. "It was the *best* Christmas." She grabs her cat, who is always by her side, and holds her up. The poor kitten looks absolutely miserable wearing the bow on top of her head. "Pickles loves her new headband."

Hayes laughs. "Pickles looks like she's plotting world domination."

"She is," Flora says with a shrug.

"Well, before she gets too far into her plans, do you want to open your last present?" I ask her.

She whips her head to me. "I have another present?"

"Yep." I grab the box I've been keeping hidden behind me, then hold it her way. "Here."

She eyes it warily before grabbing it with lightning-fast speed. Like the others, she takes her time peeling up the edges, and I sit on pins and needles the whole time. When she finally pulls it out, she looks confused.

"But I already have a Serpents jersey."

"I know. Look at the back."

She flips it around, and I hear her gasp before I can see the look on her face.

"Just Quinn! This is amazing!" She spins it back around to show me. "Look! I'm Little Flower!"

I grin at her. "You *are* Little Flower, and now you have two different jerseys to choose from when you go to Serpents games."

"I'm going as Little Flower all the time."

"Hey! What am I? Nothing to you?"

She rolls her baby-blue eyes. "You already know you're my favorite Serpents player."

"I am, huh?" He grins smugly. "Wait until Lawson hears about this."

I laugh, shaking my head at him as I rise from the floor and begin picking up the trash. With the amount of paper and boxes stacked everywhere, you'd think we had ten kids living in this place, but nope. It's just Flora. Hayes even worried if he bought her enough at one point. I pinched his nipple for being so silly.

We've been searching—together this time—for someone to come in and help with Flora while I'm in school, and we have it narrowed down to two candidates. It's crazy to think I'm looking for a replacement for my old job, but I'm okay handing off the torch. Besides, I'd rather be their someone special instead of just their nanny.

"Hang on," Hayes says. "Looks like we missed something under the tree."

"There's no way. I checked three times."

But when I glance over there, yep—there's a box

sitting right in the middle. I look at Hayes, who just shrugs, a small smile playing on his lips.

I walk over to the tree and grab the box. It's addressed to me.

Unlike Flora, I do *not* have the patience to carefully unwrap the present. I practically shred it, paper landing all over the newly cleaned floors, but I don't care. When I pull it from the box, I'm surprised to find *another* Serpents jersey sitting inside.

I turn it around to read the back. It's so over the top and so ridiculous I can't help but laugh.

"What does it say? What does it say?" Flora asks, practically bouncing on her knees.

"It says Honey."

"Honey?" She scrunches her nose up. "But your name isn't honey."

Oh, but it is.

Hayes winks at me, and my cheeks get so hot I have to hide my face in the jersey. When I look back up, he's right there in front of me, grinning down at me wickedly.

"Do you like it?"

I shake my head, wrapping my arms around his neck. "I *love* it. I love *you*."

"I love you too. Merry Christmas, Quinny."

"Merry Christmas, Adam."

I press up on my tiptoes and slant my mouth

against his in a chaste kiss when what I really want is to wrap my legs around him and beg him to take me back to our room and make love to me.

"Yeah, yeah. You love Uncle Adam. I love Uncle Adam. We all love each other. Get a room," Flora gripes, her attention back to her books.

Mine hasn't shifted. No. I'm too busy watching Hayes, and he's too busy watching her. She just said she loves him—a first.

"Breathe," I remind him softly, and he sucks in a stuttered breath.

When he looks back over at me, his eyes are glassy and red, and he's barely able to blink away the tears.

"You okay?" I whisper, and he shakes his head.

"I don't know. That was... I wasn't expecting that."

"I could tell. She does, you know? She doesn't say it, but I know she does."

He nods. "Yeah. I know. It's just...I've waited my whole life to be loved, and now I am. By the two best girls in the world, and I can't believe it."

"Well, believe it because it's true. We love you."

"I love you too. Both of you. Thank you."

"For what?"

"For giving me the best Christmas gift of all time— you."

"Oh, Hayes, this isn't your Christmas gift."

"No?"

I shake my head, then put my lips to his ear. "You remember the boots from my Halloween costume? The ones you loved so much?"

He nods.

"I kept them."

He groans, burying his face in my neck as he holds me close, and I laugh. Becoming a nanny might not have been on my radar, but it's the best job I've ever had. Because in the end, I got Flora, and I got Hayes.

And it's the happiest I've ever been.

EPILOGUE

HAYES

"You're not wearing that."

Quinn hitches her brows up at my words, her hands in her hair as she styles it into a bun that somehow looks messy yet intentional. "Excuse me?"

I slide off our bed and make my way over to her, not stopping until I'm just inches away, capturing her hazel gaze in the mirror.

"If you wear that, all I'll want to do all night is rip it off you, and I really doubt our friends want us to fuck in their bathroom."

"Why, Adam Hayes, are you saying you can't control yourself around me? Because that's kind of hot."

"Yes." I lean forward, pressing my lips against her exposed shoulder in a soft kiss before sinking my teeth lightly into her skin.

She tilts her head to the side, sighing. "You're killing me."

"And *you're* killing *me* in that dress. You look *too* good in it. It's unfair."

I drag my hands up the back of her legs, taking the form-fitting deep pink dress right along with me until I'm greeted by the sight of her perfectly pert ass in nothing but a lacy, black thong.

"Fuck," I mutter, looking down at her.

She giggles. "Thank you."

I run my finger under the lace material, pulling at it softly. "You have no idea how badly I want to sink to my knees and get a taste of you right now, have you press your hands against the mirror while I eat you from behind." I smack her ass roughly, and she gasps. "I'd fuck you hard after, just the way you like. I'd bury myself inside you until you're so full you can't stand it."

She runs her tongue over her bottom lip, then presses her top teeth into it.

"Would you want that, Quinny? Would you want me to slide my cock into your pretty, pretty cunt and make you go to the party with my cum leaking out of you for the rest of the night?"

She's panting now, her chest turning red with the heat that moves through her, and with my hard cock pressing against her ass, there's no way she doesn't know I mean the words I'm whispering in her ear.

"Yes," she begs. "Please."

"I want it so fucking bad I can't stand it."

"Me, too. So, so bad."

I believe her.

For a moment, I worried when Quinn officially moved in, we might grow tired of one another, worried the thrill we got from sneaking around was the real glue that kept us together, and without it, we would break.

That couldn't have been further from the truth. I'll be the first to admit it—Quinn Benson isn't what I was expecting. She's better. And man am I fucking crazy about her. Being with her is everything I never thought was possible.

It's coming home to someone who actually gives a shit about me. It's having someone to talk to and who listens. It's having someone believe in me for me and not just the money I make. It's being loved in a way I've never been loved before.

When Flora came to live with me, I never anticipated this was how my life would turn out, but now? Now, I can't imagine it any other way, and I really don't want to, either. I have the best girls anyone could ask for, and I wouldn't change a damn thing about any of it.

"Maybe just a taste won't hurt…"

I move to drop to my knees and deliver on at least

half of what I promised I'd do, but Quinn has other plans, grabbing my hair and pulling me back up to full height. I jut my lip out in a pout, and she laughs, spinning and circling her arms around my neck.

"As amazing as that sounds, we really do need to get going, or we'll be late."

I don't give a shit about being late. With my hockey schedule and her classes—which she's totally killing—in full swing, I feel like we hardly get to see each other anymore, and when we do, it's never enough. To be fair, I don't think any amount of time will ever be enough with Quinn, but I really don't want to share the one evening I have with her with my teammates.

"So?"

"*So*, I'm trying to be a punctual adult, remember? *We're* trying to be punctual adults. Set a precedent for that kid out there we both kind of love."

"She ruins everything fun."

I roll my eyes, but we both know I don't mean a word of it. If life with Quinn is fun, it's ten times better with Flora around too. Yes, she still has her moments of being the shy and quiet kid she was when she first got here, but she's changed so much it's almost like I don't even remember the first few hard months with her last year. We're so far past that now it's like a whole new chapter in our lives. She's doing great in school and making friends. She's even asked about joining a hockey league.

I still worry about her constantly—and I think I always will—but my anxiety isn't nearly as bad as it once was, and that's in large part thanks to Quinn and Gertie, the new nanny we hired, who lives in Quinn's old bedroom.

"Fine," I relent. "We'll go be adults. But when we get home, after Flora goes to bed, I'm fucking you until *I'm* content, got it?"

"Is that supposed to be a threat?"

"No. Maybe. I don't know." I press a quick kiss to her full lips, knowing if I linger, I'll want to kiss her more, and *apparently*, we don't have time for that right now. "Now come on. The sooner we get this over with, the better."

"Be nice," she warns, untangling herself from me and pulling her dress back down over her ass before opening our bedroom door. "Or I'll make sure you get no cake."

"There's cake?"

Flora appears out of nowhere, her eyes wide with excitement. "How come you didn't tell me there'd be cake, Just Quinn? Uncle Adam?"

I look to Quinn with a shrug. Her eyes say *I got this.*

"Because, little flower, I didn't want to ruin the surprise," she explains.

"Well, it's ruined now. Pickles, we're getting cake!" Flora shrieks, taking off through the house to the front door.

"No running!" I holler after her, shaking my head with a sigh. "Remind me again why we're going to this party and not staying here in our big comfy bed."

"Because," Quinn says, patting my chest, "Fox is your teammate, and this is his engagement party. We *have* to attend."

"I still can't believe he's getting married," I mutter. "Or who he's marrying. It all seems so…sudden."

"Hey, when you know, you know, right?" She winks at me as she brushes past.

She's right—when you know, you know.

But what I know and she doesn't? I intend to marry Quinn Benson and truly make her mine. For forever and for always.

OTHER TITLES BY TEAGAN HUNTER

SLICE SERIES

A Pizza My Heart

I Knead You Tonight

Doughn't Let Me Go

A Slice of Love

Cheesy on the Eyes

TEXTING SERIES

Let's Get Textual

I Wanna Text You Up

Can't Text This

Text Me Baby One More Time

INTERCONNECTED STANDALONES

We Are the Stars

If You Say So

STANDALONES

The DM Diaries

Stay on top of my new releases, cover reveals, sales, and more by visiting:

www.teaganhunterwrites.com

THANK YOU

My husband, Henry. Thank you for existing. I love you.

Laurie. This industry is so wild sometimes, and I couldn't be happier to have an incredible person like you in my corner. Thank you for not just being a good PA, but a damn good friend too.

My editing team. Caitlin, Julia, Judy... Thank you for all your incredibly hard work! I know the schedule for this book was a bit of a roller coaster, and I appreciate you never abandoning me on the ride.

Kim, Nina, Meagan, and the VPR team. I couldn't imagine having a better team standing behind me. You are rockstars. Truly.

Shannon, Katie, and Emily. Thank you for the most incredible covers. I can't get over your talent.

Tidbits. Thank you for always standing behind me. I know this journey can be a mess sometimes, but your support really does get me by some days.

sMother. I love you.

You. You might know this and you might not, but I had to push the release of this book back by a lot of months due to some health issues I was having. I was terrified to make the announcement. It was the first time I ever had to push a release back but there was just no way I was going to be able to do this book justice. Now that it's finished, I'm so glad I gave it the time it deserved. And I'm so glad YOU gave me the time to finish it. I appreciate your support and your understanding more than you could ever know. Thanks for sticking around. I hope Hayes was worth the wait.

With love and unwavering gratitude,

Teagan

TEAGAN HUNTER writes steamy romantic comedies with lots of sarcasm and a side of heart. She loves pizza, hockey, and romance novels, though not in that order. When not writing, you can find her watching entirely too many hours of *Supernatural*, *One Tree Hill*, or *New Girl*. She's mildly obsessed with Halloween and prefers cooler weather. She married her high school sweetheart, and they currently live in the PNW.

www.teaganhunterwrites.com

Made in the USA
Monee, IL
04 November 2024

69343815R00249